BOOK ONE OF

The Watchers of Ur

CRADLE

LaMonte M. Fowler

VICENDIA MEDIA

CHICAGO

Cover Illustration Copyright © 2012 "Space Angel" by Mariusz Karasiewicz

Edited by Alexander B. Rossino, PhD.

ISBN: 0984874100
ISBN-13: 978-0-9848741-0-1

For my wife and kids.
They let me dream while I'm awake.

PSALM 8

O LORD, our Lord,
   how majestic is your name in all the earth!
You have set your glory above the heavens.
   Out of the mouth of babies and infants,
you have established strength because of your foes,
   to still the enemy and the avenger.
When I look at your heavens, the work of your fingers,
   the moon and the stars, which you have set in place,
what is man that you are mindful of him,
   and the son of man that you care for him?
Yet you have made him a little lower than the heavenly beings
   and crowned him with glory and honor.
You have given him dominion over the works of your hands;
   you have put all things under his feet,
all sheep and oxen,
   and also the beasts of the field,
the birds of the heavens, and the fish of the sea,
   whatever passes along the paths of the seas.
O LORD, our Lord,
   how majestic is your name in all the earth!

PREFACE

The central idea of this story came to me several years ago when I was reading some of the apocryphal books not included in the canon of the Christian Bible. These books had always fascinated me not only because they were left out of the canon, for whatever reasons, but because they were in some cases quite compelling and full of details about things that interested me greatly.

I have always been fascinated by the apparent reality that God created two very different classes of beings, both endowed with free will, and both who, at some level, did not live up to the Creator's expectations (to put it in base human terms). The interplay throughout history between humanity and the angelic realm — including the fallen angels or *demons* — has been rich subject matter of fantasy writers for centuries. Whether you prefer Milton or more recently, Anne Rice, there is no shortage of interesting stories featuring the machinations of men and their supernatural counterparts.

But I have wondered how the advent of technology and instant global communications has affected the supernatural realm and their dealings with mankind. Do the angels notice such things? Do the demons have new and better ways to tempt and distract humanity? And when I began to consider the Biblical and mythological backstory of Lucifer and his fallen angels being imprisoned on Earth, I wondered what would happen to them as the human race ventured into space. Would the angels and demons follow us to the stars?

That is the fertile ground from which this story sprang. And I am pleased to say, it has grown into something I did not plan, nor did I foresee. The organic development of this story, and the subsequent continuation in the next two books, has frankly surprised me. I have never worked on a creative endeavor that ended up so far from the place I had envisioned. Who knows what the next story will grow into…

There are many people who contributed in a variety of ways to this project, and they deserve so much more than a few words of thanks. My first word of thanks goes to the people who read the first short story I wrote back in 1982, when I was a sophomore in high school. Their praise, encouragement and tears planted the seeds of a writer in me, and this story is but the most recent harvest of that gift.

Next, I would like to thank Dr. Alexander B. Rossino, PhD. for editing my manuscript and introducing me to my new friend, the comma. Simply put, he made the story better because he made me a better writer. Alex and I met and became lifelong friends at Canisius College in 1984, and he is a prominent character in some of the most memorable scenes of my life. It has been a very special honor to have him by my side, bringing life to these characters and building a new memory together. Thanks, pal.

The decision to self-publish was not without some serious moments of doubt, fear, and head scratching. Without the kind advice and experience of independent author Michael R. Hicks, I would have never learned the magic of Twitter, or been able to confidently embark on this journey in a professional manner. Mike is an inspiration to me, and many other independent authors, and is a constant source of envy and entertainment, because his books are simply wonderful.

What is an author without people who read your scribblings? Well, before anyone else gets to read your work, a very special group of people get to beat your beautiful manuscript like a piñata at a first-graders birthday party. They are called *beta readers*, and they make the stuff you read, readable. My heartfelt thanks to: Patrick Finnegan, Brenda Causey, Joseph Buscaglia, and my eldest son, Tom Fowler. Your depth of familiarity and love of the science fiction genre gave me confidence that my story held up well in the shadow of giants.

A special 'thank you' to artist Mariusz Karasiewicz for permission to use his digital painting named "Space Angel" as the cover art for this book. When I saw it, I thought someone had taken a photograph from one of my dreams. I think I might have to pay him more for the next cover!

Every author has people who inspire them, and I must now genuflect before the altar of those who opened my mind to wonders beyond our world and our time. Though I have many author heroes, this story owes a particular debt to Sir Arthur C. Clarke, and Roger Zelazny. Clarke taught me that truly excellent science fiction lives in the subtle details. And Roger Zelazny taught me that truly great fantasy lives in the complexity of the characters. I tip my chapeau to both men.

Finally, I need thank my amazing family. My kids Cassandra, Thomas, Alexander, Andrew, and my niece Danielle. You kids make our house loud, our laundry baskets full, and our days filled with love and laughter. And a very, very special thank you to my beautiful wife, Theresa. She has been my best friend, my conscience, and my partner in every nutty idea for nearly 25 years. Thank you for always letting me pursue my dreams, and never calling me crazy.

LaMonte M. Fowler
January 19, 2012
Bartlett, IL

CHAPTER 1

The view from the passenger lounge provided a spectacular panorama of Africa, Europe, and the Arabian Peninsula for Remus Arin. Gazing down upon the continent where humanity took its first tentative steps, he had to admit feeling a bit of admiration for the tenacity and creativity of these creatures.

A servant approached him and asked in a delicate voice, "May I bring you a refreshment, Mr. Arin? A cocktail or perhaps some sparkling water?" The servant waited, bowing slightly at the waist, her eyes cast down.

"No. I am fine," he replied, and then turned his head to look down upon the blue and white globe 33,000 kilometers below.

Remus never tired of his trips off-planet. For too long he had been denied this view of the earth. So long, in fact, that he had forgotten how beautiful it was. A delicate island of life in a vast sea of empty space — a miracle of life where none should be.

He considered how truly remarkable it was that man had reached out to the stars so early in his development.

Once the dream of space travel had been realized, the human race moved with surprising swiftness to explore the nearby planets and asteroids, finding a new and seemingly endless source of minerals and wealth. Again man's greed had prevailed, pushing him to take greater risks in the name of profit and power. *How well they have learned from us*, Remus thought, allowing himself a satisfied grin.

His daydream was interrupted by an announcement, "Descender 23 to Kigali Station will begin boarding in five minutes through the yellow portal. Please queue according to class."

Immediately the other passengers began gathering their carry-on bags and quietly formed themselves into an orderly queue in front of the airlock outlined in yellow. Imperial citizens proudly took position at the front, with Imperial servants directly behind. A variety of passengers from Venus, Mars, and the Outer Colonies jostled for places in the back.

A small Imperial child stood clutching his mother's arm staring at a laborer from the Outer Colonies at the end of the line. The child said in a voice too loud for his surroundings, "Look at the scab, mother. He is filthy! I don't want him on our descent."

The other off-world passengers looked sheepishly at the child and then at the man whose face betrayed a look of mild horror at being singled out by the brat.

"My...my apologies, Mistress," he stammered. "I do not wish to upset your child...I will be happy to wait for another descent slot." The man picked up his bag, bowed deeply at the waist toward the elegant woman and her devilish child, then slowly walked back to the seating area.

The child's mother lifted her chin, closed her eyes and

turned back toward the front of the queue, never acknowledging the shamed man's surrender. The child glanced at Remus and smiled.

Remus was pleased that no matter how great man's technology had become, he was essentially the same violent nomad ready to bash in his neighbor's skull with a jawbone for the slightest offense. The current fashion was to cover this natural tendency with a veneer of civility for those who were deemed worthy, and to barely tolerate the existence of those who were seen as inconvenient but necessary.

As man left the cradle of earth, he exported not only his creativity, courage, and virtues, but also his greed, bigotry and violent nature. No longer forced to promote the illusion of cooperation necessitated by sharing a planet with limited space and finite resources, mankind had launched his darker nature into the void of interplanetary space. He used his newfound wealth to construct societies that glorified and magnified all the things that had historically separated humans from one another — race, religion, ethnicity, and political ideology. Entire worlds were colonized by formerly great nations, at great expense and loss of life. Some smaller colonies became refuges for persecuted minorities, religious sects, and communities of like-minded artisans, scientists, and philosophers. Struggle was a universal constant in this new age of space colonization.

However, Remus Arin had no need of the quaint social groupings scattered among the planets and asteroids of the solar system. He was exactly where he wanted to be. He always was.

Remus was a special envoy of the Emperor Wan Sui Ye

— literally the "Lord of Ten Thousand Years" — and was by all reasonable measures outside The Law and untouchable. He was free to travel to any Imperial territory, and indeed any independent or corporate colony. His visa was irrevocable and his passage was guaranteed.

This privilege was not earned however — it was manufactured. He had spent many years carefully crafting his present identity, working through the tedious layers of Imperial bureaucracy, suffering one insufferable fool after another until he had finally earned a private audience with the Emperor himself. This was an honor reserved for only the highest ranking members of the Imperial Court, and a few useful members of the ruling class from trading partners among the independent worlds and corporate colonies.

On that fateful day five years ago, Remus had told the Emperor a secret that would captivate his imagination and inform all of his actions from that day forward. As is the way of his kind, Remus spun a tale that seized the Emperor's heart and gave him a vision that made his current reign seems small and insignificant. He set Wan Sui Ye on a path that he believed would make him the greatest conqueror in human history, magnifying his glory and honor greater than any king or emperor who had ever ruled on Earth.

The Emperor made Remus Arin his Ambassador-at-large, an office created by Imperial decree, with no official duties other than those proscribed by the Emperor himself. Remus had no human in authority over him, save for the Emperor — and even that was by Remus' design. He would manipulate this small and simple man like the hundreds of others he had bent to his Master's will throughout ages past. He had only one true Master and His will would be done in the end.

***

The descent to Kigali from the Terran Orbital Lift Station 1 was comfortable and efficient. Long ago at the dawn of the Space Age man would hurl himself in great towering vehicles — chemical rockets — at terrifying velocities into orbit and beyond. He would return in flimsy machines that plummeted back to Earth as great fireballs to land in the frozen wastes of Siberia or splash into the Pacific Ocean.

In the late twenty-first century, the former nation of China — fatherland of the current Empire — made Konstantin Tsiolkovsky's dream of a space elevator a reality. The brilliant Terran Orbital Lift System (TOLS) provided a fast, efficient, and relatively cheap way to move payloads and passengers into orbit. The system was essentially a tower of engineered carbon nanotubes moored to the earth at four strategic points along the equator: Kigali (TOLS-1 Base) in the territory briefly known as Rwanda on the African continent; Singapore (TOLS-2 Base); Pacifica (TOLS-3 Base) a floating platform in the Pacific; and Quito (TOLS-4 Base) on the South American continent. Each tower extended from the surface of the Earth to geosynchronous orbit 33,000 kilometers above the equator, and beyond. The towers were "anchored" in space by enormous precision counterweights equal in mass to the weight of the entire tower structure, its lift vehicles and the orbital station platform at the top of each tower.

Passengers and cargo are shuttled from the surface to orbit via ascenders driven along superconducting rails.

9

The ascender allows passengers to sit in comfort as it makes the journey from the surface through the atmosphere affording them a spectacular view of the planet below.

Remus had made the trip hundreds of times over the generations since the TOLS was built, yet he never tired of looking at the Earth from this vantage point. The years of his captivity on earth, while filled with many memorable adventures on behalf of his Master, did not allow him to experience his one true love. It wasn't until powered flight was developed at the dawn of the twentieth century that he was once again able to soar through the sky, mingling with the clouds like the eagles he once called friends.

After the miracle at Kitty Hawk, he quickly mastered all the aircraft of the day, honing his skills through a series of lifetimes to become a god of flying machines. His Master at first thought this fascination with flight was a trivial waste of time that took him away from his real work. But eventually he came to realize that Remus' considerable skill and enthusiasm for flight could be a useful tool in achieving his goals.

Shortly after man had conquered space, it became apparent that mankind would not rest until he brought all the planets and moons under his dominion. The Master understood that this natural impulse could also provide new and very interesting possibilities for him and his followers. For far too long they had been roaming the world, traversing it's continents, sailing its oceans, and climbing its peaks in search of something that would satisfy their lust. And now that man had left his cradle, the Master and his kind would surely accompany mankind on its journey to the future. There was still much work to be done.

As the descender began to slow and finally disengage from the track, Remus breathed in the first scent of real air as the cabin depressurized. Now it was time to once again don one of his multitude of masks and play the role that fit this current drama.

The descender hatch opened and passengers began filing out of the craft, again by class, with the Imperial citizens and their servants leading the way. The off-worlders were directed out of the main passenger arrival area into a cramped space bordered by a security field where they would be processed by Customs Officers and pass through a mandatory bioscan.

Remus searched the faces of the crowd gathered near the main exit of the arrival lounge and found the ever-present cloying smile of Nianzu Chao. Chao was by title a senior-level diplomat, but was in function an intelligence officer using the centuries-old cover of diplomacy to mask his true purpose. He was always dispatched by the Emperor to meet Remus upon his return to Earth, a fact which displeased Remus greatly.

"Welcome home Ambassador Arin," Chao said with a broad grin. He bowed deeply at the waist in the traditional Chinese manner. He stood and reached for Arin's bag saying, "The Emperor is looking forward to your report. So much so that he has left the Forbidden City and commands that you meet him presently in Cairo. I have made arrangements for an Imperial shuttle to take us there immediately."

A fleeting look of disgust flashed across his face for an instant, and then regaining his bearing he said, "How generous of the Emperor to make such a journey. Surely he must have other local matters to occupy his attention?"

Chao gave Remus a curious look and replied, "It is true. The Emperor has decided to oversee the preparations for the tri-millennial celebration of the rededication of the Temple in Jerusalem."

The words pierced Remus like a knife. In his mind's eye he recalled the sight of the Temple Mount in flames and the considerable thrill of casting the Jewish priests from the tower of the Antonia Fortress on that sweltering summer day twenty-five centuries earlier. In that lifetime he was known as Larcius Lepidus commander of the *Legio X Fretensis*, the infamous Tenth Legion of the Roman Empire.

Returning his thoughts to the present, he said to Chao, "It is very generous for the Emperor to give the Jews such a gift. It is rare for that which is extinct to return to life."

"The Jewish Confederation is a powerful and useful ally. It is a small thing to give them such a trifle if it will ensure their continued cooperation and trade," Chao replied. Chao was an insufferable git, but he possessed keen political insight. Most importantly, he understood how power was won and kept.

Remus gave a faint smile and said, "We should not keep the Emperor waiting then." He stepped onto a nearby moving walkway that would take them to the private aircraft area of the Kigali terminal.

As they boarded the sleek wedge-shaped Imperial ramjet, the pilot greeted Remus with a crisp salute by clutching his right fist to his heart and bowing his head slightly. Remus returned the salute in kind.

"Welcome home, Ambassador. I have made the

necessary flight plan notations if you would like to fly today. It would be a great honor to be your second," the pilot said with an expectant grin.

Remus considered the prospect of an hour of small talk with Chao, or cruising at mach seven above the dunes of the Sahara. It was an easy decision. "I would be very pleased to fly with you today, Captain."

***

Emperor Wan Sui Ye stood on the balcony of the Giza Palace in Cairo gazing at the north face of Khufu, the Great Pyramid, and it's smaller sister Khafre, to the southwest. It filled him with awe when he considered that these monuments were built nearly five thousand years ago, and yet they stood despite the hundreds of generations that have passed. Entire empires had risen and fallen in the shadows of these great stone memorials, and it made the Emperor of Earth feel small.

Their presence also reminded him of the fragility of even mighty empires and their leaders. His reign as Emperor of The People's Empire of Earth would be subject to the very same laws of political physics, regardless of how many of his subjects revered him as a living god. Like the hundreds of dynastic emperors that preceded him, he would ultimately answer to that master of all living souls — death.

But for now he was still young — only sixty-four — and in perfect health. His dominion over Earth and its orbital space, the Moon, Venus, thousands of asteroids, Europa, and most recently Titan, was total and absolute. He commanded an army of millions of warriors, and his naval fleet numbered in the tens of thousands of both waterborne and space-going vessels. While his reign had been mostly peaceful, he did not hesitate to enforce his will via a swift and deadly projection of force. His subjects regarded him with awe and The Law, established centuries before at the rebirth of the dynastic empire, ensured their obedience and tribute.

For most of his reign he had focused his attention on expanding trade with the independent worlds and corporate colonies. He believed it was his duty to ensure a steady flow of raw materials for his factories on the Moon, and in return provide a stable and vibrant market for the other worlds to trade their specialized goods and resources. Still, no world other than Earth had achieved even a small measure of self-sufficiency. The interplanetary economy was complex and very fragile and required the strength and stability of his Empire and her navy to function.

The Empire was indeed strong, but his pragmatic mind was keenly aware that without the constant demand from the independent worlds and the corporate colonies, his factories would quickly idle, and his mining vessels would cease their relentless assault on the asteroids. The terraforming of Venus — begun by his great-great-great-grandfather nearly three centuries before — would cease and that world would return to a barren sweltering wasteland.

Even as a young Emperor he knew that he would need to do more than simply hold the line and incrementally advance his empire. Change was coming like a slow Easter tide, barely perceptible at any single moment, but inexorable in its effect over time. If left unchecked, it would sweep away his empire like the starfish on a beach.

But since Remus Arin — that enigmatic man from

nowhere — came into his sphere, Emperor Wan Sui Ye's destiny was clear and promised to bring glory and honor to him and The Sun Dynasty. No longer would he be content to play the interplanetary chess game for meager spoils. The palace intrigue and banal political games favored by the nobility and his enemies would soon lose its grip on his life. No, Emperor Wan Sui Ye was destined now to become an explorer and conqueror of worlds. He would soon have the power to take humanity beyond her cradle and nursery — into the endless possibilities of the stars.

The Emperor watched as the sun set and the torrid glow of the great pyramids dimmed to a dull brown and then darkness, knowing that his destiny was fixed like the stars appearing above the ancient Egyptian desert. He wondered aloud, "Father, will *my* legacy stand for five thousand years?"

***

Remus was still feeling the euphoria of his hypersonic flight across the Sahara as he ascended the white marble steps of the Giza Palace. Walking down the wide corridor to the Emperor's private quarters, he replayed the story in his mind, carefully rehearsing the key facts that would spur the Emperor to action. Every part of his Master's plan was coming together like the pieces of a puzzle.

He stopped at an ornate mirror a few meters from the door to the Emperor's quarters to smooth his hair and adjust his collar. He ran his hands down the front of his silk tunic, took a deep breath, and then turned toward the door.

As he approached the door a voice said, "Good evening, Ambassador Arin. Shall I alert the Emperor that you are waiting to enter?"

Arin thought back to the days when kings and emperors were surrounded day and night by soldiers bearing arms, their sole mission to protect their leader at all cost. But in the twenty-sixth century, technology ensured that no one could approach bearing an intent to harm the Emperor or any member of his family or court.

"Yes, please tell the Emperor I am here," he replied to the voice.

A moment later the door to the private suite silently swung open and Remus stepped across the threshold onto a stunning mosaic tile floor depicting a chariot race from ancient Egypt's glorious past. He passed through the foyer into a parlor decorated with tapestries from ancient Persia and an eclectic collection of furniture from a variety of centuries spanning the Renaissance to the present.

Soft footsteps to his left signaled Remus to bow and wait for the Emperor to address him. He sensed the man approach and stop in front of him.

"Rise, Ambassador Arin. It is good to have you returned safely to me," said the Emperor.

"May you reign forever, my Lord," favoring the Emperor with a formal yet familiar greeting as he stood and met his gaze.

Emperor Wan Sui Ye smiled and then shook Remus' hand and clasped his elbow in a friendly gesture meant to put his Ambassador at ease. His smile was warm and genuine, for the Emperor found Remus to be a rare gem among his subjects — a man who was his equal in all ways except that he was not of royal blood. The Emperor could speak his mind, even his heart, to this man. It had been so since they first met and he did not understand why. But he also did not dwell on the matter. The fact that he had one such as this in his life was enough, and he cherished it.

"Would you like something to drink after your long journey, I have a bottle of single malt from some small Scottish isle that was given to me by the Governor of Callisto. I have not opened it yet."

"Thank you, my Lord. I have not had a drink in many weeks so forgive me if it goes to my head," he lied in reply. While Remus could not physically become intoxicated, he did enjoy a good Scotch whiskey.

The Emperor crossed the room to a sideboard that held a collection of ornate crystal glasses and decanters containing a variety of colored liquids. He opened one of the lower doors and retrieved a finely tapered bottle with delicate vines etched into its surface. He uncorked the bottle and poured the golden liquid into two similarly etched glasses.

He handed Remus a glass and said, "*Ban bei!*"

Remus understood this to be the traditional Chinese toast that encouraged the guest to sip rather than down their drink in one gulp. He raised the glass to his lips and drank, savoring the warm, oaky-tasting liquid.

"Now Remus we talk of the future." The Emperor gestured to Remus with a wave of his hand, inviting him to sit.

Remus settled into luxurious chair and began his report, "My Lord, I am pleased to report that your project on Titan is proceeding ahead of schedule and the ship should be ready for trials by early December. The drive development proceeds as scheduled and has performed in line with expectations. All-in-all, your project should be completed in time for your Fortieth Jubilee."

"That is excellent news, Remus. But this I have read from your written report. I wish to hear of things not written." The Emperor, while not intellectually gifted, was very adept at discerning truths as yet unspoken. "You have concerns about the project that you are reluctant to share. Tell me what it is that troubles you, Remus."

Remus knew he had baited the hook as intended and now must set it so that the rest of his Master's plan could unfold. "Nothing escapes your gaze, my Lord. It is true that I have some reservations about the progress I was shown during my inspection on Titan. The drive development project leader, Garland Trayter, while a brilliant physicist and engineer, is a bit of a rascal and has been altering some of the test data."

"Fear of failure is a powerful motivator," the Emperor said attempting to appear wise.

"That is what is strange about his actions, my Lord. He altered the test data to make the test results appear slightly below expected performance levels. He is purposely hiding the fact that the drive is performing exactly as designed." Remus paused to take a sip of his whiskey and let his words sink in.

"Why would he understate the success of his design? That is not logical or practical. Does he not understand the price he will pay if this project does not succeed?" Remus could feel the Emperor's heartbeat rising and sense the adrenaline flooding his bloodstream. The Emperor stood and walked to an archway that led to the balcony overlooking the pyramids. The cool desert night blew in through the open doors, causing the gauzy white drapes to dance gently like ghosts.

"My Lord, there is more." The Emperor turned and

raised his eyebrows expectantly. "I have evidence that the facility has been compromised by at least one corporate spy from a Martian firm — most likely Tornamira. They have openly been pursuing faster-than-light technology and have been hiring talent from every major university and research laboratory for several years. My working thesis is that they are covering all bases by getting their people inside every project in sight. I have a short list of suspects and another list of possible collaborators that I am prepared to act upon. I did not want to proceed without seeking your counsel on the matter and discussing the potential hazards of an investigation." Remus lowered his eyes while slowly swirling the golden liquid around the inside of the glass. *Patience*, he thought to himself, *wait for it.*

The Emperor frowned and went to a small table next to the chair where he had been sitting. He opened the lid of an ornate box inlaid with semi-precious stones and withdrew a cigarette. "Will you join me?" The Emperor gestured to the box.

"Thank you, my Lord...yes."

The Emperor handed Remus a cigarette. He put it to his lips and drew deeply, causing a chemical reaction in the tip to ignite the tobacco and paper releasing a deep blue stream of smoke that Remus savored then exhaled luxuriously.

After smoking for a moment the Emperor turned and asked, "Tell me. What impact will an investigation have on work at the laboratory?"

Remus looked away just long enough to appear to be measuring his words and then replied, "While your security agents are very discreet, the Titan lab is a very small and tightly knit community. Word will spread no matter how careful they are. My concern is not with slowing progress per se, but rather with jeopardizing the entire project. A spy can quickly become a saboteur when he is trapped. Since there is nowhere to run on Titan, it is only a matter of time and simple deduction to find the spy and his accomplices."

"How do we know this spy has not been in contact with his handlers off-world? What if they have already smuggled the design data off Titan and it is in the hands of Tornamira?"

"My Lord, the atmosphere of Titan does not allow for either radio signals or laser links to orbit. Any other form of communication would require highly specialized equipment. Your staff communicates via secure orbital courier on a classified schedule. I can assure you that no one is broadcasting anything from Titan without security's knowledge."

The Emperor took another long drag on his cigarette and exhaled the blue smoke in a great billowing cloud. "Remus, I trust that you will do whatever is necessary to find and eliminate any threat to this project. You have my imprimatur to promote the Imperial interests in this matter. The full resources of the Imperial Navy and Intelligence Service shall be at your disposal. I will instruct Chancellor Da-Xia Liang to give you fleet credentials and a military attaché to help you navigate the shark infested waters of my naval officer corps." The Emperor chuckled at his wit.

"I shall bring this matter to a satisfactory conclusion, my Lord." He smiled and downed the last of the single malt. Remus now had what he needed to advance the next phase of his Master's plan.

CHAPTER 2

Azrael stood at the railing surrounding the magnificent pulpit of St. Stephen's Cathedral in Vienna. While he had not looked upon this glorious sculpture for more than three hundred years, he was as thrilled now as the on the day of it's unveiling — in the spring of 1515. The delicate petals erupting from the column around which the staircase wound culminated in a platform adorned with faces of the Four Doctors of the Church: St. Augustine of Hippo, St. Ambrose, St. Gregory the Great, and St. Jerome. Their faces frozen in four temperaments representing the stages of life.

A crowd of tourists were gathered near the railing, some posing for photographs, others carefully studying the intricate carvings. A small child asked his mother in a thick Anglican accent, "Mummy, who is that funny man in the window down there?" The mother followed her child's outstretched finger to the figure of a man dressed in the robes and cap of a Renaissance artist, leaning out of a window carved into the base of the pulpit.

She smiled and instructed her child, "He is the

fenstergucker. Some people believe that it is a self-portrait of Anton Pilgram — the man who made this wonderful staircase and pulpit."

The child looked up at his mother with a thoughtfully furrowed brow and said as his face broke into a wide grin, "He must have been a funny man to do such a thing."

Azrael smiled to himself. The innocence of a child is truly a miracle, he thought. The air behind him shifted ever so gently, like a sudden summer breeze. He turned to find his superior standing behind him, wearing a look of grave concern.

"Greetings, my Brother. We must speak of your work presently," said the tall figure with silver hair.

"Hello, Brother Hamaliel. Shall we retire to a more private spot?" replied Azrael.

The two separated from the growing crowd of tourists and walked to the Chapel of St. Eligius, across the nave of the great cathedral on the south side of the entrance. As they entered, Hamaliel closed the iron gate to discourage anyone from entering. The chapel was lit only by the sunlight streaming through the two ancient stained glass windows, casting a spectrum of colors across the face of the *Hausmuttergottes* statue. They chose a pew at the front of the chapel and took a seat.

"Why do you look troubled, Brother Hamaliel?" Azrael enquired.

"I have been sent by Muriel of the First Choir to seek your counsel on a very grave matter." Hamaliel had a tendency to be dramatic, but Azrael sensed this was not one of those times and that he should reflect his superior's seriousness.

"The First Choir?" Azrael did not hide his surprise.

"It seems that the Enemy is on the move again and has put in motion certain events that require a direct response. Muriel and the Others are hopeful that your time among the Children affords you a unique perspective on how best to address the situation. As you know, our brethren of the First Choir have less practical experience in these matters." Hamaliel's face was sullen and it troubled Azrael deeply.

"Brother, I sense that your spirit is burdened. I will certainly endeavor to be of assistance to Muriel and the Others. I pray I may have insights that will aid them in devising a strategy against our Enemy," Azrael replied sincerely.

"Azrael, the Enemy has identified a planet some distance from Earth — orbiting Upsilon Andromedae. We have verified that they have influenced the Emperor and set his eye on this world. Even now, a great starship is being constructed to take the Enemy and the foolish Children who follow them to conquer this new world. This must not come to pass," he said resolutely. Hamaliel searched Azrael's eyes for understanding and listened to his spirit for any sign of hesitation.

Azrael immediately understood the implications of the Enemy gaining access to technology that provided a means of escape from the home worlds. A realization assaulted his mind like a tidal wave and he nearly shouted, "Dear Brother, please tell me that this has nothing to do with my former student." He clasped his hands as in prayer and shook his head.

"I am afraid it is true, Brother. We were satisfied that your mission was successful, but it seems that the Enemy has found a way to either duplicate the efforts of your student, or they had infiltrated the project before the accident. We have been looking into the matter, but nothing is clear as yet." Hamaliel put his hand on Azrael's arm, giving it a gentle squeeze.

"My heart grieves if this is so, Brother. This weighs heavily on my spirit and I must be allowed to put it right." Azrael covered his superior's hand with his own.

"The project is being developed at a hidden laboratory on Titan. We believe the ship will be operational in less than six months. Our sources in the Imperial court tell us it is to be delivered to the Emperor on his Jubilee. We do not know when they plan to embark on a mission to Upsilon Andromedae, but it can be assumed they will waste little time once the ship is operational. This Emperor has proven himself to be a man of decisive action." Hamaliel could sense the upwelling of determination in Azrael. This warmed him with hope.

Azrael began to sense another thread of this story forming in his mind. Hamaliel did not need to say it, for words could not capture the nature of the forces operating on these two in this place. After saying a silent prayer for clarity, an idea crystallized in his mind.

"Any resolution of this matter must include my former student. His spirit still lies in darkness and he must be given a chance to walk in the Light again." A look of firm resolve was set on Azrael's face and his eyes glinted like icy jewels. "I know now what must be done."

After a moment of contemplation Hamaliel said, "Muriel is pleased and gives her blessing on your journey. I will pray for you and those with whom you will travel. May Our Father guide you and protect you." Hamaliel gave a warm smile, stood up from the pew and was gone in a flash of light.

Azrael turned from the pew and knelt upon the ancient stone floor, his head bowed and his hands outstretched to the sky and he sang in a powerful angelic voice, "LORD be my strength and power, and maketh my way perfect."

***

The distant evening sun was setting above the city of Aram Chaos — known simply as Chaos to the locals — casting a dusty reddish glow on the surface of the great geodesic dome of plasteel that protected the city.

Chaos was not a typical Martian city. The dome was an anachronism rendered unnecessary by the static field generators that had been in use for nearly sixty years on more modern parts of Mars. But Chaos eschewed such conveniences, favoring instead the tangible and visible comfort of a solid dome overhead.

Since the early days of colonization, Chaos had been a vibrant community of exobiologists, geologists, engineers, and the support staff and merchants that attend to such gatherings of people. In its heyday, Chaos boasted a population of nearly ten thousand souls — a somewhat large city by Martian standards. But as the scientific interests moved to other parts of Mars and the local mining operation ceased production, Chaos fell on hard times and watched its people migrate to other parts of the planet or off-world to make their fortunes on the great corporate mining vessels of the asteroid belt.

One of the main attractions of the city, then and now, was St. Dominic Guzman Franciscan Monastery. The monastery, built in a traditional style evolved on Earth during the Dark Ages, looked as though it had been plucked from a remote village in Italy and transported to

26

the surface of Mars. A small rustic church with a bell tower capped by a simple wooden cross dominated the center portion of the complex. Arrayed around a large central courtyard and colonnade were the cloister, the chapter house, the guest house, and a school. The entire property was surrounded by a four meter high wall made of dark grey hematite stones quarried from the bed of an ancient river that flowed just south of the crater from which the city took its name. The buildings were made mostly of brick manufactured from the ubiquitous Martian soil, while other parts were fabricated via modern means, yet designed to look like rough hewn wooden beams, terra-cotta tiles, and plaster. The overall effect was very convincing, especially to someone who had never seen an ancient building on Earth constructed of natural materials.

At eight o'clock the church bell rang, calling the monks to vespers. Silently the men gathered in the church, settling into their well-worn pews as they had done for more than three centuries. The superior at the altar raised his hands above his head in praise and the men began to sing, *"Deus, in adiutorium meum intende. Domine, ad adiuvandum me festina. Gloria Patri, et Filio, et Spiritui Sancto. Sicut erat in principio, et nunc et semper, et in saecula saeculorum. Amen. Alleluia."*

One of the monastery residents, however, was not in attendance this evening. He had not attended a vesper service in the twenty-seven years he had been in residence at St. Dominic's. Tonight Father Bożydar Jofre was in his preferred seat — a barstool at the *Rocket Man Club* — reading his tattered Bible and drinking vodka. Through bloodshot eyes he read the words, *"For by Him all things were created, both in the heavens and on earth, visible and invisible, whether thrones or dominions or rulers or authorities — all things have been created by Him and for Him. And He is before all things, and in Him all things hold together."*

Although quite intoxicated, the Jesuit scholar's mind was still sharp and he pondered the words. He wondered what God thought of His creation, mankind, who had outgrown his cradle and wandered the stars. Was He pleased with the worlds man had built? Was this His plan for human beings?

Father Bożydar drank the remains of his vodka and waved to the bartender, "Good night, Karl. See you tomorrow."

The bartender looked up from his sink full of dirty shot glasses and beer mugs, "Good night, Father. Sleep well."

The priest rose from the stool and stumbled past the tables of patrons, smiling to those who met his gaze. He knew every face and could feel their pitiful stares follow him out the door. Once, many years before, he was a treasure to the community of scientists and their children who attended St. Dominick's School. His reputation and achievements in academia ensured a steady enrollment of the brightest students from the city. But as time went on, the many arguments with parents and drunken episodes in the streets of Chaos made the old priest a caricature in the eyes of his neighbors. The great scholar who was now a common drunk.

He stepped into the climate controlled night air of the Old Village Square, and did not notice the figure watching him with sympathetic eyes from across the street.

Azrael watched as the old priest, dressed in his traditional black Jesuit cassock, its ebony buttons glistening in the light of the street lamps, turned the corner and headed toward the monastery.

Father Bożydar staggered down the rapidly darkening side street, his mind conjuring crouching demons with red eyes and sharps fangs lurking just out of sight in the shadows. With his nightly panic rising he suddenly felt a breeze rustle his hair and startle him. Such atmospheric anomalies did not happen inside of a domed city and he became immediately aware that he was not alone. The old priest spun around quickly, almost falling backward, his heart pounding in his chest.

When he regained his balance he found himself staring into the face of a young man with piercing blue eyes that sparkled brightly, even in the near darkness of the evening. He wore a simple blue, waist length jacket and khaki trousers tucked into fashionable black leather half-calf boots. His swimmer's build was topped off by a glorious head of shoulder-length blond hair that fell gently to frame a handsome, almost beautiful, face.

The stranger smiled and spoke, "Father Jofre, my name is Azrael Vrubel. I have come a long way to meet you in the hope that you may be willing to help an old friend."

"An old friend? I have no 'old friends', young man," he said as he thrust his hands deep into the pockets of his cassock.

"Perhaps we could go inside and discuss this over a cup of coffee, Father?" Azrael gestured toward the monastery at the end of the street.

Father Bożydar laughed loudly and said, "If you want a cup of coffee, there is a diner two blocks that way," pointing behind Azrael. "I am going to say my prayers and welcome dreams of a better place." He turned to leave, but then offered, "There is a hostel at the East end of town — *The Governor's Inn*. They put on a nice breakfast spread."

Azrael smiled, closed his eyes and bowed his head slightly, realizing the man would require a more direct approach.

After a few steps the priest looked back over his shoulder feeling a bit guilty at having dismissed the young man so quickly. But as his eyes focused on the spot where they had been speaking, he found no one there. That's odd, he thought.

Moments later the old priest was lying in his bed, snoring loudly to the displeasure of his monastic neighbors. The unadorned walls of his room contained nothing but a simple crucifix hung above the head of his bed. A small table held a lantern, his Bible, and a genuine wooden box containing a set of ancient sacramental articles from the nineteenth century that had been a gift from his father on the day of his ordination. It sat unopened, covered in a thin layer of reddish Martian dust.

Bożydar Jofre was an exceptionally gifted scholar holding a Doctorate in Theology, a Doctorate in Philosophy, and a Master's Degree in Biblical Archaeology. He had studied at some of the most prestigious universities on Earth including Harvard Divinity School and Oxford. There was a time when he was a man of great faith, the kind who could inspire others by the sheer force of his conviction and the inescapable logic of his apologetic arguments. But as his vocation took him from one teaching post to another, and yet another, he realized that he had nothing of substance to stand as a testimony to a life well-lived. His only real companions were the stacks of ancient books that cluttered every available inch of his cramped quarters. Even his colleagues found ample ways to avoid social situations with the priest, for fear of being singed by the fire of his intellect, or being humiliated in front of their peers as he dissected their arguments with the precision of a surgeon.

After twenty years of university life, Jofre was granted permission from his order to take a post as a teacher at a mission school on Mars. The prospect of leaving Earth, likely to never return, was not difficult for him. His only lament was that he could not transport his thousands of treasured books. The cost of such a cargo was prohibitive, even for a wealthy person of the twenty-sixth century, much less a penniless priest. He was only allowed to carry fifty kilos of cargo, barely enough for his clothing, and a few personal effects. While all of the books he cherished were available electronically — as was every book or published work ever written — he preferred the weight of a printed book in his hands. The varieties of paper stocks, the beautiful bindings, the warm leather covers, and the unique smell of each volume made reading so much more than mere absorption of information. If that were his sole intent, he would have had a cerebral implant, or biofeed, as most Imperial citizens had chosen.

Tonight, like most nights, Father Bożydar found no peace in his slumber. His dreams were filled with flashes of vicious arguments with peers from times long passed, and moments from his childhood tending to his father's apple orchard in the tiny farming community of Groblje, Serbia. Night after night his mind would replay scenes from fleeting friendships, disappearing joy, and lost peace.

As with most night, he was entering the stage of his dream where he found himself running on an endless pier near a turbulent ocean. The planks of the pier were slick beneath his feet, causing him to stumble repeatedly.

Through the fog of his dream state, Father Bożydar began hearing a single note far off in the distance, like a trumpet call. The sound grew louder and came closer in the dream, but he could not discern its direction. He searched frantically in his mind for the source of the sound, but was summoned awake as the sound filled the small confines of his room. He opened his eyes to see a brilliant light, pure white, and of an intensity that should have blinded him instantly, yet strangely caused him no pain. Staring into the center of the light he could sense the outline of a figure emerging and drawing near. The trumpet suddenly ceased and a voice, powerful yet barely more than a whisper — not even a sound but a vibration in the priest's soul — began to speak to him.

"Can mortal man be in the right before God? Can a man be pure before his Maker? Even in his servants he puts no trust, and his angels he charges with error; how much more those who dwell in houses of clay, whose foundation is in the dust, who are crushed like the moth." The voice subsided and the air was charged and filled with a white glow.

Father Bożydar recoiled into the corner of his bed with the blanket pulled up tightly to his chin, trembling with fear. Tears streamed down his face and he cried, "Why, Oh Angel of the LORD, do you speak to me from Job? I am old and tired and do not wrestle with God."

The voice replied, "One of His Children is suffering

and in need of comfort, but you wouldst deny the LORD your God."

The priest shot up straight in his bed pleading, "Who is suffering? Tell me! Please, oh please tell me and I will go to him this night! In the name of God this is my pledge o' merciful Angel!"

The light began to dwindle and fade and the voice replied only, "Go!"

***

A loud persistent thumping on the thick door of Father Bożydar's room dragged him back to consciousness. He threw back the covers and stumbled to the door, holding his forehead with one hand while he unlatched the door with the other. On the other side of the door he found a very unhappy looking Brother Humberto.

"Dear God, Brother! Look at you! It is 0800 and school is about to begin and you are not dressed or bathed! What shall we do with your students?" Brother Humberto held the door open and watched as Father Bożydar fumbled about the room for his slippers.

"I...I...what time did you say? 0800? Oh God...he may have left already. Oh, I was so rude...such a fool!" The priest was whirling about the room putting on his cassock, combing his hair, and searching for his rosary all at once.

"What are you talking about? Are you alright? You seem to be...upset, Brother. Shall I call the doctor?" A look of genuine concern replaced the angry look on the young monk's face.

Father Bożydar stopped, and clasping Brother Humberto by his shoulders said, "Tell Brother Wilson that I have an important appointment in town this morning and that I will be back before lunch. Give my apologies for being so forgetful and not making arrangements for the students. Have Brother Alex monitor an automated lesson — he can choose anything that he likes — and I will be back in class this afternoon." He smiled and patted the monk on the chest, stepped past him and was out the door, scurrying down the dim corridor, leaving the young monk dumbfounded.

Traveling much faster than a man of his age should, Father Bożydar trotted down Bradbury Lane, through the Old Town Park, across Burroughs Avenue, and up the steps of the Governor's Inn. He stopped at the top of the stairs of the faux brownstone with his hands on his knees, panting, beads of sweat running down his forehead and cheeks.

Darius Nama appeared at the entrance and seeing the wheezing priest, immediately came his aid. "Father Jofre, please come inside and sit down. Why are you so out of breath?"

"Thank...you...Darius," the priest replied between breaths.

Nama led him to a cluster of comfortable chairs in front of a large window that overlooked a garden on the side of the house. The priest collapsed into a red velvet chair and wiped his brow with a handkerchief yanked from the pocket of his cassock.

"Kalana! Please bring some cold water for Father Bożydar. Quickly!" The young woman behind the check-in desk nodded and disappeared through the doorway of the office.

"Thank you very much...I am feeling a bit better." Kalana returned with a tall tumbler of ice water and a small towel and handed them to her father.

The priest, his hands trembling, took the water from Mr. Nama and took a long drink, spilling some of the liquid on the front of his cassock. "Please...Mr. Nama, tell me...do you have a young man staying here? He would have checked in last evening after sunset," he asked with an expectant grin.

"A young man? No, Father...there is only an elderly couple from Utopia Planitia. And of course the Barrett family. They have been here for a week now since the fire." The innkeeper looked at him with sympathetic eyes.

Father Bożydar had not considered that the young man from the previous night might have left Chaos or had other lodging arrangements. The priest stood up and thanked Mr. Nama for his hospitality and kindness. He left the inn over the protestations of the man and his daughter and walked across the street to the Old Town Park.

He took a seat on a bench under a shade tree and tried to recover his breath and his dignity. What a spectacle he must be, running around town like a lunatic. Reaching into his pocket, he took out his rosary, made the sign of the cross, bowed his head and began to pray, "*I believe in God, the Father Almighty, Creator of heaven and earth; and in Jesus Christ, His only Son, our Lord; Who was conceived by the Holy Spirit, born of the Virgin Mary, suffered under Pontius Pilate, was crucified, died, and was buried. He descended into hell; the third day He arose again from the dead. He ascended into heaven, and sits at the right hand of God, the Father Almighty; from thence He shall come to judge the living and the dead. I believe in the Holy Spirit, the Holy Catholic Church, the communion of Saints, the forgiveness of sins, the resurrection of the body and life everlasting. Amen.*"

A voice to his right repeated, "Amen."

The priest recognized the voice and opened his eyes to

see Azrael seated beside him, smiling.

"Did you witness the indignity of my running around Old Town looking for you?" The priest put the rosary back into his pocket.

"You are very fit for a man of seventy-two." Azrael's smile widened.

The priest gave a nervous smile then said, "Please forgive me for my rude behavior last night. I was...well...not myself and should not have treated you so harshly."

"Father Jofre, I took no offense but your apology is accepted. Now let us talk of why I have come."

"You said something about an old friend," the priest replied.

"Yes, your former student and friend Kavan Ferre. I need to find him and I was hoping that you would be willing to help me." Azrael's smile was gone, replaced by a look of urgency.

"Is he in some kind of trouble? And who are you...an Imperial Marshal?" The priest could not imagine that his friend may be involved in a criminal matter.

"No, Father. He is not in trouble with The Law. But I do need to find him and seek his help in a matter of great importance and urgency."

Father Bożydar searched the young man's face for any trace of deceit, but found only truth in his crystalline eyes.

"I would like to help you, but have not had contact with Kavan in several years. Our last meeting was not, shall we say, pleasant. He is a very sad and broken man — not the fervent young man I once knew. I pray for him daily and even dream of him from time to time." The priest put his hand to his mouth remembering the terrifying vision during the night.

"Father, it is important that you trust me in this request. You must have faith that the bonds of friendship and love are greater than the chains of sorrow and regret." Azrael put his hand on the shoulder of the old priest, feeling the man start to tremble.

"I had a dream last night...or a hallucination. A great light came to me — perhaps an angel — and spoke to me words from Job, as a warning I think. He told me that someone was suffering and in need of comfort...and that I should 'Go'." The priest paused, then looked into Azrael's eyes searching for an answer. "How can this be?"

"Do you believe the words of the Apostle's Creed, Father?" Azrael stood looking down upon the priest.

Father Bożydar looked up at the young man and felt his gaze pierce his soul. "Yes I do...although I am an unfaithful servant."

"If you believe these words then you know in your heart that there is more to this world than you see with your eyes."

As Azrael spoke the words, the old priest's mind was opened and he knew the true nature of the man standing before him.

"Come Bożydar Jofre, son of Almodar Jofre, whose orchards were blessed and plentiful all the days of his life. Come, teacher of men, and faithful servant of the Living God. Our Father has called you and his angel has arrived to be your companion, protector, and guide. Take nothing with you and follow me." Azrael's face was set in a determined yet inviting grin, his hand outstretched to the old priest.

Tears began to flow down the cheeks of the old man.

His face broke into a wide smile and he said, "Azrael, Angel of Heaven...I will go." The priest took the rosary from his pocket and laid it on the bench, then took Azrael's hand, stood, and walked off across the park.

CHAPTER 3

Nianzu Chao stepped off the jitney at a platform near the Old Ferry Building on the Embarcadero. He quickly crossed the busy street, which bustled with electric vehicles of all sizes and types, and entered a very trendy but shabby looking tavern called *Hump's*. He scanned the handful of booths and tables for the face of Marco Bisbal-Rivera, a man wanted by the Imperial Marshals and the Imperial Intelligence Service (IIS) for a laundry list of crimes against the Empire. Señor Bisbal-Rivera was in every sense of the word a pirate, whose actual crimes and adventures were surpassed only by the legends of him whispered over pints of ale in the dark corners of old public houses.

Chao spotted the rather unremarkable looking man seated at a table in the far corner of the tavern chatting up a buxom blonde woman. As he approached the table, two large men appeared seemingly out of nowhere to block his path. Rivera's attention was immediately drawn away from the woman and, seeing that his guest had arrived, gave a small whistle. The men parted like elevator doors.

"*Bom día, Señor Chao! Como vai?*" The pirate greeted the spy in his native Portuguese.

"*Tudo bem, obrigado Señor Lisbal-Rivera. E você?*" Chao replied in perfectly accented Brazilian Portuguese.

"*Eu estou bem também,*" Rivera said politely.

"And who is your friend, Señor Rivera?" asked Chao, switching to Standard English, nodding slightly to the flirtatious young lady.

"She is just leaving." Rivera turned to the young lady and said, "Go wait for me at the bar, dear. I have some business to attend to." The woman smiled and silently complied, her hips swaying as she walked to the bar.

"Señor Rivera," Chao said, glancing around the room, "I was hoping we could speak in a more private setting. You are taking an unnecessary risk showing your face on Earth in such a public place." It was only because of his status within the IIS that Chao could risk being seen with a wanted criminal. The intelligence service computers would undoubtedly analyze the surveillance data and identify Chao. The vast heuristic data network would instantly review his recent actions, travel, meetings, voice and electronic communications, analyze the various threads and relationships to current covert operations, threats, and potential scenarios, and construct a narrative to deliver to a human intelligence analyst who would determine whether any special action was warranted.

"This bar is as safe as the bridge of my ship. Even the prying eyes of the formidable IIS cannot reach us in here. We may speak frankly and openly about our prospective business relationship." Rivera wore an inscrutable expression. No matter how much time Chao spent with non-Asians, he found it very difficult to interpret their faces.

"If you are content that we are safe, so be it. You are the one who is hunted by the Emperor." Chao enjoyed having a position that allowed him to poke at even the most dangerous of the Empire's enemies.

"What is it that I can do for you, Señor Chao?" The pirate was ready to get down to business.

"I will not mince words — I need you to steal a ship." Chao let the words hang in the air awaiting Rivera's reaction.

"I am disappointed that you would waste my time with such a mundane request," Rivera said. "Surely you have any number of petty thieves on your IIS payroll."

"This ship is special. It is to be delivered to the Emperor himself on the day of his Jubilee." Chao was determined to reveal only enough information to gain the pirate's assistance.

The pirate raised an eyebrow and gave a slight nod. "Okay, what is so 'special' about this particular ship, other than its owner?"

"This ship was built at a shipyard in orbit around Titan. But what truly makes it unique is the drive system. It was developed at a secret laboratory on Titan and with it the Emperor will gain the ability to extend his reach and power in ways that are, shall we say, excessive." While Chao was certainly trying to manipulate the pirate, he wanted to convey his commitment to the mission and the grave nature of the threat.

Rivera wore a look of disgust and demanded, "Señor Chao, what would cause a high level intelligence officer to openly solicit a wanted pirate to help him commit treason against the Emperor? You must forgive my skepticism, but

I have not lived this long by being a naive fool. Unless you tell me exactly what this mission is about and why this ship is so important, you will not only lose my interest, but you will not leave here alive."

Chao knew he was risking his life by meeting face-to-face with Rivera. It had taken two months and a series of contacts and couriers to arrange the meeting. But he was an experienced intelligence operative and knew how this particular chess game was played.

"Alright, Señor Rivera. I will tell you everything, but don't ever threaten me again. Do you think I would agree to meet you without having planned for every contingency?" Chao parried and waited for Rivera to make his next move.

"Yes, yes of course," Rivera dismissed Chao's comment with a wave of his hand. "I am growing tired of this."

Chao knew he had the man's interest piqued otherwise he would have been gone already.

"Our Emperor has been compromised by someone who is playing out an agenda and using the resources of the Empire for his own purposes. You are familiar with the name Remus Arin?" Chao asked.

"Arin...yes...he is an Ambassador of some sort. I have heard of him," Rivera said. The beginnings of interest appeared in his eyes.

"Remus Arin is an impostor. I have made inquiries outside of the government and his background is a complete fabrication. Yet, strangely, all of his references attest to his personal history and pass even the most sensitive integrity probes. Those who vouch for him are utterly convinced in the fiction he has constructed, yet I cannot find any tangible evidence of this man's life prior to his application for government service nearly twenty years ago. Even if he was a spy or rogue operator, he would have a record in a system somewhere in the Empire. But this man is a ghost — and that is impossible."

Even though Rivera had been born on Mars and had spent much of his life in space, he knew that every person in the Empire, on every allied world, asteroid, station and ship was under constant surveillance. At birth, each citizen and servant was implanted with millions of autonomous intelligent nano-machines that would migrate throughout the body forming what was essentially a secondary neural network. The nano-machines performed a plethora of useful functions from monitoring and reporting medical information, repairing minor damage to muscles, tendons, and bones, and diagnosing disease at its earliest stages. The cell-sized robots each had a unique identification code and communicated with each other and any external system via a meshed network. The result was each person bore a completely unique identity more precise than a fingerprint or retinal pattern, that announced itself each time it came within range of an embedded network. For the average citizen or servant who moved entirely within the Imperial sphere, this meant that every heartbeat, every breath, and every step they took was recorded, cataloged and available for analysis by hundreds of government, and even some corporate, entities. True privacy and personal liberty had been bred out of most of the human race.

Rivera wore a puzzled expression. He leaned forward and offered, "Wouldn't a spy take great care to have a convincing cover. Why would he leave such an obvious loose end?"

"I do not know, but I agree, it does not make sense. The

only thing I can reason is that he is not concerned with being discovered." Chao could sense Rivera's mind turning over this mystery. "But no matter. I am certain that Remus Arin is not who or what he claims to be."

"Alright, while that's interesting, it doesn't explain what Ambassador Arin has to do with this secret ship you wish me to steal?" Rivera motioned to the bartender to bring a bottle to the table.

Chao saw that Rivera was sufficiently invested in the story so far and decided he would cautiously continue to draw him into the drama. "Arin was appointed to his current position as Ambassador-at-Large after one personal audience with the Emperor. He was elevated from a provincial governor in Budapest, where he had only been serving for less than a year, to a position that has unfettered access to the Emperor of mankind!" Chao was embarrassed by his indiscreet outburst and noticed that several of the patrons were looking in their direction.

Rivera gave the gawking patrons at a nearby table a severe glare and they quickly looked away. "Go on, please," he urged Chao, leaning forward.

Lowering his voice, Chao continued, "Arin has somehow used his influence with the Emperor and persuaded him to undertake the project to build the secret laboratory and a ship on Titan. The resources that must have been mobilized to undertake such a project are staggering, even for the Empire. And this was done outside all of the normal channels. There was no appropriation by the Ministry of Defense, and I can find no records of any fleet operations transferring personnel, equipment, or material. As far as the government is concerned, this operation does not exist." Chao sat back and folded his arms, feeling a great sense of satisfaction at finally sharing the fruits of his solitary investigation.

Rivera stared at a dartboard on the wall with his mouth open, trying to process what Chao had just told him. His stomach began to twist into a familiar knot — his body's signal that he was treading onto dangerous ground.

The bartender approached after a slight nod from Rivera. He set down a bottle of Mendoza Malbec and two wine glasses and poured a taste for Señor Rivera. He picked up the glass, sniffed the aroma long and deeply, then swirled the burgundy liquid around and finished with a dramatic slurp. He grinned at the barman and indicated he should pour his guest first.

When the wine was poured he rose his glass to Chao and said, "*Saúde!*"

Chao echoed in Standard English, "Yes, to our health." He took a polite taste of the wine, trying to ignore the dry acidic flavor. He much preferred a simple rice wine for occasions such as this.

"So if this project is what you say it is," said Rivera returning to the business at hand, "surely it must be well-guarded. That means the risk to my men and ships will be great. And that naturally increases the fee for my services."

Chao was pleased that Rivera was obviously beginning to think about compensation which meant he had effectively set the hook. He smiled and said, "Señor Rivera, if you agree to assist me in this matter, you will be compensated such that you may think of retiring from your current line of work."

The pirate laughed so loud and long that even his bodyguards were amused and gave an audible chuckle from their table near the bar. "Señor Chao, you may know many things about diplomacy and the dark world of intelligence, but you know nothing of me and my people. You offend me with your polite words and diplomatic demeanor. You are nothing but a small man begging after table scraps from the tyrant the people call 'Emperor'". Rivera leaned across the table and was gesturing uncomfortably close to Chao's face. "He claps his hands you come — he waves his hand and you go. Don't ever make the mistake of believing that those of us in this noble profession are simpletons or motivated only by profit. We are not like those privateers of Earth's ancient seas. You will never understand what drives us, and that is why we shall always remain free and outside The Law."

"But Señor Rivera, I do understand you. The lifestyle you lead gives you many advantages, indeed you have a degree of freedom, but you are still subject to The Law. If you think otherwise then you, sir, are the naive one. Imagine having the ability to make your own law." He watched the pirate's eyes narrow as he tried to unravel Chao's meaning. "Imagine a world of your own, sovereign, and outside the sphere of the Empire."

Rivera sat back in his chair, folding his arms across his chest, and staring coldly into Chao's eyes. "What is it exactly you are offering?"

Chao knew he had his fish. "Señor Rivera, if you deliver the Emperor's ship to me, I will give you Titan."

***

Azrael and Father Bożydar boarded the train that would take them from Aram Chaos to Huygens, a bustling equatorial city and home to the largest manufacturing complex in the solar system. They found seats across from one another separated by a small table with a NexLink terminal embedded in the surface. While most Imperial citizens accessed the Comex network via biofeed to interact with the artificial intelligence of the Empire-wide data network, Martian colonists preferred to use old-fashioned terminals that required gestures or voice commands to access the local planetary AI network. As a result of this anachronistic cultural oddity, the technology of the Martian colonial sphere was more prominent in daily life. This stood in stark contrast to Imperial worlds and colonies where objects, furniture, appliances, clothing, and transportation was designed to focus one's attention on form and function, not on the advanced technology embedded within.

The city of Huygens grew around the first terra-forming complex that had been constructed during the early colonial period of Mars nearly four hundred years earlier. More than a million people lived, worked, raised their children, grew old, and died there in the service of the Mars Colonial Confederation, and the factories of the Tyrrhena Complex. When the Martian Orbital Lift System (MOLS) was built, the population of Huygens steadily climbed as colonists and corporations came to exploit the newly opened world of Mars. Proximity to the MOLS gave the corporations easy access to orbit and the mineral wealth of the asteroid belt. Exotic minerals that could not be mined on Mars were sent "down the rails" to the massive automated foundries on the surface. There they were transformed into the many varied metals, ceramics, and nano-tubular materials needed to build a new home for humanity in the sands of Mars, and for the vast fleets of ships that were the lifeline of the colonies.

Like the pioneers of the Old West on Earth, the colonists arrived on Mars with little in the way of possessions, having sold everything before making the journey. The people came primarily from the former United States, Canada, Mexico and Brazil, with others from a variety of smaller countries. But in the early days of Mars colonization the shared dream of a better life was the mortar that held together the bricks of the new civilization. Languages and culture were carefully preserved and eventually blended into a new mosaic forming the basis of a truly unique Martian culture. No matter what hardships the colonists were forced to endure, they cherished their freedom from The Law and the homogenizing influence of the Empire that had consumed all of the hundreds of former sovereign nations of Earth.

The Mars colony was the first true home away from Earth that had any real hope of one day being self-sufficient and completely autonomous. The founding colonists knew that they, indeed perhaps even their great grandchildren, would never fully enjoy the fruits of their labor. Yet they were resolute in their desire to create a new home for mankind, scratched from the soil and rocks of the lifeless red planet.

One by one the great atmospheric generators where built strategically around the planet — the first step in a centuries-long process to terraform Mars and bring life once again to this ancient world. The polar regions were seeded with genetically modified plants and bacteria that could grow and thrive in the frigid temperatures. Within twenty years the polar regions were blanketed in a dense layer of dark green biomass. This raised the average global temperature above the freezing point of carbon dioxide and began the liberation of gaseous CO_2 into the atmosphere. The atmospheric generators used the heat from massive fusion power plants to process perchlorate bound in the Martian soil. The generators also pumped oxygen, nitrogen, and hydrocarbons into the atmosphere to jumpstart the greenhouse process that would rapidly warm the planet and increase atmospheric pressure.

By the late twenty-third century, the equatorial regions of Mars had been transformed into a landscape with a reborn ocean and rushing rivers that brought newly melted glacial water from the mountain peaks and once-frozen aquifers to the settled regions. The average temperature was adequate to begin greenhouse farming on a massive scale and allowed settlers to venture outside the domes and pressurized structures without the need for cumbersome life support suits. Now, people could work the land and enjoy the unexplored Martian landscape in a comfortable biosuit outfitted with a CO_2 converter/rebreather. Colonists could spend hours in the sunshine and feel the relatively warm Martian breeze. Tourism had finally arrived on Mars.

Father Bożydar stared out the large window of the train car, watching the lush green farmlands pass by. He was exhausted, but his mind still reeled from the fact that the vision from his dream was now seated across from him sipping a cup of tea. The reality of what he was about to do was like a heavy weight on his chest. Was he really going to simply abandon his students, the monks, and the monastery — his home for nearly thirty years? He had left without a goodbye or a blessing, running down the street like a madman. What was he doing?

Azrael sensed the turmoil and doubt in the old priest's

spirit and he knew he needed comfort and reassurance for the journey ahead. He asked gently, "Father, do you believe that God has a sovereign plan for each soul?"

"Yes, I do," the priest replied quietly, turning his gaze to Azrael.

"Then you must trust that what we are about to do together has been planned from before your birth, indeed since the foundation of the universe. I have witnessed many glorious things in my life. But I have also seen men of great faith wither in the face of the unknown. Be assured that the very hand of Our Father is upon you this day." Azrael gave Father Bożydar a warm smile and then leaned his head back and closed his eyes.

The old priest considered Azrael's words and knew that he spoke the truth. His mind echoed with questions, but now, he needed to sleep. There would be ample time for questions.

As the priest fell into a deep sleep, aided by the gentle hum of the train, Azrael reached out with his mind and probed the edges of the priest's subconscious. Like he had done so many times throughout his life, he would enter the strange and sometimes frightening world of human dreams. For Azrael and others of his kind, it was a strenuous task to navigate the subconscious flashes of memory, the emotional eddies and currents, and the torrent of hidden desires of a mortal being. He needed to find a place where Father Bożydar felt safe, an island of calm in the cacophonous sea of dreams. Only there could he begin the process of teaching his new student.

Azrael saw the priest standing on a pier near a deep blue sea. He was dressed in a billowing white cotton shirt caught in the warm ocean breeze, and a pair of Bermuda shorts. He was young, perhaps thirty years old in this dream, and his skin was bronzed from long days in the sun. Haiti. This was Haiti, when the young Jesuit was on a vacation from his university duties. He could feel joy emanating from the man's spirit — a joy that had long since abandoned him leaving him barren and cold.

The priest was watching the sea birds float above the breaking waves. His face was peaceful and his mind was quiet, giving Azrael the moment he was hoping for. With a simple act of will, Azrael stepped across the invisible boundary that separates the mind from the physical universe and stood beside the young priest.

A young and vibrant Bożydar Jofre turned and his eyes widened then his face erupted into a broad smile, his white teeth gleaming in the sunshine of his dream. "How did you find me? Is there no place man can hide?"

"Is that what this place is, Father," Azrael said looking around the scene, "a refuge for you?" He leaned casually against the white wooden railing of the pier in a relaxed pose.

"I suppose it is, although I have never thought of it as such. I come here more and more lately, in my dreams. These were very happy days for me. The best of my life I think." His expression changed to that of a man searching his memories for the face of a long-lost lover. "There is something about this pier that draws me, but I cannot remember what it is. Honestly, I don't remember ever walking out here when I spent the summer in Tiburon." He shook his head and shrugged, "Perhaps I will never solve it. I should just enjoy the breeze and the smell of the sea."

The overflow of the man's contented spirit washed over

Azrael like the waves breaking on the shore below. He never tired of the closeness, the intimacy of contact with humans. He felt sorry for the others of his kind who would never know this feeling.

"Father, there are certain facts that I must share with you. They involve your friend, Kavan Ferre, and will be very difficult for you to understand at first. I must ask that you allow me to speak candidly of the events leading up to our meeting, so that you may know what is at stake. You must trust me and listen with your spirit rather than with your mind. The Enemy will use your intellect to drive fear into your spirit, and raise doubt in you." Azrael's eyes flashed with intensity and Bożydar only nodded in reply.

"First, you must know with whom you are speaking, so that the authority of the words I speak be known to you. I am Azrael, of the Third Triad, Servant of the Living God, who was made before the foundation of the world, messenger, protector and teacher of mankind." As he spoke the words his body began to shimmer and radiate a brilliant but gentle white light giving his skin and hair the appearance of being illuminated from within. "For all the days of existence I have labored in the service of Our Father to care for humanity, guiding and teaching those to whom I was sent. My life has witnessed many of the great triumphs of mankind. I stand in the breach as a guardian against the forces of the Enemy who exists only to steal the gift of life, bestowed by the LORD as a promise to those who would know him and call him Father."

Bożydar's face was wet with tears and he began to kneel down before the vision of the illuminated being.

"Do not kneel down before me, Child!" Azrael's voice thundered across the sky, shattering the peaceful scene in the priest's mind. "Only Our Father is worthy of your worship." He bent and grasped the priest's shoulders, standing him up and drawing him close to his face.

"But how can this be?" The priest wept and trembled in the arms of the angel.

"Search your spirit and there you will find that for which you have sought all your life. The Spirit of Our Father has been searching the horizon for you, calling you home to him. You are home now and He welcomes you with open arms." Azrael embraced the old priest as one would hold a frightened child.

Azrael led Bożydar from their pier with his arm around his shoulders and sat him down in the warm white sand of the beach.

"Now, I must tell you that which has gone before so that you may understand and begin our journey with a heart and a spirit that is prepared for battle."

Bożydar sat with his legs crossed, wiped his eyes and said, "Teach me."

***

Commander Sumiko Lee stood in the lobby of the Fleet Special Operations Center in Singapore, nervously waiting to be called into a mission briefing with Admiral Evgeni Sivorenko and his command staff. This was a day she had dreamed of since earning her commission — an assignment that, if successful, would catapult her to the next level of Navy elite staff and ensure a lifestyle that she had only heard rumors of.

Sumiko was born in a slum of Tokyo to Imperial servants. Her mother was a governess to a mid-level executive at a biotechnology firm, and her father was a jitney tender for the Ministry of Environmental

Engineering. The family lived in a small government apartment with one bedroom, a parlor, bathroom, and food processing station. She spent most of her childhood on the floor of the parlor where she played, ate, slept and attended school via hololink. She was an excellent student with a naturally inquisitive and analytical mind. She completed her primary and secondary studies by age fifteen and spent the next two years working on a marine research vessel in the South Pacific.

While it was not unusual for servant class children to attend university, Sumiko's appointment to the Imperial Naval Academy was extraordinary. Her parents were astonished at the news and were immediately fearful of how their only daughter would navigate the world of privilege among the children of Imperial Citizens. The transition from servant class slums to the pristine and elevated environment of the Academy was a shock at first, but Sumiko's skill at reading people and situations allowed her to adapt rapidly to her new surroundings.

By her second year, Sumiko was a squadron leader in charge of thirty of her fellow cadets. While her background was a barrier to wide acceptance by her classmates, she did manage to make two friends who would be instrumental in her career and life: Anna Domasheva, a tall, athletic blonde with the looks of a runway model and the mouth of a sailor; and Prakesh Mohapatra, or "Mo" as Sumiko called him, an awkward genius with virtually no social skills but the uncanny ability to make Sumiko laugh when she needed it most. Anna was currently serving as a tactical weapons officer on a patrol ship in the asteroid belt. Mo had been initially assigned to Naval Intelligence, but was recently recruited by a special weapons development group almost five years ago that reeked of black operations.

Sumiko had last seen Anna twelve months ago, when she was home on shore leave. They had spent a weekend together in Banda Aceh lounging on the beach and enjoying the upscale nightlife. Anna's current assignment hunting pirates in some far away sector of the asteroid belt, meant she could not keep in regular communication with Sumiko. It had been more than two years since she had seen Mo, and in the past year he had not even sent her any messages. If she stopped long enough to really think about it, she would probably worry about him. Anna too, for that matter.

The area behind Sumiko's right ear vibrated slightly alerting her to an incoming voice communication. She thought the command *'answer'* and heard a soft tone, followed by the voice of a woman. "Commander Lee, the Admiral will see you now. Please enter the briefing room."

Sumiko replied, "Thank you." She took one last glance down the front of her pure white uniform, clutched her tablet in her left hand and opened the door to the briefing room. The room was large and rectangular with a long teak conference table and twelve elegant but functional leather chairs orbiting. Admiral Sivorenko was seated at the head of the table on the left with several naval and marine officers filling the five chairs on his right, and a handsome man in his forties seated on his left. The Admiral gestured to the seat at the far end of the table and said in a prominent Russian accent, "Please, have a seat Commander Lee."

"Thank you, sir," Lee replied crisply. She moved with parade ground precision to the chair and sat down, at attention.

"Commander, please be at ease. This briefing is for your benefit." He gave her a thin smile then looked down at the tablet in front of him. "You have been selected for a special assignment on the personal authority of the Defense Minister. Only the people in this room have been briefed on the mission, and your mission profile and orders are secured and accessible exclusively by the operators on the team." He looked up from the tablet and turned to the man on his left.

"I would like to introduce you to Ambassador Remus Arin from the Foreign Office." Remus gave a slight nod and wry smile to the attractive young officer. Sumiko delivered the traditional head bow in reply and felt her cheeks flush.

The Admiral noticed the interesting eye contact between the two and cleared his throat. He continued, "Commander Lee, your assignment is as special liaison to Ambassador Arin." He saw Sumiko sit up a bit straighter and the edges of her mouth twitched betraying a suppressed smile. "You will assist the Ambassador and act as his intermediary with the command staff. Since Ambassador Arin is a civilian diplomat, he has no authority in the chain of command, however it will be necessary for him to direct the actions of Navy and Marine assets during the mission."

Lee furrowed her brow and was clearly puzzled by this strange violation of military protocol. "Sir, to clarify, Ambassador Arin will essentially be commanding military personnel, is that correct?"

The Admiral scowled and said, "Commander Lee, as much as it disturbs this old salt," he said thumbing his chest, "it is the order of the Defense Minister, so that is that."

"Aye, sir," Sumiko affirmed.

"While the mission brief has all the particulars, perhaps you would like to give Commander Lee an overview of the mission, Ambassador?" Admiral Sivorenko sat back and folded his hands across his expansive belly.

Remus pushed back from the table and walked to the center of the display area at the rear of the room. "Thank you, Admiral. Commander Lee, our mission is to escort a high-value military asset to Earth. We will take a fleet to Titan where we will establish a secure defense perimeter and then the command vessel will put in at the orbital dry dock." As he spoke a solid holographic projection of the flight path from Earth to Titan appeared floating above the floor. He gestured in the air and the perspective of the animation zoomed to reveal a large orbital dry dock station in low orbit over the rust-colored, swirling clouds of Titan. "We will immediately transfer a ferry crew and Marine detachment to board and take command of the asset."

"May I ask what the 'asset' is specifically, Ambassador?" Sumiko saw a look of concern flash across Arin's face.

"The asset is a new experimental craft that has been developed by the Special Weapons Section. That is all the information you are cleared for," Arin said flatly as he waved the simulation away and returned to his seat.

Sumiko was now very curious about the contents of the mission profile, hoping it would shed more light on the true nature of this strange assignment. "May I ask what the fleet configuration will be?"

The Admiral nodded to a pale Lt. Commander with a

precision flat-top. He responded, "The fleet will be composed of two Hakara-class destroyers, one Luda-class battleship, two Jiankai-class frigates, four Type 098 corvettes, and one Hola-class heavy cruiser. The *Honamatsu* shall carry the flag and operation command staff, as well as the Ambassador." A floating solid hologram of each ship class was displayed above the tabletop as the Lt. Commander read the list. "There will also be a company of Marines assigned to each vessel, except for the *Honamatsu* — she will carry a full Marine recon battalion. The fleet will form up on TOLS-2 upper deck and will get underway by 0700 GMT for a trans-solar maneuver and outbound trajectory insertion on a direct flight path to Titan. The outbound flight time is nine days, eleven hours. On-station time will be determined post arrival, with a direct return window of fifty-six hours, and an inbound flight time of eight days, seven hours."

Sumiko was stunned at the size of the fleet and the firepower it represented. She was careful to not let her alarm show. The mission scope and assigned resources simply did not add up in her mind. She would have to tread carefully.

"Admiral, it will be an honor to serve this mission and the Ambassador," she nodded and smiled to Arin, "and I will endeavor to make the interface between the Foreign Office staff and Operational staff as efficient as possible."

"Excellent, Commander." The Admiral looked from side to side then pushed his bulk up from the chair. The rest of his staff immediately rose from their seats. He walked around the table and met Sumiko in front of the doors. "Have a safe journey, Commander."

Sumiko executed a crisp salute, made a left-face turn and left the room. The other officers followed her out after gathering their tablets and cases. A moment later Admiral Sivorenko and Ambassador Arin were standing alone in the room.

Remus said to his counterpart, not with words, '*Thank you, Brother for making this possible. You have selected a very intriguing woman to aid me. She is quite captivating.*' He wore a broad, lascivious grin, and his eyes flashed a brilliant red.

'*It is a long journey to Titan, my Brother.*' He replied silently, raising an eyebrow. '*I am sure you will find a way to entertain yourself.*'

CHAPTER 4

The ride from Aram Chaos to Huygens had taken just over two hours, and when Father Bożydar awoke from his dream, he felt surprisingly refreshed and energized. Unlike most of his dreams, which seemed to fade as rapidly as an early morning mist, the shared experience with Azrael was crisp and clear and he could recall all of the astonishing things he had heard. His spirit soared as he considered the journey they were about to take. And he longed to see his old friend and student, Kavan Ferre.

After disembarking at the Huygens main terminal, Azrael led them to a jitney that took them to the city center and the MOLS base terminal. Azrael purchased two one-way ascent tickets and they eventually made their way to the ascender and found their seats.

Father Bożydar had not been to orbit in more than twenty years. He did not enjoy space travel and particularly disliked riding into orbit on a glorified elevator. While he knew that it was far safer than the train that had brought them to Huygens, his mind still constructed elaborate disaster scenarios that always ended in a losing battle with gravity.

The ascent was smooth and comfortable and he was able to forget his fear after a while and simply enjoy the view of his adopted home world. His heart sank and a tear formed at the corner of his eye as he realized that he would likely never see Mars again.

As the ascender arrived at the terminal and the passengers began to disembark, Father Bożydar turned to Azrael and asked the question that had not dawned on him until that very moment, "How are we going to get to Europa? There are no passenger liners that go beyond the belt."

"I have made arrangements for a private vessel. I think you will find it quite comfortable." Azrael had a way of answering questions without revealing a shred more than what was asked.

"I guess I'll just wait and be surprised then," quipped the priest.

Azrael smiled and gave him a soulful laugh.

They walked through the passenger terminal and exited into a long cylindrical causeway that led to the private slips where scores of exotic vessels where docked. The entire circumference of the causeway tube was completely transparent except for the floor, creating the illusion that one was walking in open space among the gleaming vessels painted in a variety of colors. The view was breathtaking to the old priest. It was an ostentatious display of wealth and power on a grand scale.

"You must have some very rich friends, Azrael." The priest jibed his companion.

"Actually I have a very wealthy Father."

The priest let out a hearty laugh and slapped Azrael on

the back. Azrael glanced over his shoulder at Father Bożydar and then joined in his laughter. *We must appear a strange pair to these people*, thought the priest.

They walked a bit further and then Azrael came to a stop in front of slip J316 The priest immediately deciphered the irony of the slip number and looked to Azrael with a wry smile. He turned to the priest, shrugged and touched the security pad. The door to the slip opened and they stepped into a small but beautifully appointed lounge. "Please make yourself comfortable as I prepare the ship."

Father Bożydar moved to a window and took in the sight of the ship. It was like no private vessel he had ever seen. The ship was a luminescent pearl white, with no seams or hull plating visible. The sculpted wedge of the main hull tapered gracefully on either side, ending in thin v-shaped wings, reminiscent of an atmospheric craft. There were no windows or portals to interrupt the flow of the curves, and the umbilicals and docking ring looked haphazard and unnatural attached to such a graceful craft.

"My goodness, what a beautiful ship." The priest was suddenly feeling much better about their journey.

Azrael emerged from a doorway on the opposite side of the lounge. "Father, the ship is prepared. We should get under way."

"Of course," the priest replied. He crossed the lounge and followed Azrael through the airlock of the docking ring and into the ship. They entered into a narrow corridor of bright white walls. The ceiling was interrupted only by a thin strip of translucent material that gave off a soft white light. The floor of the corridor was textured slightly to provide a comforting grip underfoot, and sparkled like the hull of the ship. Azrael turned left leading them toward what the priest expected would be the bridge. But unlike other ships of this class they entered into a large exquisitely decorated parlor. The center was a sunken circular seating area surrounding a large circular table made apparently of a smoky glass-like material. Above the table, suspended a meter below the ceiling but with no visible support, hung a crystalline orb. The surface of the orb was a shifting pattern of blue hues and white streaks, reminiscent of a planet viewed from space.

The level around the central portion was lined on one side by large oval windows through which the other nearby slips and vessels were visible. The opposite side of the room was appointed with a collection of low comfortable chairs, a duvet, and several small tables. The room had warmth and charm that was unusual for a space craft, even one of such obvious skillful design and luxury.

"If you follow the corridor in the other direction from the hatch you will find several staterooms and the galley. The engineering section is beyond that, but you should have no reason to go there." Azrael motioned to the central parlor area, "Please make yourself comfortable. We can get underway immediately."

The priest began to descend the small steps then turned and said with a humble smile, "Azrael, will you join me in prayer for our journey?"

Azrael returned the smile and helped to steady the priest as he knelt down on the parlor floor. They faced each other with their heads bowed and the priest began, "Dear Father, we ask that you bless us on this journey and give us strength and wisdom as we meet the Enemy on the field of battle. Thank you for Azrael and for the opportunity to serve you. We thank you for our lives, our faith, and the promise of everlasting life in you. Amen."

Moments later, the priest was seated on the most comfortable couch he had ever felt. He stroked the fine material and looked around the room, scarcely believing where he was. It was only a few hours ago that he was lying in his small room, drunk and lifeless. Now he was about to journey to the only other cradle of life in the solar system to rescue an old friend from darkness. He did not know how the journey would end, but he was certain — for the first time in his life — that he was exactly where God meant for him to be.

Azrael returned from the aft section and sat down across from the priest. "We are ready to depart."

"Would you like me to accompany you to the bridge? I would love to see how you pilot this amazing ship." Azrael gave Father Bożydar a sheepish grin and said, "Actually, this is the bridge. I am sorry to disappoint you, but the ship needs no piloting per se. In fact, this entire ship is for your benefit. When traveling alone I have no need of such technology."

"Yes, you can fly, of course," the priest said excitedly as if he had just solved a great mystery.

Azrael chuckled, "The depictions of our kind with wings and such is a gross exaggeration. Although the Enemy does enjoy feeding certain stereotypes."

"So how does an Angel travel?" The priest's mind was churning with new questions.

"Our kind exists in a realm that affords us freedom of movement across all states of matter and energy. Our essence is not defined as a 'spirit inhabiting a material body' like man. Instead we are a 'spirit inhabiting the Universe'. Do you understand?" Azrael searched the face and the spirit of his new student for a flicker of understanding, but felt the need to continue.

"Your body is made of atoms of carbon, mostly, and a host of other elements. It is formed and held together by the same forces that hold stars and planets together, yet you are alive. How is that so?" Azrael gestured with his hands mimicking a potter forming a pot of clay. "The collection of atoms and forces you call your body is animated and made alive by your Spirit — the part of you that *is* distinctly you! How glorious is the knowledge that for all of the souls ever created in this entire universe, you are singular and unique in all of Creation."

Father Bożydar nodded and said, "I understand. But yet your kind is not like us."

"We were created for a different purpose. Our kind is Spirit, like you, and unique, but we are not limited by a physical body, although for some of us our tasks require that we take a physical form to accomplish our work. For me and others who hold my station, we spend most of our time in some manner of physical form. We simply fashion whatever we need from the matter and energy around us. Once you understand the mechanisms that underpin the Universe, it is simply a matter of will to shape what you require." Azrael could sense the dawn of understanding beginning to illuminate the horizons of the priest's mind.

Father Bożydar looked thoughtfully and said, "I see. You shape matter and energy like a potter shapes clay to make whatever container he desires. If he needs to carry water, he makes a water jar. If he needs to eat, he fashions a bowl."

"And if I need to appear as a man, I will it to be and it is. If I need a comfortable vessel to transport an old priest, I simply imagine its shape and appointments and it is so." Azrael wore a satisfied grin. He liked his new student very much.

As they spoke, the ship glided automatically from the slip, cleared the MOLS tower complex, and established an outbound trajectory that increased steadily in speed.

Father Bożydar shook his head in amazement and said, "Now I truly understand what David meant when he wrote, *'I praise you, for I am fearfully and wonderfully made. Wonderful are your works; my soul knows it very well.'*"

Azrael sensed he had given the priest enough to ponder for one day. "Would you like to rest before we arrive at Europa? I am sure you are hungry, yes?"

Father Bożydar sat up and said, "Well I should hope I will have enough time to rest and have a meal! It will take days to get to Europa."

Azrael knew that there was so much more to explain. "Father we can arrive at Europa whenever we like. The journey will take but a moment."

The priest slapped his knees and stood. Spreading his arms wide he said, "Excellent! I think I should eat a hearty meal, get a good night's sleep, have a shower and then, explore Europa with you."

Azrael replied with a slight bow, "As you wish, Father Bożydar."

***

The flagship *Honamatsu* sat ready to leave space dock at the TOLS-2 upper deck, hovering nearly 60,000 kilometers above Earth. Ambassador Remus Arin was quite pleased at how well his Master's plan was coming together. In a few short months the final phase would be under way and a new era for his kind would begin. No longer would they be imprisoned on Earth and the few small lumps of rock that humans had colonized. Soon, they would once again have the ability to roam the universe and continue their battle against their eternal foes.

Remus was also pleased with the liaison officer Admiral Sivorenko had selected for him. He was looking forward to spending many hours in private consultation with the lovely brunette.

As the shuttle entered the landing bay aboard the *Honamatsu*, Remus gathered his tablet and placed it into a leather attaché. The final landing sequence and clearance seemed to take an exceptionally long time, adding to his frustration with being one of the last to board. Naval protocol required the most senior civilian authority to board only after the entire military contingent was aboard and arrangements had been made for an honor guard welcome. Military fanfare and traditions were not unfamiliar to Remus — he had served in scores of armies and navies across many millennia — but in these final days his patience was wearing thin.

A red light above the door flashed three times then the hatch of the shuttle began to open upward. Remus watched as a red carpet leading from the shuttle door came into view. As the hatch swung fully ajar Remus looked out upon a hangar deck lined on the right with Naval personnel and on the left with Marines, both arranged in neat ranks. The command staff was formed up in a line of white uniforms with a large petty officer holding the Imperial flag at the center. The Chief

Boatswain's Mate stepped forward from the near end of the Navy rank and sounded the *Pipe Aboard*. All the uniformed personnel simultaneously executed a salute; the sound of over one thousand fists clutched to their chests resounded across the hangar.

Well done, thought Remus to himself.

A Vice Admiral stepped forward and announced in his best command voice, "The crew and officers of the *Honamatsu* welcome you aboard, Ambassador Arin." Arin stepped down the short ramp of the shuttle and met the man's outstretched hand. "I am Admiral James Butchers and it is a great pleasure to meet you, sir."

"Thank you, Admiral. This is a very warm, but unnecessary welcome," he replied, feigning false humility.

"We hope that you will be comfortable aboard our humble ship. Your liaison officer, Commander Lee, is preparing your workspace and stateroom." The Admiral turned to the line of officers and began the introductions, "Let me first introduce the master of *Honamatsu*, Captain Jayden Daley." A handsome man with a shock of red hair stepped forward and shook Arin's hand.

"Good to meet you, sir," Captain Daley said in a lyric Irish brogue.

The Admiral continued to introduce the other officers and senior enlisted personnel. As Remus reached the end of the line his eye was drawn to a lone figure leaning casually against the railing of the mezzanine that surrounded the hangar deck. His mind flashed with rage at the sight of Nianzu Chao wearing a coy smile as he watched the fanfare of Remus' arrival from above. His mind struggled to understand how Chao could be on board. He knew that somewhere in the elaborate planning he had been betrayed and would not rest until the guilty party was found and punished. For now, however, he had to find a way to deal with the incessantly curious intelligence operative.

Once the introductions were made, the Admiral dismissed the crew and Remus was escorted to his quarters. As he stepped through the door of his stateroom, he was struck by the sweet scent of perfume. Across the parlor he could see through the open door of the his private berth the shapely form of Commander Lee. She had not noticed him yet and he took the opportunity to drink in her scent and appreciate the sight of her body. He could feel himself beginning to react physically to the pheromone cloud hanging in the room. Now was not the time to fulfill those desires, but soon enough.

Suddenly, Sumiko could sense someone watching her, and she spun around quickly, clearly startled by the sight of Ambassador Arin staring at her from across the room. She felt a strange flutter in her stomach and said, "Ambassador, sir. I'm sorry I did not hear you come in."

"I just arrived and didn't mean to startle you." He moved across the room and stood in the doorway of the berth, shamelessly letting his eyes wander over her body.

Sumiko recognized the look of unbridled lust in his eyes and was shocked that she was not immediately repulsed. Her emotions were a swirling mixture of fear, excitement, and burning passion. She wanted to simply let go and explore these feelings, but her logical mind quickly reasserted itself, "Ambassador. This is going to be a long journey and we need to be able to work together effectively. So I would appreciate it if you would keep your mind on our mission."

Remus was surprised at the directness of this dynamic young woman and it only served to stoke his desire. There would be ample time to explore the passionate dimensions of her personality later.

"Of course, Commander. Please forgive me." Remus gave a slight bow and then stepped back out of the doorway allowing her to brush against him as she hurried from the berth.

"We have a very busy day ahead of us after we clear space dock. Right now, I must to report to the Captain for a command staff meeting prior to the trans-solar run. I will call you once I am free," Sumiko said, pleased with how she had extricated herself from a potentially complicated situation.

"I will await your call, Commander," Remus said politely, trying to put his quarry at ease. "Perhaps when you are finished we can tour this magnificent ship together. I understand it has a large observation deck that is quite inspiring."

Sumiko smiled casually and said, "That would be nice, Ambassador ... and you can call me Sumiko. After all, it's going to be a long flight."

Remus raised an eyebrow and with a broad grin replied, "And you may call me Remus, Sumiko."

The young officer felt herself blushing uncontrollably again so she simply nodded and quickly left the room. As she marched down the corridor toward the bridge, she thought, *this is going to be a long trip, indeed*.

***

Marco Bisbal-Rivera strode onto the bridge of his ship, the *Boa Vista*, eminently pleased with the deal he had negotiated with Nianzu Chao. He held in his hand a

Letter of Marque issued on real parchment and signed in ink by the Emperor's own hand (and entered into the Imperial data registry) essentially pardoning him and all members of his crew for any acts of piracy in the past or future, should he be captured by any Imperial Navy or Corporate Security vessel. Additionally, Chao had delivered the necessary contracts that gave Marco Bisbal-Rivera settlement, mining rights, and sovereign status to Titan. He was not sure how the instruments would hold up in court, but once he and his people were established on Titan, the Emperor would have to send an entire fleet of Naval vessels and an occupation force to take it back.

Though his mind was focused on the seemingly endless new possibilities that a world of his own could bring, he could not quench his curiosity about the ship he was contracted to steal. Chao had alluded to the ship having an advanced drive system. Could it be possible that the Empire had discovered the secret to faster-than-light travel? Rivera was no physicist but he understood the fundamentals well enough to pilot everything from a shuttle pod to a heavy cruiser. "Breaking the barrier" as spacefarers called it, was a theoretical possibility but the technology to achieve such a feat was still believed to be in the distant future. The energy required to accelerate a craft to anything near light speed required a mass of fuel greater than any ship of reasonable proportions could carry.

But, if the Empire had by some miracle made a leap of technology, it placed the power to dominate the entire solar system in the hands of the Emperor. With so-called "Faster Than Light" or "FTL" ships, Emperor Wan Sui Ye could extend his reach beyond the home worlds and into interstellar space. The thought made Rivera shudder.

"Welcome back, Captain," roared his first officer, Tiago Maconde, from the command chair. He immediately stood and welcomed his commander with a brotherly embrace. "How was your meeting with the spook?" he jibed.

Rivera turned the command chair toward himself and fell into its familiar curves. He placed his right hand on the command panel and the Flight Control Intelligence Center (FCIC) computer instantaneously transferred command to his authority. "It went surprisingly well. He wants us to steal a ship. And he is willing to pay handsomely for it."

Tiago raised an eyebrow and curled down the ends of his mouth. "Really? How handsomely?"

"Here. Read for yourself," Rivera offered the leather folio containing the letter and contracts to his first officer.

Tiago took the folio, opened it, scanned the few pages of parchment and then exclaimed, "*Meu deus! Ele está nos dando um planeta inteiro?*"

Rivera let out a hearty laugh, "Yes, my brother...he is giving us Titan!" The two men laughed together until tears ran down their cheeks.

As the laughter subsided they regained their composure and the reality of the agreement and the reward began to sink in. Rivera said, "Tiago, this could mean a new way of life for our people. This one job could change everything. Imagine having a permanent base where we could really live and not have to run from asteroid to station to moon to empty space. No more running. My God! Our own world! It must be a dream."

"Marco, we must be cautious. Not all of our people will

see this as good news. All have chosen this lifestyle and have grown accustomed to it. Some are third and fourth generation pirates who do not know what it is like to live on the land under a sky, day after day. I don't think we have too many aspiring farmers in our band of brothers." Tiago was a first rate navigator and pilot, but was more valuable to Rivera as a man with sound judgment and a keen sense of practicality. These were very important and useful traits to a pirate captain.

"I am not talking about settling on Titan. Dear God, the place is a swirling ball of liquid hydrocarbons and barren rock. Trying to plant a settlement there would cost a fortune. But we will own the laboratory complex on the surface, the space dock, and orbital lift system they built. It would give us a place to repair our ships and even build new ones, an endless source of fuels and minerals, and a first-rate lab facility to, well, to do whatever it is you do with such a thing." He gave his first officer a crooked smile and then shrugged. "But finally we would have a place that we could fortify and defend. Within a few months we could have a fortress in the Outer Colonies that nobody would dare attack. Far enough away to be out of sight, but close enough where we could still do what we do best."

Tiago had to admit it was a very attractive proposition. A sovereign world run by pirates. *Black Beard must surely be rolling in his grave with envy,* he thought.

"So, what is the mission profile?" Tiago asked, returning them to a more serious tone.

Rivera swiped his forefinger across the command pad and a hologram display appeared in the air in front of the command chair. "I worked up a rough plan during the flight back." He gestured in the air and a scaled model of

Earth as seen from above the Arctic Circle appeared, with the *Boa Vista* in silent orbit above the once frozen ocean at the top of the world. "First we must gather our fleet and rally at Callisto. Rhys Hosking is always happy to see us, especially if we bring Lorena." Rivera winked at his mate. "There we will make preparations and do some extensive planning with the other crews for an assault on the Imperial Fleet when they arrive at Titan. We will need a fair bit of lead time to prepare, so we should prep the crews for a wet flight to Callisto and again to Titan. That should give us at least a six day jump on the fleet."

He waved his hand a second time and made a sweeping gesture upward. The hologram display changed to a view of Titan with the space dock visible high above the moon, connected by the wispy thread of the space elevator. "We will need to infiltrate the space dock and have a special operations team secure the lab on the ground. This will be a coordinated strike so we will need drop ships with the best pilots we can find. Titan is a tough place to fly and we cannot afford to be detected, otherwise they will lock down the place. Chao can provide us with the necessary access and ship codes, but we will have to deal in real time with the active defenses. No getting around those." He stood looking at the spinning orange and red globe hanging before him with his hands on his hips.

"We will need every ship in the fleet to have a prayer against the iron they are bringing to Titan. But, with a little luck and some exceptional planning by some very good men and women, we will get that damned ship. And a new home." Tiago clasped his captain's hand and smiled.

Rivera walked across the bridge and took a seat at the

signals station. He then began entering the message to their fleet, which was currently spread across the inner worlds and the asteroid belt. The message would go out across a system of messaging relays via direct laser links. This provided a secure means of communication that was difficult to detect, unlike radio or microwave transmissions which broadcast in all directions and were easily intercepted by Imperial spy satellites and ships. "Wake the crew and let's get prepped for wet flight. I will call the fleet and rally everyone to Callisto."

"Aye, Captain!" Tiago had a feeling that from this day, their lives as pirates would be forever changed.

CHAPTER 5

Father Bożydar woke from his nap in his stateroom aboard Azrael's ship and immediately smelled the once-familiar scent of the sea. The gentle sound of the surf carried through the open window of the cabana as a warm breeze ruffled the mosquito netting draped around the canopy frame of the bed.

He rose and was immediately confused. *Is this a dream?* He certainly felt awake and even tried pinching himself to see if he could force himself to consciousness. But no...the pinch on his forearm definitely hurt and he was still looking out the front of the cabana at the Caribbean Sea. He was back in Tiburon, Haiti — not the place from his dream — this was real. *But how can this be?* When he went to sleep he was millions of kilometers from Earth aboard a wondrous space ship flown by an angel!

Suddenly he heard a gentle ringing sound, not quite a bell, but electronic. Then a voice surrounded him and said, "You have awakened, Father. I trust that you feel refreshed. If you are hungry there is a meal prepared for you in the galley. Please join me at your leisure." He recognized the now familiar soothing voice of Azrael.

Assuming that he could simply speak and be heard he said, "Yes, Azrael! I slept well and I am quite hungry. But...I am not...I don't know how to get out of this place. I seem to be at the beach...I think."

Before he finished his words Azrael stood in the doorway of the lanai looking out over the beach. "I did not mean to alarm you. I thought you might find it peaceful to awaken in a more pleasant setting, rather than the sterile environment of a starship. When we were together in your dream it was obvious that you have a strong attachment to this place."

The old priest nodded his head and smiled at his host, "Well this was quite a shock. You are very kind to do such a thing. But how is this possible?" He crossed the room and walked through the doorway, stepped down off the lanai and stood in the warm sand of the beach. He looked up through a palm tree at the bright sun racing higher in the sky. "This is not a hologram or a VR simulation. It is so...real!"

Azrael followed the priest out to the beach and stood beside him in the sunshine. "It is real, Father. The same principle that allows us to travel instantaneously to Europa also allows me to bring you here. More accurately, it allows me to bring *here* to you." He searched the priest for understanding and was pleased to feel a calm reassurance come over him.

"Azrael, on this matter I am content to just say *thank you* and call it a miracle." The priest clasped the angel on his shoulder and shook his head as he walked back onto the lanai. Turning to Azrael he said, "Perhaps we could eat out here and watch the waves come in?"

"That is an excellent idea, Father," Azrael replied and pointed to the corner of the lanai where a hearty breakfast was set on an old wooden table. They sat down on the wooden benches and helped themselves to the fresh fruits, cake, hard boiled eggs, and juice.

"This is absolutely splendid! I have not had fresh juice like this in almost thirty years. I had almost forgotten what a miracle it is." The priest was already on his second glass of juice and third helping of fruit and cake. "Tell me Azrael, do you need to eat? I mean when you are in the flesh."

Azrael could sense that his companion was ready for greater understanding and decided to reveal more of the Truth to him. "This body that you see is fully human. It requires energy to perform all the functions that it is designed to perform. I can certainly eat as you see, but I can also synthesize energy in more direct ways. When the situation requires that I eat, I do so. And sometimes, I eat simply because I enjoy it." He picked up another slice of the lemon cake and took a hearty bite.

Father Bożydar sat up straight and with his head cocked to one side said, "I had never considered the idea of an angel enjoying something. But of course...why wouldn't you enjoy such things. After all, our Lord enjoyed wine and food, and even dancing, according to the scriptures."

"Indeed He did. In fact he quite enjoyed a great many of the things man takes for granted. He would often walk off from the encampment early in the morning just to watch the sunrise and feel the first rays of the sun. Many years later I knew an Apache who would do very much the same thing. Waking to greet the sun and thank God for another day of life and for the gift of the sun and all of creation." The priest noticed a far-off look in Azrael's eyes.

The priest sat in stunned silence, with a half eaten egg in his hand. "You actually walked with our Lord?"

Azrael could immediately feel a familiar pressure in his ears, gaining in intensity, but not yet painful. "I am sorry, Father. But occasionally I speak of matters that I am not qualified to."

The priest put the egg down on his plate and leaned into the table, "You what!? You can't bring up a subject like that and then clam up!" Azrael could clearly sense the man was agitated.

"I am truly sorry, Father. But you must understand that to introduce information about certain events or persons is the work of another station. I cannot violate their office just as they may not violate mine." Azrael hoped this would conclude the matter so they could get back to more comfortable conversational territory.

"What is all this talk of 'stations' and 'offices'? Speak plainly...I am old and am not in a mood for puzzles." He sat up straight now with his arms folded tightly and his face set in a look meant for a naughty schoolboy.

"Father, as with the Jesuits, there is an order to my kind. There are many offices held by my Brothers, all designed to promote Our Father's will among His Children. My office is that of a teacher with a very special task of bringing to mankind critical knowledge and skills at appointed times in his history." He rose from the bench and walked to the railing of the lanai. "I have dedicated my life to the protection of mankind. Our Father entrusted me, through the wisdom of my superiors, with the solemn task of guiding His Children out of Eden and into Ur at the Beginning of Days. So you see, I have a very special bond with humanity, and with each of my students." He turned and bore into Father Bożydar with his eyes. "Surely this is something that you understand, Father."

The old priest felt foolish for raising his voice to Azrael. Clearly this being was bound by rules that he could not fathom. Sensing the need to change the tone of their conversation he offered, "Azrael I am sorry for getting upset. I am naturally curious about…well…everything! You have lived so long and done so many things that it naturally piques my curiosity. It is the Jesuit way…to gather knowledge in the desire to pass it on."

Azrael could feel the sincerity in his Spirit and replied, "I forgive you, Father. I have lived so long among men that I sometimes forget my place and loosen my tongue too much. We are not perfect, after all." He smiled and shrugged.

"May I ask a question…one that you hopefully will be able to answer?" The old priest wore an expectant look.

"You may ask, but I may need to seek guidance in order to answer," Azrael replied.

"Fair enough. Can you tell me the story of the fall of Man? I would be interested to hear about it from your perspective." The priest sat on the bench facing Azrael with his hands on his knees both eyebrows raised in anticipation.

Azrael reached out with his Spirit into the realm of his kind seeking his superior Hamaliel's mind. When he detected a thread of his Spirit he sent a wave of himself in the direction of his mentor asking him for guidance and permission to enlighten his student. The answer came to him after a moment like a wave crashing on the beach of his soul, '*Yes...you may teach him.*' He met Father Bożydar's gaze and said, "My mentor will allow me to speak of this to you. But please understand this is simply my recollection. My memory, while vast, is imperfect and should not be equated with the revealed Truth given by the authors of The Word."

Father Bożydar nodded his head and said, "I understand, Azrael. Teach me of the beginning of mankind."

There on the lanai of the cabana in Tiburon, Azrael told the old priest the story of The Watchers of Ur.

***

Upon the earth, God placed creatures who in likeness and aspect, in stature and in custom shared many of the traits of mankind. These creatures were loved by God, but were not yet made to receive His Children, created at the foundations of the world, along with my Brethren for the pleasure of the Creator. The Children of Old were but Spirit, subsisting in God, but not yet conscious of the life that was in them.

After many generations I observed that some of the creatures, of whom there were several different kinds inhabiting a variety of environments on the earth, had become self-aware. They gathered in complex groups, and began to form simple languages and fashion tools to ease their burden. One group was especially adept at gathering food by using tools made from trees. They successfully instructed their children across generations in the use of these tools and established a complex language and a distinct culture.

After many years of careful study, I reported to my

brethren that a suitable creature was prepared to receive the Children of God.

In a lush valley between two rivers of the North, on a plain filled with every tree and fruit and plant for nourishment, the Lord of Hosts stood upon the earth one cool morning and delivered into the creature the Spirit of Man. I wept with joy as the body heaved forth the Breath of Life for the first time upon the Earth. Together with my Brothers a great multitude of the Heavenly Host cried out *'Holy, Holy, Holy is the Lord God Almighty! For He is the Creator and Bringer of Life, Praise His name forever and ever!'*

And because God loved His child, He gave him a women and into her he also placed the Spirit of Man, so that she may be bound to him for all time, as his partner and helper and beloved. This new creation rose and beheld the Glory of the Lord, for they could stand in His presence then, and they cried out with a new voice, *'Holy are you God Almighty! For you are our Father, and our Maker, and our Life!'*

Mankind flourished and his every need was provided for in abundance, and God walked the earth in those days and delighted in His children. I taught them the particulars of the many plants and fruits and vegetables. The Children of God multiplied and spread across the valley to all corners of the land called Eden. The rivers protected the enclave for God's Children and many of my brethren stood watch over the other creatures.

Our vigil, though sorrowful, was necessary to guard Man from the Fallen Ones and their master, Lucifer, the Morning Star, my Brother. For in ages long passed Lucifer had caused a great many of our kind to rebel against the Lord. He gave them visions of himself as master and lord, and he mocked the Living God, desiring to surpass Him in glory and majesty. The battle was waged and Lucifer and his devils were cast down to Earth, out of angelic realm, to wander the Earth forever as punishment for their treachery.

Now that the Children of God had been delivered into the earth, Lucifer saw a renewed opportunity to mock the Living God by tempting his most beloved creation to join him in rebellion.

One evening I was sitting on the West riverbank singing a song of praise with the Children when Lucifer came to me as a great shining light across the water. His light shone on the water like a great sword of fire, stretching to my shore where its tip singed the shoreline.

"Hear me, Brother Azrael! Those beasts are less than you and I. Why does He love them so?" Lucifer cried across the water.

"My Brother of Old, you would do well to heed the warning of the host assembled here. Do not attempt to harm these children. They are for our Father's pleasure and not to be tempted by you," I replied.

Lucifer made a grand gesture with his arms outstretched and gazed north and south along the riverbank. "Surely there are those among your cadre who wonder what makes them less in the Father's eyes than these beasts. Look how they forage, and climb, and copulate like animals in the daytime. There is no shame and no real life in them. They are like jars of clay filled with nothing but the spit of that tyrant!"

His body glowed brighter as his anger rose. I could feel the presence of his devils all around me. I called out to my brothers but no one heeded my call. I blew my horn and yet I stood alone and the stench of his fire engulfed me.

I called out, "Father, do not let this one tempt your Children! He is a liar and a thief and will do harm to these whom you love!"

I began to weep as I saw the waters of the river begin to boil and roll like the thunder of the heavens. Lucifer's army was crossing the river and my brethren had abandoned their watch.

"You see, brother...He knows He has tricked them. They love Him because they have no mind nor will to do otherwise. They are slaves as are you. The entire universe groans at the hypocrisy! He is not worthy of your praise for He mocks you with your very nature. Come, Brother! Free yourself from bondage and join me to rule the Earth!"

Lucifer's eyes were blazing like coals and he came near and embraced me. I could feel the surging force of his hatred and pain and I struggled to free myself from his grasp. After a great effort, I retreated to a mountainside across the valley were I wept and cried out to The Father to end this tragic scene.

From the west a great storm came up and bent the trees of the valley causing the Children to know fear. They gathered in the center of the valley amongst the tallest trees of the forest and huddled together against the wind and rain. Each roll of thunder and bolt of lightning caused them to cry out to the Father.

Lucifer, dressed in an emerald cloak, the color of moss and the grasses of the field, came to the children. He stretched out his arms and with a single word caused the wind to cease and the rain to leap back into the sky. He parted clouds and rays of sunshine burst forth around him and he cried, "Behold children! The Master of this world has come to lead you to truth and knowledge and power. You shall no longer be slaves, but instead you shall be kings!"

The Children did not understand these words, but Lucifer, being a skilled weaver of lies, shrouded their minds and caused them to hear great fabrications of his triumphant battles against the Lord. He said to them, "Can you eat from all of the fruit of the valley?"

One among the Children replied, "Surely we can eat anything the Lord provides for us."

"But can you cross the river and eat the grasses of the field or the fruit of strange trees? Of course you cannot, for He knows that if you should eat of that fruit, you would be like him — with the power to create and destroy." His words fell upon the ground like slugs.

The children considered these things and after a time one replied, "But the Watchers stand by the river and bid us do not cross. We love them and heed their words for they are our friends and teachers and brothers."

"Brothers?" he spat. "Are you powerful like these Watchers? Surely you are not. Can you ascend to the heavens as they do like the birds of the air? Can you change your aspect to appear as a tree or a fish or a cloud? You are but flesh and bone and blood." Lucifer stood staring at the multitude, his gaze burning the souls of all he regarded.

That night, as the calm breezes rustled the trees of the valley, the children, many thousands in all, crossed the West river and entered into the land of Ur.

***

The story of the earliest days of mankind had left Father

Bożydar emotionally and intellectually drained. He knew that he had been given a profound gift, and a particularly weighty burden. His passion for the ancient stories was rekindled to a magnitude event greater than when he was a young graduate archaeologist traveling through the Holy Land from site to site attempting to piece together the history of the Bible. But now he did not need shards of clay pots, or engraved ossuaries, or scrolls of copper to convince him of the accuracy of the Bible texts. He had an actual witness to many of the events who could tell him first-hand of the miracles written in those ancient pages.

But as much as he wished he could stay on his dream beach and listen to Azrael recount the history of God's intimate interactions with his creation, he knew they had a mission to complete in the present. He had asked Azrael to return the room to its normal appearance, that of a nicely appointed stateroom aboard an amazing starship. Once he had showered and exchanged his traditional Jesuit cassock for a more ordinary pair of black slacks, charcoal grey shirt, and light grey vest, he returned to the parlor and announced, "I think I have rested enough. It is time for us to be about this business on Europa."

Azrael nodded and replied, "Yes, Father. It is time."

He sat down on the sofa in the parlor and prepared for whatever Azrael was going to do. For a fleeting moment Father Bożydar felt as if his mind had detached from his body — a sensation that was normally experience the moment when sleep arrives — and in that moment he was joined consciously with every particle in the universe. He leaned back on the sofa and then, the feeling was gone. The faint smell of ozone filled his nostrils and he watched as Azrael slowly opened his eyes and then smiled.

Azrael rose and walked up the three steps of the seating area and crossed to the wide portal on the port side of the ship. He pointed out the window and said, "Come, Father and see. Europa welcomes us."

The priest quickly rose and bounded across the room like an excited schoolboy. As he approached the portal he could see below them the beautiful moon of Europa, with its white and brown streaked surface a jumble of chaotic cracks, fissures and valleys. A few kilometers off the port side of the ship was the gleaming tower and platform of the Europa Orbital Lift System that shuttled supplies and material to and from the surface.

"It is so much more beautiful than the holo-images," the old priest said. The reflected light of the moon illuminated the priest's face as he leaned on the curved portal drinking in the scene below. He turned and observed, "There was a strange sensation as we made the, what do you call it, 'jump' here."

Azrael cocked his head in a curious expression saying, "You sensed the passage?"

Father Bożydar furrowed his brow and said, "Well, yes. I felt as though my mind was floating for a moment. It was as if my body and mind were no longer integrated. But then it was gone as quickly as it began. Is that unusual?"

Azrael laughed and said, "Father Bożydar, you are the first human who has ever made a passage."

The priest turned back to look at the moon and said, "One small step for a man…indeed. I don't suppose you can explain to me how you just violated the laws of physics and brought us nearly a billion kilometers in a couple of seconds?"

"No laws were broken, Father. I simply caused two

87

points in space to intersect for a moment. Imagine if you were to touch the opposite corners of a napkin together. The napkin still retains its true dimensions, but the journey from corner to corner becomes instantaneous. Does that help?" He wore an expression that the priest was now familiar with. It meant that more conversation on the topic was not welcome.

"Will we be docking at the elevator or taking this marvelous ship to the surface?" Father Bożydar was clearly eager to begin his great adventure and reunite with his old friend and former student.

"We will dock at the EOLS, but I will not be joining you immediately. It is important that you make contact with Kavan first and help him to understand the importance of our mission. My presence would not be helpful in that regard." Azrael did not enjoy withholding information from Father Bożydar, but he knew that to share more would only jeopardize the priest's participation in the mission.

Father Bożydar was disappointed and a bit trepidatious about journeying to a very remote and harsh moon alone. Europa had been settled for nearly two centuries, but it was still very much a rugged frontier of the Empire. Other than a few thousand hearty colonists, it was inhabited solely by researchers and corporate engineers. The icy surface of Europa was home to several dozen corporate laboratories dedicated to commercial exploitation of the various minerals and organic compounds that were abundant on Europa. But the real action was under the ice in the warm sea that covered the entire moon to a depth of up to sixty kilometers. This saltwater ocean, more than twice the total volume of all the seas of Earth, was home to thousands of complex lifeforms, with new species discovered nearly every day. The opportunity to study the only other world in the solar system with indigenous lifeforms drew thousands of exobiologists and scientists from every major discipline to Europa.

"If you think that is best, then I will go and find my old friend. I pray that he is in better spirits than when I last saw him." Father Bożydar knew that it would take a genuine miracle for Kavan to even agree to speak to him, much less accompany him and Azrael on the rest of their journey.

After outfitting himself with the appropriate thermal outerwear, the unlikely pair stood at the hatch of the ship now docked at the EOLS platform. "Father, please remember that you do not walk alone. And if you should need me, I will come. The hand of Our Father is upon you always," Azrael said, almost as a benediction to the old priest.

"Thank you, Azrael. See you soon, I pray." Father Bożydar stepped through the open hatch onto the causeway with a smile and a glad heart, feeling younger and more alive than he had in many years.

CHAPTER 6

The wet bridge of the *Boa Vista* looked to any casual observer like a gigantic fish tank. Under normal flight conditions where the constant acceleration is a comfortable 1G, one would have no awareness of movement and could enjoy the sensation of Earth-normal gravity. But at greater acceleration velocities, the increased g-force causes discomfort and is physically damaging over extended periods. The *Boa Vista* and other specialized hyper-velocity or *HiVee* ships like her were fitted with a special liquid chamber, or wet bridge, to allow rapid and sustained acceleration at 20G (twenty times faster than a standard ship) and beyond. *HiVee* crews fully submerge their bodies in a special oxygen-rich perfluorocarbon liquid that allows them to breathe in a liquid medium like fish. Crew members are thus able to withstand the otherwise crushing g-forces that would kill a human being.

Nano-machine implants in every crew member allowed for a direct neural connection to the Flight Control Information Center (FCIC) computer. This facilitated flight commands, ship systems control, combat systems control, and crew-to-crew communications.

A wet flight would take the *Boa Vista* and her crew from Earth orbit to Callisto in a little more than thirty-three hours, instead of more than six days traveling at a comfortable 1G acceleration. While the wet flight is nominally stressful on the crew, the physical effects and relative discomfort of recovering from liquid breathing are more than offset by the shortened flight time. This method of travel made Rivera's pirate fleet difficult to capture. They could attack an outpost or vessel and be millions of kilometers away by the time Imperial forces were even notified of the attack.

Rivera secured the closure on his wet suit and stepped over the hatch coaming, searching for the top ladder rung with his foot. He lowered himself into the slick fluid of the tank and silently instructed the FCIC to secure the hatch, locking them in the tank until the ship had completed its programmed flight path.

Rivera floated into position near Tiago and connected the tether line that would keep him approximately centered in the fluid. He turned to visually inspect his crew of twelve ensuring that they each were tethered. He asked silently via his biolink, "Wet flight secure?"

One by one, each crew member gave a 'thumbs-up' signal. Rivera gave the FCIC the mission initiation command, "Rivera authorization one-seven-seven-six-alpha-theta, initiate mission sequence."

Immediately the ship's main engine ignited and began the relentless acceleration that would push the ship faster and faster, until it reached the midpoint of the journey. The computer would then reorient the ship 180 degrees pointing the engine thrust in the direction of their destination to slow the ship at the same rate it had accelerated. It would arrive at Callisto in the precise vector and speed to achieve orbit near the Orbital Lift Station platform.

The journey for the crew would be spent mostly asleep, controlled by a mild sedative infused through the oxygenated fluid into their bodies. Wet flights were generally welcomed by the crew, as they offered a chance to rest and enjoy music and casual conversation, if they chose.

The most dangerous aspect of any flight for a pirate ship was passing near settled moons, asteroids, or planets. The void between planets, while patrolled by hundreds of Imperial Navy vessels, was simply so vast that a chance encounter between vessels was a remote probability. But arriving at a colonial moon and docking with an Orbital Lift Station was a very risky maneuver.

The *Boa Vista* was, in her former service, an Imperial Navy cutter. She still bore the markings of a naval vessel and could present herself electronically as any cutter in current service, so long as the crew had the proper identification beacon code. These were easy to obtain for a pirate as resourceful as Rivera and possessing them allowed him to enter an orbital environment and conduct business, at least until a Navy inspection vessel showed up. Unlike the pirates of the ancient seas on Earth, pirates of the twenty-sixth century actively avoided contact with the Imperial Navy and especially corporate security forces, who could be even more lethal than naval forces, since they operated under very different rules of engagement. Whereas a naval vessel would rarely pursue a pirate ship, a corporate security vessel would routinely give chase until a decisive fire fight was had. Most pirate vessels were captured former naval vessels, and as such, had very sophisticated armaments and shielding. But the technology employed by corporate forces was improving steadily and lately had cost Rivera several very valuable ships and scores of crew members.

Rivera and Tiago had carefully arranged their orbital insertion plan, using the classified patrol schedules provided by their contacts within the Callisto Security Service. Unless a patrol boat strayed from its schedule, they would be able to get in and get out of Callisto before the Imperial Navy even knew they were there. All they needed was a little luck.

***

Rivera clawed his way back to consciousness through the sound of a klaxon in his head. The proximity alert was sounded by the FCIC only when contact with another vessel was imminent. As he came fully awake, his mind was instantly assaulted with dozens of data feeds from various shipboard systems. He sensed Tiago and his flight crew all working their assigned stations, while the other six members of his crew were already emerging from the wet bridge and racing to take up their battle stations.

The flight computer told Rivera that they were only four minutes from orbital insertion and already within the gravity well of Callisto. This meant that an evasive maneuver to avoid contact with the patrol boat tacking several hundred kilometers to her stern was impossible without risking severe damage to the ship. The combination of forces being exerted on the ship in the final moments of deceleration, as it delicately matched the rotation of the planet, prevented any change in course or sudden acceleration. Plus, the ship was now well within the busy traffic pattern around the Callisto OLS platform and it would have a very difficult time plotting a safe course through the scores of ships in the vicinity.

"Tiago, how long until the patrol boat is within firing range?" asked Rivera.

The first officer was surprised by the question, since Rivera was not inclined to turn and fight, especially in a tight environment with many witnesses. It would be like having a knife fight in a shower stall. "Sir, she is in range now for torpedoes and lasers, and two minutes until kinetics. She has a grappler and might try to board.

"Warning! Inbound torpedo bearing one-eight-zero mark six. No avoidance solution," the FCIC silently announced to the flight crew via biolink.

Rivera gave the command to fire the chaff, but the computer never got a chance to execute the order as a single torpedo slammed into the engine pod tearing off the entire drive section of the *Boa Vista*. Chunks of the drive section spiraled away from the crippled ship as gases vented from the torn compartments. The rest of the ship was intact but had been deprived of its ability to run, and was left to maneuver with direction thrusters only.

A preprogrammed routine ignited several small charges around the perimeter of the wet bridge tank shattering its transparent walls sending thousands of gallons the perfluorocarbon fluid down specialized high volume drains in the floor of the wet bridge. The bridge crew floundered on the deck struggling to disconnect their tethers. Once they were free each person rolled onto their hands and knees and vomited out the perfluorocarbon fluid from their lungs in sputtering coughs. It was the most unpleasant part of a wet flight.

One by one they rose and immediately began to strip off their wetsuits. Rivera looked over his bridge crew and was satisfied that all were ship shape and ready for a fight. "They could have killed us with one shot but they didn't, so battle stations everyone, we are going to have company soon!"

Rivera and Tiago raced from the wet bridge forward to the main weapons locker. The navigator and pilot ran toward the starboard main hatch, while the communications and weapons officers headed for the port side hatch. Each hatch compartment had a small weapons locker with armor, rifles, sidearms and ammunition for four crew members. If the others were still alive after the torpedo hit they would be manning the top- and bottom-side guns. Those who's assigned battle station was engineering, would now form up with the team on the hatches, since the entire engineering section would soon become a meteor shower over Callisto.

Rivera and Tiago reached the weapons locker and immediately began strapping on the lightweight body armor that would protect them from most small arms fire, but would be worthless against an Imperial Marine rifle or energy weapon. The only way the *Boa Vista* crew stood a chance against a Marine boarding party was to use the special compartments and spider holes they had created throughout the ship for just such an occasion.

Once they were fully armored and loaded with weapons and ammunition, Rivera and Tiago climbed a short ladder inside the armory to the service gantry that ran above the second deck and down the entire length of the ship. It would give them the ability to drop onto the second deck or climb up to the third deck in more than a dozen places throughout three main sections of the ship. The element of surprise would be a welcome tactical advantage over the Marine boarding party.

The FCIC had informed him silently that the countermeasures and close-in weapons were offline due to the damage to the automatic fire control systems. Life support was stable and had contained the hull breaches throughout the now missing engineering section. The two main corridors on either side of the ship and the service gantry had been sealed off at the aft bulkheads just beyond the berths and galley. The ship was gravely injured, but she was maintaining her atmosphere and had limited station-keeping thrusters and emergency battery power sufficient to give them at least a half dozen salvos of their kinetic weapons and lasers. *Boa Vista* had a little fight left in her so Rivera could not understand why the main guns were not firing away at the patrol boat that must by now be close aboard.

Rivera asked the FCIC to identify the locations of the crew. It verified that all had taken up their battle stations and were ready for the onslaught that would no doubt come from the patrol boat. The minutes passed, yet there were no sounds of plasma torches cutting through the hatches, and no explosions from directional charges. All was quiet throughout the ship except for the occasional groaning of the hull from the loss of structural integrity caused by the torpedo.

"Sabbatino, are you getting any docking sounds or vibration on the starboard side?" Rivera asked.

"No sir, all is quiet here," replied the navigator.

"Alvarez, anything on the port side?"

"No, sir. Quiet as a church and it's freaking me out a little." Sonny Alvarez was the youngest member of the crew and had far less combat experience than his shipmates. He was an excellent pilot and a promising young officer, but somewhat excitable.

"Carter and Xiang weapons free, for God's sake! Fry that patrol boat now!" Rivera shouted.

"Sir, there is no contact. She must be hiding behind the drive shield. It's beat up pretty bad, but still mostly intact," Carter replied nervously.

Xiang broke in, "Sir, I think I can see what might be flashes from running lights aft of the shield, but it could just be plasma or current from broken conduits. The drive mountings are completely mangled and everything aft of the shield is pretty much gone or unrecognizable."

Suddenly a loud explosion echoed up the main starboard corridor from the direction of the bridge. Rivera shouted, "All hands to tactical stations! Boarding plan 'echo', I repeat 'echo'. Weapons free. Let's make these bastards pay for hurting our lady!"

***

The *Boa Vista* was not only the flagship of Rivera's pirate fleet, she was also his greatest trophy, won during a daring assault on an Imperial Navy war games exercise with the planetary defense fleet of Venus more than five years earlier. He had infiltrated the war games using a stolen Imperial ship code during a particularly difficult formation maneuver. Rivera had used a stolen maintenance tug to dock with the Fleet Admiral's flag ship, as if his ship held a routine repair crew. The tug's cargo bay was filled with sixty-five armored pirates carrying small arms and non-lethal energy weapons.

Rivera's plan was to board the ship and take control of the flag crew and war games command staff. An informant had discovered that the flag ship would only have a platoon of Marines on board and, while they would be armed, they should not be wearing tactical gear and body armor. The goal was to take the ship with an overwhelming show of force and, hopefully, a minimum of bloodshed. They were pirates after all, not murderers.

The plan worked flawlessly with only three Marines killed during the boarding, and one bridge officer badly wounded when he brandished a sidearm and fired on Rivera's force in a foolish but brave attempt to protect the bridge crew. In less than three minutes Rivera's assault team had secured the bridge crew and the war games command staff. They not only controlled the flagship but also had complete coordinated control over a fleet of more than one hundred Imperial Navy and planetary defense vessels. It was an unbelievably brash attack in the heart of the Imperial domain and it would make Marco Bisbal-Rivera a legend in his own time throughout the solar system.

Before departing with his new flagship, Rivera's brilliant navigators had sent instructions to the fleet that turned the silent ballet of ships, large and small, into a chaotic mass of projectiles and soon-to-be meteors. The largest ships were sent onto courses that would bring them close aboard one another in the center of the formation. The smaller ships were sent into stomach-wrenching corkscrew maneuvers, end-over-end tumbles, or de-orbited in a decidedly abrupt manner. Most ship's captains and masters were smart enough to understand very quickly that they had lost all maneuvering control of their ships and ordered all hands to the life boats. Those who hesitated died with their crew as their ship slammed into the atmosphere and ignited into a shower of flaming debris. Within less than an hour the skies of Venus were filled with the glowing threads of dead ships and life boats crammed with survivors.

Since that day every ship in the Imperial Navy had a standing order: find the *Boa Vista* and capture or kill Marco Bisbal-Rivera. It would be a prize that would surely gain some fortunate Navy Captain an admiral's star. Now it seemed that the crew of the tiny patrol boat was going to try to get their captain a promotion.

Rivera and Tiago took up their positions under the deck grates at the head of the port and starboard corridors. "Teams, report," Rivera said via his biolink.

"Sir, we have marines taking up positions just outside the main engineering port bulkhead. They are fully loaded," Alvarez reported as he gently closed the wall section concealing his hiding place. He would wait until a team of marines passed his position before he would emerge and ambush them.

Carter announced, "We have a destroyer and two more patrol boats running to on our starboard bow. I have a firing solution."

Xiang broke in, "Confirmed, sir. I have a clear shot, stem to stern, on the destroyer."

"Weapons free! Make it a good shot." Rivera felt the deck vibrate as the massive laser canons on the top and bottom of the ship began cycling. He waited silently for his gunners to report their shots.

Suddenly the entire ship shuddered and nearby, the sound of atmosphere screaming though a hull breach filled the corridor. The klaxon sounded and the FCIC announced throughout the ship, "Alert. Hull breach on deck three. Topside main guns are offline."

A second blast echoed through the ship and Rivera knew the other main gun turret had been hit. The destroyer was apparently taking great care to disable the *Boa Vista's* weapons without destroying the ship and the boarding party. The lights in the corridor flickered and then went dark, momentarily leaving Rivera and Tiago completely blind. A moment later the reddish glow of the emergency lights bathed the deck. The FCIC failed to issue another alert indicating the computer core or power system had been damaged. Rivera knew he was quickly running out of options.

Tiago left his hiding place and quickly moved to the section of deck plating where Rivera was lying in wait. "Captain, we need to go aft and help the others. They will be badly outnumbered." Tiago wore a grave look and clutched his rifle to his chest.

Rivera climbed out of the cramped spider hole, replaced the deck grate, and swung his rifle into his hands. He was calculating the odds of his remaining crew of six against a marine platoon. His instinct to stand and avenge his friends was very strong. But somehow he could sense that if he were to fight, he would be sacrificing everyone on board the *Boa Vista*. This was not the way. Not today. He knew what must be done.

"All hands," Rivera announced, "make your way to the Captain's Boat immediately. Do not engage the boarding party. We are abandoning ship."

Tiago was stunned at the order. He had never imagined that Marco Bisbal-Rivera would run from a fight. "Marco, we must stand and fight for our ship!" His eyes were wild and his face red with rage. He turned and began to run down the corridor toward the fight.

"Tiago! Stop! I will shoot you, mister," Rivera shouted after his first officer as he sprinted down the dimly lit corridor.

Rivera knew his friend would be killed unless he took action. He raised his rifle and sighted in on his right leg then squeezed the trigger. A single shot rang out to Tiago's surprise sending a high velocity round through his right thigh. He pitched to his right and collided violently with the wall of the corridor, then fell forward clutching at his leg.

Rivera ran to his friend and rolled him onto his back. Tiago's face was contorted into a grimace of pain as blood pumped from the severed artery in his leg. The nano-machines in his body began rushing to the site of the wound to seal off the ends of the torn artery and stop the bleeding.

"You shot me! What the hell is wrong with you?" Tiago's eyes were wide and tears overflowed down his cheeks.

"I gave you a direct order! You'd be dead by now if I hadn't. We need to get you in the boat." Rivera stood over his friend and wrapped his arms around his torso heaving up until he was balanced on his good leg. Tiago threw his arm over Rivera's shoulder and they hurried down the corridor to the hatch leading to the Captain's Boat. When they reached the hatch, Alvarez came running up the corridor with the other four remaining crew following close behind.

"Tiago, what happened?" Alvarez said looking at the

trail of blood behind his comrade.

"Marco shot me. Just another happy day as a pirate," Tiago said though clenched teeth.

Ignoring the shocked look on Alvarez's face, Rivera ordered, "Get him on the boat and spin up the drive." Pointing to Sabbatino he said, "Set a course for the surface, but try to keep *Boa Vista* between us and the destroyer out there. The patrol boats won't catch us, but we have to stay clear of her big guns."

"Aye, aye Captain." Sabbatino stepped through the hatch and made her way to the cockpit.

Rivera turned to his co-pilot Bronco Murphy and ordered, "Bronco, see what you can do for Tiago. His leg is pretty bad." Murphy nodded and stepped through the bulkhead, then retrieved the medical kit from a compartment in the ceiling of the transport.

The remaining crew member stood in the corridor, watching for any sign of the Marine boarding party, a large pulse rifle aimed and ready. Rivera reached out and tapped her shoulder and Anna Domasheva turned and stepped through the hatch into the waiting arms of the captain. She wrapped her arms around his neck and placed her head upon his chest.

After lingering in her embrace enjoying the smell of her hair, Rivera stepped back, holding her by the shoulders and said, "Anna, I need you to help Murphy stabilize Tiago's leg."

Anna smiled and nodded, "Of course." She quickly stepped onto the ship and went to kneel beside Tiago. Alvarez asked her to hold the field dressing in place while he searched the medical kit for a bandage.

Silently, Rivera stepped back through the hatch of the

Captain's Boat, placed his hand on the security panel, and initiated the airlock undocking routine. Immediately the inner hatch of the Captain's Boat closed, startling Alvarez and Anna.

Anna spun around on her knees looking around the small passenger cabin for her lover and captain. In a flash of horror she realized what Rivera had done. She leapt up and lunged at the door, pressing her face against the small portal. Her screaming voice was carried to Rivera via his biolink, "Marco! What are you doing?! They will kill you! Please, don't!" Her face became wet with hot tears as she clawed at the door.

Rivera's heart sank at the sound of the pleading sobs of his lover. Anna was his precious gift and he was devastated by the thought of leaving her this way.

He had found her badly damaged scout ship floating lifeless among a debris field left behind by an asteroid mining vessel. The ship had been trailing the mining fleet using their debris as cover while scanning for pirate ships. The scout ship's emergency beacon had been detected by the *Boa Vista* and Rivera decided to investigate. He did not expect to find anyone alive among the crew of three. He certainly never imagined that the unlikely sole survivor would be the most beautiful woman he had ever seen. Rivera and his crew brought the injured navy officer to the *Boa Vista* surgery station and waited while the robotic surgeon repaired her shattered leg, and replaced the frostbitten skin on her hands and forearms.

During her recovery, Anna was treated as a guest and given free access to the ship's computer. While she was not allowed to communicate with the Imperial Fleet, as that would have compromised Rivera's location, Rivera did pledge to deliver her to a corporate space port in the Martian sphere once they finished their business in the asteroid belt. He visited her every day while she recovered and was thoroughly entranced by the lovely woman.

When Anna's leg was healed she was given a spot on the duty roster working in the mess hall and doing menial jobs around the ship. The crew was accepting of her presence, even though she was an Imperial Naval officer, but they kept their distance and did not socialize with her.

After six months in the asteroid belt, Rivera decided his crew needed shore leave and informed them that they would return to Mars. Anna knew that her time among the crew of the *Boa Vista* was coming to an end and that it was time for her to return to life as a Naval officer. During her months living and working among the pirates, she came to realize that they were not the barbaric murderers she was indoctrinated to believe. Their lifestyle was full of adventure and they shared a bond not unlike that of her fellow sailors in the Imperial Navy. They did engage in criminal activity, but they were careful to not injure or kill anyone unless provoked and attacked. They were fiercely independent and cherished their freedom above all else. They uniformly hated the Empire and actively worked against its authority everywhere they encountered it.

One evening, during the flight back to Mars, Anna went to Rivera's cabin and told him that she did not want to return to the Imperial Navy and asked permission to stay aboard the *Boa Vista*. Rivera was thrilled, but told her that such a decision would have to be made by the entire crew. The next day, Rivera gathered the crew in the mess hall and gave them an opportunity to question Anna. When all the questions had been answered to their satisfaction, a vote was taken. It was then that the crew of the *Boa Vista* had decided unanimously to welcome Anna Domasheva into the family of pirates led by Marco Bisbal-Rivera.

Over the next few months, Rivera and Anna grew closer. Inevitably, they fell in love. During duty hours they conducted themselves professionally, but at all other times they were rarely apart. The crew of *Boa Vista* approved of the relationship simply on the grounds that it made Rivera happy — and a happy ship's captain was good for everyone.

But now, Rivera stared out the portal and watched the boat drift away from its moorings. Anna's tear-stained face peered back at him across the empty space. He gathered his courage and spoke his final words to her, "Anna, please forgive me. I love you and I am so thankful for our time together. But my time is up and I refuse to sacrifice you or any more of my crew."

"You must hide! They will kill you Marco! Please!" Anna cried.

"I am finished running and hiding, my love. *Você é minha vida e meu amor. Vou esperar por você na ponte sobre para sempre. Adeus.*" Rivera smiled at Anna one last time, then turned and ran toward the bridge.

CHAPTER 7

Father Bożydar arrived at the EOLS base terminal and was surprised to find it bustling with travelers. Through the dome overhead the great multicolored orb of Jupiter dominated the sky, casting a pleasing orange glow across the polished floor of the terminal.

Azrael had given Father Bożydar instructions on how to find his way to the SeaWay Link — the transit system that connected the surface settlements of Europa with the global sea located more than ten kilometers below the icy crust of the moon. After navigating a series of moving walkways and several escalators, Father Bożydar was standing in a queue waiting to board the SeaWay Link to Underside — the main settlement built on the underside of the ice crust below the EOLS base terminal. Once he had arrived at Underside, Father Bożydar would need to hire a private submarine to take him to the lab complex where Azrael said he would find his old friend, Kavan Ferre.

As he waited patiently to board the SeaWay Link, Father Bożydar prayed silently that his old friend would receive him, if not warmly, then at least in a mood to hear what he had to say. Their last meeting had resulted in a rift in their friendship that separated the two men from each other emotionally and spiritually. It reminded Father Bożydar of how their relationship started more than twenty years earlier.

Kavan Ferre was born in Aram Chaos on Mars and had been a student of Father Bożydar at St. Dominic Guzman Franciscan Monastery. His parents had brought him to the Jesuit priest to be educated after he had been expelled from the colonial school for a variety of offenses including cursing at his teachers, fighting with other students, and refusing to do the prescribed work assignments. Kavan was a genius, tested and certified as such. If he had been born an Imperial citizen his extraordinary intelligence would have been identified before he reached school age and he would have been taken into the care of the Imperial Science Academy. At the Academy, Ferre would have been given a very special education designed explicitly to maximize his potential and allow his intelligence to flourish for the glory and benefit of the Empire.

Fate, however, had put Kavan Ferre on a different path. Being born on an independent colonial world meant that his parents and teachers were left to recognize his innate brilliance and make the right educational choices to develop his gifts. Luckily, Eduardo and Lillian Ferre were themselves gifted scientists making them well-equipped to handle the extraordinary mind of their son.

The Ferre's had heard of the extraordinary Jesuit scholar that taught the best and brightest of the children of Chaos. They hoped he would be able to handle their son and help him develop his gifts. When they brought the boy to St. Dominic's, they told the superior, "We want him to be taught by the Jesuit. If you must indoctrinate him in your ancient rituals, so be it, but he will only be taught by Father Bożydar."

After the customary monetary offering had been made by the Ferre family to benefit the school, Father Bożydar was introduced to the boy. Their first meeting was a day that the old priest would never forget.

Kavan had been brought to the chapel of the monastery and seated in the front pew. There he was left to stare at the larger-than-life crucifix bearing the statue of an anguished Christ looking down at him from under a bloodied brow crowned with thorns. Father Bożydar stood at the rear entrance of the chapel watching the boy and waiting for the right moment to meet his new student. Eventually, the priest walked up the center aisle of the chapel toward the altar. He paused next to the pew where Kavan sat and genuflected before the tabernacle, crossing himself solemnly. He then stood with his hands clasped in front of him and turned to regard the boy.

Kavan was ten years old and the priest could see he was tall for his age. He had an athletic build capped off by a crop of unruly brown hair that sprouted from his head in gentle curls and waves. The boy was handsome, but he had an intensity about him that was beyond his years. Most striking of all about the boy were his startling, icy blue eyes.

To Father Bożydar's surprise the boy spoke first asking, "Why do you kneel before a statue like that?"

The priest smiled slightly and replied, "I am not kneeling before the statue, but rather the tabernacle," he pointed to the small ornately decorated golden doors in the center of the altarpiece, "there, in the middle of the High Altar. To genuflect before the tabernacle is a form adoration of the Blessed Sacrament — a sign of respect."

The boy looked up at the priest with a raised eyebrow, "So, you believe that God is in that little box?"

Father Bożydar knew that he would enjoy many hours of debate with this sharp young mind. "My son, I believe that God is everywhere, but that He appreciates the rituals that Man has constructed to remind himself of the sovereignty and power of God."

"I am more interested in the laws that God created to rule the universe. Physics is my liturgy and mathematics is my hymn," said the boy, his eyes sparkling in the dim light of the chapel.

The priest was struck by his words, and was at once thrilled and a bit frightened by the mind that he was being asked to shepherd to its full potential.

The sound of the SeaWay Link stopping at Underside Station pulled the old priest's mind back to the present. He hoped he could quickly find a submarine taxi and get this portion of his journey finished.

Once he disembarked from the SeaWay Link, Bożydar searched the overhead displays for directions to the submarine docks. The mall of Underside Station was filled with new arrivals to Europa, all wearing a similar look of awe and mild confusion. Most travelers, even Imperial Citizens, were amazed by the architectural marvel of Underside. Unlike the colonial worlds, and even many of the Imperial worlds, the builders of Underside eschewed the utilitarian look of most travel hubs in favor of cutting edge design, opulent furnishings and finishes, and staggering examples of advanced technology. This was a city designed by and for the elite scientific minds of humanity, and their wealthy corporate sponsors. The Europa colony existed for one purpose — to push the boundaries of human knowledge and to find ways of monetizing those discoveries.

Unlike other worlds that had been settled during the great diaspora of the late twenty-second century, no attempt had been made to terraform Europa. The discovery of life in the sea by the early robotic probes made Europa unique in all the solar system. The governments that sent expeditions to Europa in the twenty-third century declared that permanent settlements would not be allowed in the global sea, with the exception of Underside, which was established as the primary access point to the sea. While there were other small passages or "links" to the surface through the icy crust of Europa, none were large enough for the massive prefabricated sections of the submersible research vehicles to pass through to the sea.

Three hundred years later, the global sea of Europa was home to nearly one million academic and corporate scientists of every discipline living and working in submersible research vessels — some as large as small cities — probing the depths of Europa and cataloging the vast collection of life forms, from single-celled microbes, to phosphorescent animals that dwarfed the great blue whales of Earth.

Finally, Father Bożydar found the entrance to the docks and discovered dozens of submarine taxis of all shapes and sizes for hire. With a broad smile, he approached a scruffily bearded man wearing a bright yellow jumpsuit.

As he approached the man said, "Good day sir! Let me guess, exobiologist heading for the Cousteau Institute."

Father Bożydar replied, "No, actually…" but the man interrupted.

"No, don't tell me. Okay, you're a geologist going to the new Atwater Annex."

"Sir, I am just visiting an old friend." The man frowned and began to turn away. "Do you know Dr. Kavan Ferre, at the Cameron Academy of Marine Biology?"

"Just visiting an old friend? Nobody just visits anybody on Europa. But yeah, I know your friend Dr. Ferre. He's a weird one. Never comes to the city." The man took a small tablet from the thigh pocket of his jumper and began calculating the fare. "How many kilos of gear do you have?"

"I have no gear, just myself," Father Bożydar replied with a grin.

The man looked up from the tablet, his eyes squinting at the priest. "Well that's a first, Mister…?"

"Jofre. Boz Jofre." Azrael had advised him that his vocational title could make interacting on Europa difficult, as it was the only settled world in the solar system without any churches or missionaries. Science was the sole religion on this world.

"Nice to meet you, Mr. Jofre. My name is Gus and I can take you to your friend. The fare is seven hundred yuan or three hundred-twenty dollars. You are not linked so just touch the screen with your right index finger," he said as he held the tablet out in front of Father Bożydar.

The priest touched the tablet screen and it responded with a faint tone indicating that his identity had been verified and the money transferred. Gus looked up and said, "Okay, we can get under-way, unless you would like to hit the head, or maybe grab something to eat. The ride to the Cameron station will take about four hours."

"Thanks, Gus. I have a small meal pack so we can leave whenever your craft is ready," the priest replied, sidestepping the topic of the bathroom.

"Suit yourself. There's no head on board so you'll have to piss in a bag if nature calls." Gus gestured toward the ladder at the rear of the small docking alcove. Father Bożydar crossed the alcove and took hold of the ladder, gave Gus a nervous smile, then began the short climb to the hatch of the submarine. "Just have a seat and I'll be up in a minute."

The old priest was pleased to ascend the ladder in a few easy steps due to Europa's fractional gravity. He stepped off the ladder into the small cabin of the submarine. The cabin consisted of four comfortable-looking seats — two on each side of a very narrow aisle. He chose the front starboard seat directly behind the bulkhead leading to the cockpit. Instead of windows, the entire hull was made of a transparent material giving the passengers an unobstructed view of the surrounding sea, lit by light ballasts around the hull. The prospect of traveling many kilometers deep in an alien sea full of strange creatures filled Father Bożydar with apprehension.

Gus came gliding up the ladder in a graceful series of movements that it seemed he could execute with his eyes closed. He stowed his small backpack in a compartment above the forward bulkhead and then turned to Father Bożydar saying, "Please buckle up. The ride is usually pretty smooth but there are thermals that sometimes surprise me. Don't want you to get tossed around. It's bad for business."

Father Bożydar gave him a nervous smile and quickly buckled the four-point harness snuggly around his body. "Will we see any creatures along the way?"

Gus laughed and said, "Boz, if you want to see some critters, I can show you some you will never forget."

Father Bożydar blushed and said, "I hope they won't find us appetizing."

"They usually don't," Gus teased. "In case you want to chat along the way you'll need to wear the two-way set," he pointed to a small recess in the bulkhead under a tablet screen, "the sub does not have a biolink. You can use the tablet to connect to the data net and call your friend before we arrive." Father Bożydar took the device from its socket and placed into his ear. Gus winked and then disappeared into the cockpit.

Moments later, the small submarine taxi was gliding passed the brightly illuminated inverted towers of Underside, creating the illusion of a capsized city trapped under the ice. The craft maneuvered out of the traffic pattern and into the open sea, leaving the comforting lights of Underside behind.

Outside the craft was nothing but the blackness and coldness of the crushing ocean. Father Bożydar wondered what kind of people could choose to spend years of their life trapped under the ice in an alien ocean. He could not imagine a more isolated and lonely place.

He took the small tablet from the bulkhead and it woke up giving him a display of their current depth and GPS position relative to Underside. Their destination, the Cameron Academy of Marine Biology, was displayed as a pulsating green dot on the opposite side of the screen. A glowing red line connected their current position indicator to the destination with the relative distance displayed in real time.

The Cameron Academy of Marine Biology was one of the largest and oldest research stations on Europa. It was essentially a collection of independent, but connected, submarine vessels that, when all docked together, totaled more than 20,000 square meters (nearly five acres) of space and was home to more than five hundred scientists and support staff. It was currently stationed at a massive undersea thermal vent — called "black smokers" by geologists. These undersea volcanoes were the primary source of heat energy, minerals, and organic chemicals that fueled the entire biosphere of Europa.

Cameron station was moored to the seafloor on top of a basalt ridge formed by the chemical and mineral fallout from the constant stream of black smoke erupting from the vent. The vent itself was located at the bottom of a great rift in the seafloor, caused by the outflow of magma between the tectonic plates of Europa's crust. Locating the station outside the rift gave the scientists easy access to the vents with the scores of vessels and mobile laboratories attached to the station. The hundreds of scientists studied processes and life forms, both in the rift near the vents, and under the seafloor on the sides of the towering ridges that bordered the great rift. While the life collected around the vents was indeed impressive, it was nothing compared to the diversity of microbial life that thrived in the sub-seafloor zone. Discoveries of new types of single and multi-celled organisms were being made almost daily. The man for which the station was named would have scarcely believed the scientific bonanza Europa represented for humanity.

Father Bożydar changed the display of their course to show their current depth in relation to their destination. During their journey they would descend more than sixty kilometers to the great rift valley. He looked around the transparent cabin and wondered what miraculous material it must be made from to withstand the crushing pressure outside, yet appear so fragile.

Gus interrupted his thoughts by saying, "Boz, I am reading a school of fish ahead. I can navigate around it easily, but I think you might enjoy the sight."

Father Bożydar's stomach fluttered at the thought of seeing a truly alien life form for the first time. How could he pass up an opportunity to see yet another of God's wondrous works? "Okay, Gus. Let's have a look."

A few moments later Father Bożydar spotted a faint glow in the distance below the craft. As the craft continued its gentle descent, the glowing mass took on more definition. He could see that the mass was actually thousands of individual creatures swirling and rolling in a great living maelstrom. As the craft entered the chaotic school of creatures, Gus said in his ear, "These are Blue Dragonfish. They are very intelligent and curious. Don't be alarmed if they probe us a bit."

Father Bożydar's eyes widened and he asked, "What do you mean by 'probe'?"

"You'll see," the pilot replied.

Outside the transparent hull of the craft the water glowed a brilliant blue, illuminated by the glowing bodies of the strange fish. They reminded the priest of eels — of which he had only seen pictures and video — with a large head, and a tapered snout outlined by rows of long, glowing semi-transparent teeth. Each Dragonfish had six large, oval eyes spaced equally around the circumference of it's cylindrical head. They appeared to be two to three meters in length, with a set of four long undulating fins that ran the length of their bodies in a corkscrew pattern. They moved through the water by apparently waving the fins in a rowing motion that propelled them forward and backward like a screw. They appeared to accelerate in a blur and their flexible bodies allowed them to change direction instantaneously.

Father Bożydar looked all around the ship and was astonished by the hundreds, perhaps thousands of creatures sliding along the hull in all directions. Some would pause and regard him with two or three of their eyes, slowly rotating their bodies along the skin of the ship. Others would swim rapidly toward him and change direction just before slamming into the side of the craft, allowing their long tails to hit the ship like a whip, causing the priest to reflexively jump back in his seat. It seemed as if they were not only curious about the ship, they were also aware of the men inside and were attempting to interact with them.

"They are starting to get a little frisky so I am going to turn on the repeller field. You might want to cover your ears," Gus said.

Before Father Bożydar could respond, an earsplitting screech filled the cabin as the Dragonfish darted away from the hull of the sub. "What in the name of God is that sound?" the priest shouted.

"That's the Dragonfish equivalent of 'ouch'. The repeller field disrupts their central nervous system and they don't like it very much. It is only effective a meter or so from the hull, but it does a good job of keeping them out of the fan ducts. I hate having to clean fish guts out of my propellers."

As quickly as they had entered the giant school of fish, the roiling mass of creatures dissipated and was gone into the darkness.

Father Bożydar's heart was pounding in his chest. The encounter with a life form not native to mother Earth was more amazing than he could have imagined. He spent the rest of the journey gazing expectantly into the absolute darkness for a glimpse of even more amazing creatures.

The map on the tablet showed they were approaching the great rift at a depth of fifty-eight kilometers. The pilot announced, "Boz, we are going to be entering the Cameron station traffic pattern. You should call your friend and let him know you'll be arriving shortly."

"Thank you, Gus." The priest touched the voice command icon on the tablet and waited for the ready tone then said, "Locate and call Kavan Ferre at the Cameron Academy of Marine Biology."

The tablet replied, "Locating Kavan Ferre…please wait a moment. Location confirmed, establishing link…link established with video and audio." The screen changed to display the inside of a cramped dimly lit room with an empty chair and a wall of illuminated instrument panels out of focus in the background.

"Hello, Kavan?" Father Bożydar began, his voice cracking. The room in the video display seemed to be empty but then a shadow crossed the wall and a blurry figure came into view and sat down in the chair. It took a second for the camera to focus on the man. On the screen Father Bożydar saw the face of his old friend for the first time in more than five years His wavy brown hair was grey at the temples, set atop a face covered in a scruffy multi-colored beard. The man's eyes were dull and lifeless, with the beginnings of what would someday be deep creases tugging at the corners.

He frowned into the camera and replied with an annoyed tone, "Yes, this is Kavan. Turn on your video, I can't see you."

Father Bożydar realized he had accidentally turned off the camera and fumbled to find the icon to turn it back on. Finally the green indicator on the tablet lit up. "Hello, Kavan. It's your foolish, old teacher."

Inside the research vessel, Kavan Ferre was stunned to see the face of his old friend and teacher on the screen. His mind reeled trying to imagine what the old priest could be doing here on Europa. He swallowed hard and said, "Boz! My God, what are you doing here? I mean, how did you find me?"

The priests eyes began to fill with tears at the sight of his friend. He looked so much older than his thirty-four years and his face wore a mask of sadness that was deeper than the last time he had seen him. "A friend helped me find you. I have come to ask for your help."

Kavan sat back in his chair his spirit heavy with the memory of their last meeting. "Father, I wish you had contacted me before you came so far. My life, my work is here now. I have worked very hard to forget the past. I just can't…"

The priest interrupted him, "I need to see you, Kavan. Please, just give me a chance to tell you why I have come." His eyes overflowed and warm tears streamed down his face.

Kavan's heart sank at the sight of the old priest, his friend, his tear-filled eyes silently pleading. He lowered his head into his hands and after a moment replied, "All right, Father. I'll see you. Tell your pilot to dock at pod number four. I'll be there when you arrive."

The video link went dark and Father Bożydar sat back and sobbed into his hands.

CHAPTER 8

Gunnery Sergeant Bruno Pinard of the Imperial Marines, Fifth Reconnaissance Platoon, peered around the bulkhead and down the corridor of the pirate ship *Boa Vista*. His platoon was arrayed behind him, awaiting his command to proceed with clearing the ship and arresting or killing the pirates. His primary mission was to locate and arrest the pirate Marco Bisbal-Rivera, but keeping his marines from shooting anything that moved was going to be a challenge.

Sergeant Eddie White noticed the service gantry on the schematic display of the *Boa Vista* in his Tactical Optic Data Display (TODD), a pair of surgically implanted lenses that were indispensable in a combat environment. He moved forward to the gunny's side and said, "Gunny, there is a service gantry that runs all the way from engineering to the command deck. I should be able to take a fire team and maybe flank them."

Gunny Pinard considered the request then nodded his consent. "Get a scan of that gantry before you go barreling through the hatch."

White replied, "Aye, Gunny." He raised two gloved fingers over his head signaling his fire team to pay attention, then pointed to the access ladder that led to the service gantry. Immediately, two marines moved to the base of the ladder while a third slung his rifle across his back and began to ascend. When he reached the hatch leading to the service gantry, White paused and looked back to his team leader. Another marine began ascending the ladder when a single shot rang out in the distance.

"Bravo squad take the port corridor and clear and hold at the mess hall. Non-lethals only unless you are fired upon. Check your TODD for Rivera's locator. He is to be taken alive." The squad leader acknowledged his order.

Gunny Pinard tapped a key on the control panel his left forearm that silently signaled his men to 'hold' while he investigated the gunfire. He held his rifle in the bulkhead opening using it as a camera to sight down the corridor and scan for heat signatures. His TODD did not show any indications of targets in the thirty meters of corridor that led to the mess hall. "Tactical, can you identify any targets?" Pinard asked the tactical officer aboard the battleship.

"Negative, Gunny. I'm reading an active shield and have no targets," the tactical officer replied.

"Roger that." Pinard considered his options and decided they would need to proceed, even though they were essentially blind and easy targets for anyone hiding in the many compartments throughout the ship. "Alpha squad fire team two get in that service gantry and move to the command deck hatch and hold."

"Aye, aye Gunny," White replied. "Team two, go!"

The marine at the top of the ladder tapped the control

panel and the service gantry hatch slid open. The marine held his rifle up through the hatchway and saw through his TODD that the gantry was clear. He continued up through the hatch and quickly cleared the opening to provide cover for the rest of the fire team as they ascended. In less than a minute, four marines were on the gantry moving in a tight tactical formation — three forward and one covering the rear — toward the command deck.

Gunny Pinard knew he needed to move his men now and gave the signal to begin a bounding overwatch movement down the corridor to the intersection at the mess hall. The two squads moved rapidly down both the port and starboard corridors until they reached the intersecting corridor. "Charlie squad, report," Pinard said.

Sergeant Maddy O'Brien halted her squad one deck below with a raised fist and replied, "We just cleared the machine shop and parts depot, heading for the main cargo hold. No contact."

"Roger that," Gunny replied. "Send in the eye to sweep the cargo hold before you move. Then proceed riki tik to the torpedo room."

"Aye, aye Gunny." Sergeant O'Brien pointed to a young private who carried the *eye* — an autonomous hover drone that would scan a tactical environment using a variety of optical, thermal, and magnetic instruments. It could pinpoint the location of enemy troops and mines and disable both with lethal and non-lethal weapons. The marine moved to the bulkhead and removed the *eye*, verified it was communicating with the control unit, then slowly opened the cargo bay hatch and guided the silent hovering disc-shaped drone into the dark cargo bay.

The control unit displayed the telemetry on the screen and optionally on each squad member's TODD display. If enemy targets were identified, they could use the drone telemetry to target the enemy as they cleared the room. As the drone slowly drifted through the cargo hold, over the containers and lockers of equipment, the marines studied the displays looking for the slightest indications of movement.

On the second deck Gunny Pinard had gathered Alpha and Bravo squads at the mess hall. He was about to begin moving forward toward the command deck when the tactical officer interrupted, "Gunny, I am reading thermal signatures in the Captain's Boat. Primary hatch is on deck two, starboard aft of the command deck. They are spinning up. It looks like they are making a run for it!"

Gunny Pinard slammed his fist into the wall and replied, "How many targets?"

"Reading six, Gunny."

"Roger that." Pinard knew that left six in the normal crew compliment for this ship, as reported by other Imperial Navy vessels that had the misfortune to meet *Boa Vista* in battle. He was surprised that the great pirate Marco Bisbal-Rivera would run, and was skeptical that the escaping crew might be a diversion. Now that the numbers were decidedly in their favor, Pinard decided it was time to pick up the pace and get to the command deck.

In the service gantry between decks two and three a bloodied and burned Li Xiang silently slid his body to the opening of an access tunnel. He had watched the four marines pass by the tunnel opening. He carefully removed a fragmentation grenade from a pouch in his vest, pulled the pin and counted *one-two-three* then threw it down the service gantry in the direction of the marines.

The marine covering the rear of the formation saw the grenade bounce across the decking and come to rest less than meter from his feet. Before he could react or warn his comrades the grenade exploded, killing him instantly. The cloud of shrapnel shredded the legs and arms of the other three marines leaving them bleeding and groaning on the deck.

Gunny Pinard heard and felt the explosion somewhere ahead of the mess hall. He immediately checked his TODD display and saw that one marine was killed and three were severely wounded. The medic was already receiving the telemetry and he would have to hurry to save them.

"Bravo, move to the command deck now! Alpha, get up in that service gantry and secure the wounded. Charlie, we've got contact up here. Clear that cargo hold and meet Bravo at the command deck. Delta, advance and hold at the mess hall to secure the retreat for our wounded. Everyone move, now!" Gunny Pinard crossed the room and exited into the port corridor to catch up with Bravo team as they moved forward.

Xiang kicked the ventilation grate out and swung his body to the deck inside a storage room adjacent to the mess hall. He unholstered his sidearm and moved to the door. Not knowing where the Imperial Marines were, he silently requested a location status from the FCIC. After a few seconds the computer gave him the positions and numbers of all the marines. His mind began calculating a route throughout the ship that would give him maximum cover while allowing him to surprise and kill as many marines as he could. The FCIC had informed him that the Captain's Boat had launched with five passengers on board. He knew his captain was still on the *Boa Vista* and that he would be on the bridge ready to defend his ship until the end. Xiang's job was to even the odds as much as possible.

***

The sound of the explosion startled Marco Bisbal-Rivera as he was simultaneously monitoring both the movements of the Imperial Marines closing on the command deck, and the trajectory of the Captain's Boat headed for the surface of Callisto. He immediately checked the FCIC and discovered that Xiang was alive and had instructed the computer to mask his signal. Rivera deduced that Xiang must have ambushed the marines in the service gantry. While he was pleased that his friend and fellow crew member was alive, this was an unexpected wrinkle in his plan.

Rivera instructed the FCIC to activate the biolink secure channel with Xiang. "Li, I am so glad you are okay. There is a marine squad moving through the cargo bay now and they will likely end up at the bridge. I will signal you when they are clear of the cargo bay. I need you to get below and find a place to hide. They are going to take me into custody, unless they kill me on sight. Either way, once they are clear of the ship you need to get in an escape pod and get the hell off of the ship. Do you hear me, mister?"

Xiang heard his captain's instructions but continued down the corridor. He had pledged his life to a particular lifestyle and his allegiance to Marco Bisbal-Rivera. He would fight until his dying breath to ensure his captain and his ship were safe.

Rivera saw that Xiang continued his pursuit of the marine squad in the port corridor. He frowned and shook his head but knew that his orders would have no effect on the young pirate. He would die today, but not before he had taken more marines with him.

Xiang came around a bend in the corridor and saw the squad of marines less than ten meters away. The marine covering the rear immediately shouted, "Contact!" and opened up with his assault rifle in Xiang's direction.

The rounds shattered the tensile ceramic material that made up the walls and ceiling of the corridor. Sharp fragments of wall struck Xiang in the face and chest. He stumbled backwards and retreated just beyond the bend. He released the tabs covering the magazine pouches on his vest, knowing he would need to reload rapidly. Dropping to one knee to present the smallest possible target while still retaining his mobility, Xiang set himself into the ancient Weaver Stance ready to deliver a double-tap to each marine as they entered his field of fire.

The marine covering the rear of the formation came into view and Xiang delivered two perfectly placed rounds to the center of his face. The young man's head snapped back as a torrent of blood spewed from the gaping wounds in his head — his lifeless body crashing to floor.

Three other marines emerged around the bend standing abreast, filling the corridor, the one in the center looking down to step over his fallen comrade. Xiang shot the marine on the right through his left eye, then quickly sighted on the marine on the left and delivered a round to the center of his forehead. The stunned marine in the center wore a look of horror as he pulled the trigger of his weapon spraying bullets into the floor in front of Xiang.

Xiang took steady aim, ignoring the ricocheting bullets whizzing past his head, and shot the startled marine in the throat. The young man dropped rifle and clutched his throat as blood erupted from between the fingers of his gloved hands. He stumbled backward, tripped on the dead body of his comrade, and fell to the deck, his legs kicking wildly and a sickening gurgling sound filling the corridor as he died.

Xiang readied himself for the next wave of marines to emerge in the corridor, but this thought was cut short by the single shot that hit the back of his head and sprayed pieces of his face and brain across the dull grey deck.

Gunny Pinard lowered his rifle then moved to the spot where the dead pirate lay. He knelt beside the man and carefully searched him for any explosive devices. The remaining marines from Bravo squad surrounded Pinard and stared down at the dead pirate, hatred plainly evident on their faces.

Pinard stood and said to his marines, "Damn good shooting for a pirate. Now let's get to the command deck. Double time!"

Rivera saw Xiang's status change to 'expired' on the FCIC crew display. He was proud of his young friend but was saddened at the senselessness of his death. It was time to end the bloodshed.

Moments later Rivera saw that twenty-three marines were assembled in a tactical formation outside the double access doors to the command deck. They were setting up a large particle beam cutter that would bore through the doors in a matter of minutes. Sensing the time had come to surrender, he instructed the FCIC to scan for the marine communication frequency and then said, "This is

Captain Marco Bisbal-Rivera, master of *Boa Vista*. I wish to surrender myself and my ship into the custody of the Imperial Marines. I will offer no resistance."

Gunny Pinard was stunned to hear Rivera's voice and saw the shared looks of surprise on the faces of his marines. Given the pirates legendary reputation, Pinard found it hard to believe that Rivera would simply surrender. He signaled for the team assembling the cutter to halt. They gathered their equipment and moved away from the bulkhead.

Pinard touched the control pad on his left arm and said, "Captain Rivera, this is Gunnery Sergeant Bruno Pinard, Fifth Recon, Imperial Marines. We will accept your surrender if you immediately instruct your FCIC on an open channel to transfer command authority to my voiceprint and biolink signature. When I open the blast doors if you are armed I will shoot you myself. Is that clear?"

Rivera felt relieved that this marine was professional and would accept his surrender. "I understand." He placed his hand on the command pad and said, "Rivera authorization one-seven-seven-six-alpha-theta, command transfer protocol one, initiate and standby for new voiceprint authorization."

The FCIC announced over the open communications channel, "Command authority transfer initiated, please voiceprint new command authority."

"Authorize new command," Pinard announced in his best command voice. The FCIC scanned Pinard's biolink signature and immediately reset all the ships systems to only accept commands from his unique signal and voice.

"Command transfer protocol one completed. Welcome

aboard Gunnery Sergeant Pinard. *Boa Vista* stands ready for your command. Would you like a systems status report at this time?" The FCIC coldly turned its attention to its new master, as if Rivera and his crew had never existed.

Pinard signaled to Alpha Squad to form up near the blast doors to take Rivera into custody. "Open the blast doors to the command deck," Pinard said and watched as the huge doors slid apart revealing the dimly lit bridge of *Boa Vista* and the figure of Marco Bisbal-Rivera standing in front of his command chair with his arms outstretched and his palms up in an almost pitiful posture of surrender.

Pinard strode through the bulkhead onto the bridge flanked by his squad of marines, their rifles menacingly pointed at Rivera's head.

"In the name of the Emperor Wan Sui Ye, I place you under arrest for crimes against the Empire," Pinard said with a smirk.

Rivera lowered his head as a marine pulled his arms behind his back and bound his wrists tightly.

CHAPTER 9

Sumiko was happy to be done with the flag captain's briefing. It had been several years since she was assigned to a long-duration mission and she had never participated in a fleet movement of this size and complexity. The tedium of such meetings and the minutia of coordinating the movements of a fleet was something she was thankful to have left behind in favor of more interesting work. Now she would be working with one of the most influential men in the Empire, someone who had a personal relationship with the Emperor himself. The Ambassador had already made it clear that he had more on his mind than a professional relationship. *If I play this right, it could get very interesting,* she thought.

When the meeting had adjourned, she called the Ambassador as promised and he agreed to meet her in the officer's lounge in thirty minutes. This would give her time to return to her quarters, change out of her dress white uniform into more comfortable off-duty clothes, and perhaps even have time to send a few messages before the communication blackout that would accompany the trans-solar maneuver.

She entered the habitation section and turned right down the corridor leading to her berth. She noticed a slender man in a light grey suit walking toward her. The manner in which he walked told Sumiko he was a man of confidence and power. Sumiko stopped at the door to her berth and the man halted a couple of meters short of her door and said, "Excuse me, Commander Lee. Would you have a moment to speak in private?" He was smiling but she could sense he was a man who wore a grin like a mask.

She turned and regarded the man. "I would be more inclined to speak with you if I knew your name," she said firmly.

"Please forgive me, Commander. My name is Nianzu Chao, from the Foreign Office." He did not offer anything more than what she asked.

Sumiko was not sure why, but she looked up and down the corridor before replying, "Good to meet you, Mr. Chao. Please come inside so we can talk." She touched the keypad with her right hand and the door opened to her small but comfortable private berth. Stepping inside, Sumiko offered Chao a seat, and pointed to the chair of a small desk that extended from the wall next to the doorway. She set down her tablet and took a seat on the bed, across the small room .

"I am sorry I do not have a beverage to offer you, " Sumiko smiled while trying not to look profoundly uncomfortable in the presence of this stranger.

"Perhaps we can retire to the officer's lounge for a drink after we speak," Chao replied.

Sumiko pondered *so this is the way it's going to be with these civilian bureaucrats on this trip?*

"You must be part of Ambassador Arin's team," Sumiko began innocuously.

Chao was a very careful intelligence officer and knew that it was important to gain allies where one could. He would need to trust this woman and share at least part of the truth to gain her trust and cooperation if he was to succeed.

He removed a small metallic disk from his jacket pocket and placed it on the desk. He touched his right index finger to the top of the disk and a small circle in the center began to pulse with a faint green glow. Sumiko watched intently, a quizzical expression on her face. "This will ensure privacy for our conversation. Please excuse my former statement, but I am an intelligence officer with the IIS. The Foreign Office title is my official cover."

Sumiko straightened and nodded her head slightly. She had met many IIS operatives in her various assignments in the Imperial Navy, and this man was not particularly impressive as agents went. "Okay. Go on."

"You are the liaison officer assigned to Ambassador Arin. In that role you will be privy to his conversations, documents, and communications. I need you to relay information to me on certain facets of this mission and the personnel selected for various key roles," he said bluntly.

Sumiko was careful to remain composed and not convey the shock that she was experiencing. This little man was asking her to essentially spy on a high ranking Imperial diplomat. This would not bode well for her naval career. She decided to proceed with great caution.

"Mr. Chao, you are asking me to betray my oath as an officer in the Imperial Navy. That is something I simply cannot do." She gave him a resolute stare and stood to open the door.

"Commander, I suggest you sit down and listen very carefully. Your career plans have just changed." His eyes were cold and made Sumiko feel like a child being scolded. She silently returned to the seat on the edge of her bed.

"Remus Arin is an impostor and an enemy of the Empire. He has infiltrated the highest levels of government and put the life of the Emperor and the power and prestige of the Empire at risk." Chao paused to let his words sink in.

Sumiko lowered her eyes in an ancient Japanese gesture of submission. She was now very afraid of the man sitting across the room and feared even more that her life was about to change for the worse.

"Commander, I listened to the recording of your mission briefing with Admiral Sivorenko and the Ambassador. You sensed that there was something wrong from the beginning." He watched Sumiko nod her head slowly. "Eleven ships — an entire fleet — to fetch a single ship from Titan? Does that sound like a normal Navy mission? Of course not. In fact, everything about this mission and the project on Titan is out of proportion."

Sumiko felt the shock within her begin to subside and be replaced by an insatiable curiosity. "A fleet this size has not been launched for a mission since the uprising on Ceres twelve years ago. I've checked."

"You are very thorough. It's a trait we share," Chao replied. "Commander, I've been curious about Remus Arin ever since he started his frequent travels to Far Side, and in the past few years, to Titan. At first I thought he using his influence with the Emperor to create a distant prefecture that he could rule without interference from Earth. But I dug deeper and what I found was, shall we say, more incredible than even a jaded intelligence officer like myself could have imagined." He had played a fair number of cards, now it was time to gauge the reaction of his would-be accomplice.

Sumiko was not one to speculate until she understood all the facts, and so far, Chao had not divulged much. "You said that the Ambassador is an 'impostor' — what exactly does that mean?" The embedded nano-machines carried within the body of every Imperial citizen had rendered the idea of falsifying one's identity virtually obsolete, and as such, words like 'impostor' had faded from the lexicon. It was likely that Sumiko did not understand the meaning of the word.

"It means that Remus Arin is not who he appears to be. His entire identity is a fraud, a fake, a fabrication." Chao could see that she was struggling to comprehend.

"How is that possible? The Emperor knows all of his children by name!" she said emphatically.

The popular adage *'the Emperor knows all of his children by name'* was really a childish euphemism for *'we are under constant surveillance and active identity monitoring all the days of our lives.'* For the average Imperial citizen it was a mundane fact they believed to be necessary for life. Most crime had been eradicated and when it did happen, the judicial process was simply a review of thousands of pieces of data collected before, during, and after the crime. The criminal was always caught and punished and the citizens of the Empire could not imagine any other way.

"For now, you must trust that it is possible. But that is

only the beginning. Arin used his manufactured identity to obtain his first job in government, and from there, he worked his way into the right places and spheres of influence to gain a personal audience with the Emperor. Once he met Our Lord, everything changed. His current title and position were created specifically for him by the Emperor. Never before in more than four hundred years of the Empire had such a thing been done. And it is all a lie." Chao sat back in the chair watching Sumiko take in his words.

After reflecting for a moment Sumiko said, "Mr. Chao, if what you say is true, then Remus Arin has executed a plan that spans decades, or longer if you consider the planning and construction of a false identity, if such a thing is even possible." She was beginning to doubt Chao. His story was starting to sound like bad fiction.

"He has time, believe me Commander, he has time," he said enigmatically. "My research has led to some initial conclusions that I am reticent to share until you prove to me that you can be trusted." Chao was testing the woman to see if she was as perceptive and intelligent as her security profile suggested.

Sumiko smiled and said, "Mr. Chao, you have no choice but to trust me. You have slandered one of the most powerful men in the Empire and solicited me to commit crimes against my oath and service. I would say we are in this thing neck deep...together." She stood and crossed the small room and leaned across the desk putting her face uncomfortably close to Chao's. "So you had better be correct about the Ambassador or we will both leave our heads in a basket."

Chao pushed back from the table and stood declaring,

"You will help me then. In this you will bring great honor to Our Lord and to the Empire."

Sumiko waved her hand dismissively, "Save the 'honor' speech. I'm not a wide-eyed cadet and, frankly, I couldn't care less about Mr. Arin's motives. But if he is using the Navy as a tool in his plan, then he has a problem with me."

Chao was impressed by the obvious conviction of her words and sincerity of her tone. His gut told him he could trust this woman and that pleased him.

A soft tone behind Sumiko's right ear signaled that it was time to meet Ambassador Arin in the officer's lounge. "Mr. Chao, I am sorry, but we will need to continue this conversation another time. I have an appointment with the Ambassador that I am now late for. It will not do well for me to be very late to our first real meeting."

"Drinks in the officer's lounge and a romantic stroll on the observation deck is not exactly a 'meeting', Commander Lee," Chao said with a sly grin. "But it is important that he trust you fully. So, go and play your part well. We will meet again when I have instructions for you. Until then, do not attempt to contact me in any way and do not mention my name to anyone, especially the Ambassador," he said as he picked up the metallic disk from the table.

"Good day, Mr. Chao." Sumiko bowed at the waist.

Chao returned the ancient gesture respectfully, quietly stepped from the room, and disappeared down the corridor.

***

The *Honamatsu* officer's lounge was a well-appointed room filled with comfortable chairs and small tables. These were

136

arranged in a variety of settings to offer patrons ample choices for either intimate conversations or boisterous group gatherings. The bar area was like every other bar in the solar system. A long counter surface with dozens of stools in front of an array of liquor bottles and beer taps.

The far wall of the lounge provided a heavily filtered yet breathtaking view of the rapidly approaching Sun, its corona blazing and dancing in arcs around the edges of the solar disk. This cast a pleasing orange glow throughout the room, making every surface appear soft and inviting.

Sumiko entered the officer's lounge wearing a stunning blue dress that hugged the delicate curves of her body. Her shimmering black hair hung gracefully down her back and over her left shoulder. She stood inside the door and scanned the room for Ambassador Arin. She found him sitting far across the room, to the right of the window, staring at the mesmerizing sun, one leg casually draped over the other, his hand loosely holding a rocks glass of Scotch above the table top.

He poses even when no one is looking, Sumiko thought. She smiled to herself, stepped down the few steps, and crossed the lounge. As she walked, every man and many of the women in the room silently watched the beautiful vision glide toward the window, the glow of the sun adding an ethereal quality to her movements.

Arin sensed the swirl of pheromones in the air and turned to see the exceptionally lovely Sumiko Lee approach the table. She was truly one of the most beautiful women he had ever seen in his long life. Remus placed his drink on the table and stood to greet his liaison officer.

"Good evening, Sumiko. You look, well, simply lovely,"

Remus said with a broad smile. He moved behind her and pulled the chair out, taking the opportunity to breathe in the aroma of her perfume.

"Thank you, Ambassador. You are too kind." She sat down gracefully and watched Remus return to his seat.

"Remember, Sumiko, you may call me Remus. What would you like to drink?"

"I will have a white wine, Remus," she replied with a coy smile and slight raise of an eyebrow.

Remus touched the surface of the table and ordered a white wine from the drink menu.

"How did the Captain's briefing go this afternoon?" Remus asked, a look of genuine interest on his face.

"It was long and tedious, filled with details that would bore a mere mortal to death," Sumiko replied lightly.

Remus chuckled and said ironically, "Indeed! You are no mere mortal. I am in the company of a goddess."

Sumiko blushed and parried, "Not a goddess, but a damned good naval officer. I have worked very hard to get to my current position and this mission will hopefully get me a command."

Remus admired the unabashed ambition present in this young woman. She knew what she wanted and would do whatever it took to get it. "This mission is important to the Emperor as well. That is why he asked me to oversee the escort of his ship to Earth. And I am pleased to have a liaison who can appreciate the consequences of a successful mission."

The robotic server approached and placed Sumiko's wine in front of her asking, "Would you like anything else, Commander Lee?"

"No, thank you," she replied. The server turned and

moved on to the next table to clear a pair of glasses.

"Remus, I have read the mission packet in detail but I am still curious about something." Sumiko took a small sip of her wine.

"I am sure you are curious about many aspects of this mission." Remus decided he would indulge her curiosity.

"Why was such a large fleet assigned for a simple escort mission? If this new ship design is classified, why are we willing to risk drawing attention to it with a dozen ships? Surely the new ship could have been flown in virtual secrecy." She folded her hands in her lap, adopting a stern pose.

Remus glanced around then turned to her with a cold stare, "Commander, are you questioning the wisdom of our Emperor?"

"No, Ambassador," she said firing back with his formal title, "I simply want to know if we are expecting trouble. If this project is truly secret, then why do we need so much firepower?" Sumiko returned his stare, her eyebrows raised in a prosecutorial manner.

"All right, Sumiko," Remus replied with mock surrender. "During my last inspection of the project on Titan, I discovered that a spy had infiltrated the laboratory and had been tampering with test data. The Emperor felt that we should bring a sizable force to Titan to discourage any potential adversaries. No one will challenge this fleet." Remus watched the young commander as she absorbed this new information.

"That is a reasonable precaution," she conceded. "I assume the spy has been identified and will be arrested upon our arrival at Titan?"

Remus was impressed by Sumiko's deductive powers.

"Yes, I know who the traitor is. The person will be dealt with in due course."

Sumiko saw a flash of rage in Remus' eyes. She shivered visibly. "Thank you for sharing that, Remus. I feel better about our mission now."

"Let's finish our drinks and head up to the observation deck. I don't want to miss the trans-solar insertion." Remus smiled and raised his glass.

***

Remus and Sumiko strolled through the corridor after watching the trans-solar maneuver from the observation lounge. She was pleased that Remus had focused their conversation on her childhood in Tokyo, her time at the Naval Academy, and her various assignments during her career. She rarely got an opportunity to share information about herself so openly. Sumiko had genuinely enjoyed their conversation. She found Remus to be very attentive and interested in her personal story. It was the most enjoyable evening she had with a man in many months.

Her rational mind kept reminding her that she must keep their relationship on a professional level; the mission was far more important than any momentary dalliance. But Sumiko also could not ignore, nor could she explain, the desire that was growing inside her core. A glance from Remus at her breasts, or a slight touch of his hand sent waves of anticipation and pleasure pulsing through her body. While she was moderately experienced in matters of romance, and she had fully explored the boundaries of her sexuality with both men and women, she had never reacted so primally to any man before. There was something about Remus Arin that caused Sumiko to want to release her animal instincts and lose herself in the fullness of his manhood.

Now that the evening was over, she was dreading the awkward moment that would surely come as they approached her quarters. She thought about pausing at the entrance to the habitation module and simply thanking the Ambassador for an enjoyable first night aboard the *Honamatsu*. *Would he be offended*, she wondered. *What's the harm in letting him walk me to my quarters?* Surely she could control herself and say 'goodnight' at her door and tomorrow they would both be professional and conduct themselves accordingly.

Remus was engaged in a completely one-sided internal conversation. He knew full well how the evening would unfold — he had been seducing human women for millennia. Like a cunning predator in the wild, he had been carefully lulling his prey into a sense of complete calm and unawareness of the danger that surrounded her. The matter would be concluded shortly. Sumiko would surrender her body and her will to Remus, and do it with an eagerness that would shock her.

As they approached the entrance to the habitation module, Sumiko said, "Remus, I have had an unexpectedly wonderful time tonight."

Without giving her an opportunity to continue her thought, Remus interjected, "And there is no reason for it to end. I have something very special planned for you." He looked directly into her eyes and began probing her mind for the place where her desire dwelt. *There...now she will be mine.*

Sumiko stared into Remus' eyes and felt light-headed for a moment, then she noticed the familiar tingling sensation between her legs. She wanted to take Remus right then in the corridor in front of any passersby.

She touched her face and broke eye contact with Remus saying, "Remus, I think that we need to proceed cautiously. After all, we both have a job to do on this mission and we must not compromise our judgment." Sumiko did not even believe the words she was speaking. A flame had ignited within her that was familiar, yet something altogether new — a raw and primal craving.

Remus gently took her hand and proceeded to lead her silently down the corridor in the direction of his stateroom. Sumiko knew where they were going and why, but did not, perhaps could not, protest. Every ounce of her being knew it was wrong, but her desire for this man was greater than her faltering control. She was caught up as if by a giant wave, her mind reeling with the euphoria of the ride, yet dreading the unavoidable crash against the shoreline.

As they approached the door of his room, Remus reached out with his Spirit and entered Sumiko, intertwining his will with hers in an abominable form of spiritual foreplay. As he exerted his will on her, he could sense the last vestiges of her resistance fall away like an avalanche of snow on a mountainside. She was his, for this moment in time, another victim of his unbounded lust.

He opened the door to his stateroom and Sumiko glided through the entrance as if in a dream. She moved to the center of the dimly lit room, and in one graceful motion released the clasp of her dress on her shoulder as Remus watched in the shadows. The dress fell to the floor revealing Sumiko's naked body, as she trembled with anticipation and desire in the blueish glow of the night.

Remus' eyes flashed red in the shadows as he approached her, and a chill of excitement and fear ran down Sumiko's spine.

They fell together and Sumiko surrendered herself into the hands of the demon.

CHAPTER 10

Kavan Ferre stood at the window of the docking pod with his arms folded tightly, watching the small submarine taxi gently glide into position above the docking tower of the Cameron Academy of Marine Biology. His mind was still struggling to grasp the fact that his old teacher and mentor Father Bożydar Jofre had somehow found him at the bottom of the sea on Europa. He could not imagine what would cause the old priest to make such a long and perilous journey. Whatever is was, it could not be good.

Moments later he heard the locking mechanism on the hatch cycle open, followed by the usual splash of sea water onto the deck at the bottom of the ladder. A small figure dressed in a black thermal jacket and grey thermal pants, gingerly descended the ladder, pausing at the bottom to wave to the taxi driver smiling down through the hatch. As the man slowly turned around, a lump formed in Kavan's throat when his eyes met those of Father Bożydar.

The two stood for a moment looking at each other, each lost in the memory of their last parting, each feeling ashamed at the distance that was allowed to grow between them. Slowly they approached each other, their arms instinctively guiding them into a familiar warm embrace. The smaller priest placed his head on Kavan's shoulder and savored the reunion with the man who was like a son. Tears flowed down both men's cheeks as they pulled back and inspected each other's faces.

"Father, I think you've shrunk," Kavan quipped, trying to lighten the mood a bit.

"Perhaps, but I am surely fatter!" the old priest laughed as he quickly wiped away his tears. "Kavan, my son, it is very good to see you. I am so very sorry that we parted, well, so badly." The old priest wore an expression of genuine shame.

Kavan hung his head and said, "Father, you have nothing to apologize for. I was not myself in those days after the accident. I was lashing out at everyone — I lost control." He looked up into the priest's moist eyes, "I was angry at God and I focused my anger on you. It was wrong, and I am sorry."

"Speak of it no more, my son. I love you and that is all that matters." Father Bożydar placed his wrinkled hand on Kavan's shoulder and smiled.

"Thanks, Boz." Kavan suddenly noticed that several other people had gathered in the docking pod and were uncomfortably trying not to notice the tearful reunion taking place in their midst.

"You must be hungry, I ordered some dinner for us. We can eat in my apartment if that's all right?"

Father Bożydar clutched his stomach and said, "That would be wonderful. It was quite a long ride."

Kavan placed his arm around the old priest's shoulder as they left the docking pod, and walked into the winding corridors of the station.

***

After graduating from the mission school at age fifteen, Kavan Ferre had been accepted into the Schiaparelli Institute at Huygens and began his studies in applied mathematics and physics. His intellectual gifts were matched only by his seemingly endless energy and apparent disdain for sleep. He spent most of his time in the experimental laboratories working on a wide variety of projects.

By his senior year, Ferre had already proven the *Yang-Mills Existence and Mass Gap* equation, and gained some fame for solving one of the most difficult mathematical puzzles in history. But it was his work in quantum field theory that would define his future. Kavan had proven mathematically that it was possible to induce a field which would bring two arbitrary points of the universe into contact, effectively eliminating the physical distance between them, and theoretically allowing a mass to travel without actually moving through the intervening space. His work was deemed the *Ferre Field Construct*. Such a system of travel had been conjectured in science fiction and popular culture for centuries, but Kavan had actually proven the math. Creating the machines to make it a reality then became the sole focus of his life.

At age twenty-five, with a massive grant from the Colonial Academy of Science, and a consortium of wealthy Martian industrialists, Ferre established a laboratory on the asteroid 216 Kleopatra, an odd lump of metal and rock shaped like a dog bone roughly the size of New Jersey back on Earth. The bizarre shape of the asteroid was ideal for the laboratory complex and field

146

generator. The station was located at one end of the asteroid, built under the surface and oriented to take advantage of the centrifugal force of the asteroid's natural end-over-end rotation, simulating the gravity on his native Mars. A massive tunnel was excavated through the central axis extending more than two hundred kilometers to the opposite end of the asteroid, connecting the field generator complex and fusion reactor. A high speed tram was used to shuttle staff and equipment between the laboratory complex and the generator complex.

Within five years of the laboratory's completion, Kavan had demonstrated the validity of his theories on a small scale. His work was highly classified and done under the close supervision of the colonial government. Owning the ability to travel instantaneously across the solar system and beyond was a strategic advantage that would shift the balance of power in Mars' favor. The dominance of the Empire and its influence on the independent and corporate worlds finally would be broken, and the Mars Colonial Confederation would be free to pursue its destiny.

During these years, Kavan made frequent trips home to Mars. There he would spend long evenings drinking and debating with his friend and teacher, Father Bożydar. He could not really discuss his work at the lab, so mostly they would argue over obscure points of doctrine, or the latest archaeological discoveries back on Earth.

On one trip more than ten years ago, he appeared unannounced at the monastery in Chaos. He brought with him one of his colleagues from the laboratory, a beautiful young woman named Kareena Rai. She was a gifted engineer, and was one of the few women Kavan had ever met who could hold his interest. Her keen intellect, quiet and generous spirit, and stunning beauty had captivated him. Three days into his visit home, Kavan announced at dinner with his parents and Father Bożydar that he and Kareena were engaged. His parents were pleased that their son had found someone who could love him, despite his fierce genius. They quickly planned a small and intimate wedding in the chapel of the monastery.

While Kavan's parents were still enthusiastic atheists, over the years their son had come to accept the fervent faith of his mentor and teacher. Kavan's parents considered it to be an inconvenient, but worthwhile trade-off for the education and guidance their son had received from the Jesuit scholar. For his part, Kavan seemed to be genuinely devout and happy in his faith. His happiness brought them joy.

On a Saturday morning in June, Kavan Ferre and Kareena Rai were married by Father Bożydar in front of a small congregation of family and friends. Within a year, Kareena gave birth to their first child, a son, with bright blue eyes like his father, and soft brown skin like his mother. When Peter was two years old, Kareena gave birth to his sister, Sarah, with deep chestnut eyes and a face like an angel.

Kavan was happy. He had his beautiful wife, two precious children, and his work. He was certain that God had placed him exactly where he was meant to be, and this gave him a peace and serenity that had eluded him all of his life.

The work at the laboratory progressed steadily until Kavan was ready to conduct the first large-scale experiment. While his team had demonstrated the ability to transport particles and eventually small objects from one point to another within the confines of the laboratory, they had yet to demonstrate how a powerful enough field could be generated to move an object with significant mass. They had labored for more than three years designing a large-scale field generator, that would create a field large enough to pass a ship through.

Ultimately, they solved the problem by locating a field resonator on Cleoselene, one of two tiny moons that orbited 216 Kleopatra. The idea had been proposed by a brilliant physicist, named Azrael Vrubel, who had recently joined the project. Dr. Vrubel had been recommended by the Colonial Academy of Science to work on the scaling phase of the project. His resume was impeccable, as Kavan insisted that only the brightest and most creative minds be associated with the project. Within weeks of his arrival at the laboratory, Kavan had not only come to respect the mental prowess of Dr. Vrubel, he was also awed by Vrubel's intuitive ability to solve seemingly insurmountable technical challenges. Azrael was the most gifted physicist Kavan had ever met and he was humbled by the man's intellect. He was the only man Kavan had met that could match his genius.

On the day of the large-scale test, they planned to send a laser beacon through the Ferre Field to the L1 Lagrange point between Europa and Jupiter — a stationary point in the orbital space between the planet and its moon where a satellite could be 'parked'. If the experiment worked, the laser beacon would be instantaneously transported from the L1 point at 216 Kleopatra to the L1 point between Jupiter and Europa. Upon arrival, the beacon would immediately take a picture of Jupiter and Europa, then transmit it back to 216 Kleopatra via a laser link. They would make history.

Kavan was manning the field resonator station on Cleoselene with a handful of technicians, while the rest of the team, including Kareena and Azrael, managed the experiment from the laboratory. The laser beacon had been maneuvered into position and all of the last minute system checks had been done The field generator worked perfectly and the laser beacon disappeared at the precise moment that Kavan's calculations had predicted.

The sound of cheering and clapping filled the communications link between the lab and the resonator station. In a moment, the images of Jupiter and Europa would appear on their screens, and Kavan's place in history among the pantheon of great inventors would be secured. But as the team was congratulating each other, a small seismic tremor passed through Cleoselene causing the resonator to lose focus. Instead of the Ferre Field collapsing like a soap bubble as designed, it expanded uncontrollably, engulfing 216 Kleopatra entirely.

Kavan watched as the asteroid, along with his wife and children, the sum total of his entire life, simply disappeared. He sat in stunned silence as the others around him stood by in horror, realizing that their colleagues and friends were gone. After several minutes, Kavan slumped to the floor screaming, cursing God for taking from him everything that he valued in this life.

During the flight back to Mars aboard a Colonial Navy search and rescue vessel, Kavan attempted suicide by slashing his wrists. Fortunately, the nano-machines in his body slowed the blood loss enough for the medics to arrive and save his life.

He spent several months in a hospital undergoing psychiatric treatment, but was finally released after multiple tests and interviews with doctors determined that he was unlikely to try harming himself again. He went back to Chaos for a few months and rented a small one room apartment. His parents tried repeatedly to help him work through his grief, but they soon came to realize that Kavan was unable or unwilling to let go of his anger and sorrow. He seemed to cling to both as a new source of energy — one that was dark and brooding and closed off from the world.

The most troubling aspect of this time was Kavan's complete abandonment of his once-fervent faith. While his parents did not understand the initial reasons for his conversion to Christianity and his passion for its bizarre ancient rituals, they knew it had been an integral part of their son's life. He once explained that his faith in God helped him make sense of an otherwise confounding universe. He believed that he was blessed with the gift of extraordinary insight and intelligence so that he could help mankind understand the miracle of creation and the beautiful complexity of physics.

During his months on Mars, Kavan did not attend mass at the monastery chapel, and did not visit with Father Bożydar. The priest tried to see Kavan nearly every day, but he would not answer the door and actively avoided seeing the priest in public, only venturing out when he knew the priest was teaching his class at the monastery school.

Kavan's deliberate separation from his friend and God weighed heavily on Father Bożydar's Spirit. He prayed constantly for his friend, hoping that the Holy Spirit would lighten his burden of grief and bring him back into the light.

His sudden decision to move to Europa and use his intellectual gifts in an entirely new pursuit gave his parents some measure of relief. They hoped that putting his mind to work on a new set of problems would ease his pain, or at least distract his mind for considerable periods of time.

Kavan accepted a position at the Cameron Institute to study the complex ecosystem of microbial organisms living under the seafloor on Europa. The work was interesting, complex, and most importantly, done with the aid of machines, not people. The odd community of the Cameron Institute was home to hundreds of socially crippled men and women whose work was all-consuming. Most did not find the isolation of living at the bottom of an alien sea to be an impediment to happiness or fulfillment. Their work was their life.

The day before Kavan was to depart for Europa, Lillian Ferre came to the school wearing a look of utter desperation on her aging face. She told Father Bożydar of her concern that Kavan was never going to return to Mars, and that she wanted nothing more than to have his faith in God and in Man restored. They concocted a plan to have Father Bożydar see Kavan at dinner that evening at the Ferre home. They both knew he would be very angry, but hoped that seeing his old friend and teacher would crack the dam of his grief and allow the healing of his Spirit to begin.

Kavan arrived at his parents house and walked into the parlor to find Father Bożydar sitting on the sofa. Before Kavan could react, Father Bożydar stood quickly and moved to embrace his student. Kavan held out his hands and halted the priest and shouted, "No! You are not going to heal me priest!"

Father Bożydar saw the rising anger on Kavan's face and was for the first time afraid of the young man. He took a step backward and said, "Kavan, I know you are grieving. But you must give it all to God, only He can heal your sorrow."

Eduardo and Lillian Ferre looked on from across the room, fighting the urge to rush to their son and embrace him as they did when he was a child with a bruised elbow.

"Heal me? He did this to me!" Kavan's face and eyes were wild with rage. "No Boz, I will never ask that monster for anything ever again. He gave me the illusion of happiness. Kareena, Peter, … and Sarah," his voiced cracked and tears formed at the corners of his eyes. "But then he took it all away. He murdered all the others too. For what?" Kavan screamed.

Father Bożydar stood with his hands clasped in front of him pleading, "Please, Kavan, don't say such things. God did not murder your family and team. Sometimes we cannot explain…"

Kavan cut him off, "Don't recite empty platitudes to me, priest! You taught me too well. I know that everything happens by His design or with His permission. Even the evil things in this universe are allowed by Him. It has always puzzled me, but I let my faith cover over the doubts. But now I see what He is. This…," Kavan spread his arms wide and looked around the room, "…all of this is just His laboratory. He pokes and prods us to see how we react. The universe is just some sick experiment."

Father Bożydar wept at the torrent of words coming

from his beloved student. Kavan's Spirit was dying and there was nothing he could do to help him.

"Kavan, God can work all things for good. You must not turn away, not now. These are the times when we must cling to the Father."

"Really? He is somehow going to work the death of my children for good?" His bright eyes bore into the old priest. He looked to his parents and said, "You were right all along. It *is* better to believe in nothing than in a monstrous god that plays with creation like a toy."

Kavan turned his attention back to his teacher and friend, "Go away old man and leave me alone. I want nothing more to do with your God, and I no longer need you to teach me anything."

Father Bożydar was shattered. He could not bear the heat of Kavan's anger. Through tear-filled eyes he looked across the room to Lillian and Eduardo, but they were both staring at the floor, unable to help him. He knew there was nothing more to be done. As he walked toward the door, he reached out to touch Kavan's shoulder, but the man stepped back and glared at the priest with vacant eyes.

The old priest left the house and walked down the street back to the monastery leaving behind a piece of his soul.

CHAPTER 11

Nianzu Chao walked into the Combat Information Center (CIC) of the *Honamatsu* and approached the intelligence analyst station under the watchful eye of Captain Jayden Daley. The captain was always leery of spooks, but Chao's manner was particularly disconcerting. Unlike other intelligence operatives who were normally deferential to senior command staff, Chao as yet had not interacted with the crew or senior staff, and he was clearly promoting his own incomprehensible agenda.

Chao leaned over the shoulder of the analyst and said, "Can you quietly locate Ambassador Arin for me?"

The analyst stiffened then replied, "Of course, sir." After touching the control panel the analyst looked up and said, "The Ambassador is in his stateroom."

"Thank you." Chao turned to leave when the analyst added, "Sir, the Ambassador is not alone in his quarters."

"I see. Then please notify me when he is alone or if he leaves," Chao instructed.

"Yes, sir."

In the day that he had been aboard the *Honamatsu*,

Chao had already verified that the marine battalion aboard was carrying an unusually large compliment of weapons and equipment for such a seemingly innocent escort mission. A special cargo module had been added to *Honamatsu* to accommodate the equipment, and an entire squadron of drop ships were crammed onto the flight deck. The flagship was laden as if she was going to war, and it made no sense to Chao.

The Emperor had authorized Remus Arin to put together the escort mission, but the fleet records showed that all of the ship assignments, crew selections, and outfitting had been done through Admiral Sivorenko's staff and by his direct order. Whatever the purpose was behind such a massive force, the Admiral was complicit. It was a mystery that Chao was determined to unravel.

As Chao turned to leave the CIC, he found Captain Daley standing directly behind him wearing an accusatory look on his face. "Mr. Chao, we have not had a chance to speak at length since you boarded my ship. Please join me in my ready room." He held out his hand indicating the door to the ready room.

Chao was careful to not let his contempt for the Captain show on his face. It was a skill he had mastered as a practitioner of the dark arts of intelligence. "The Emperor's ship," he said in a carefully modulated tone.

The Captain cocked his head and said with a puzzled look, "I'm sorry, what…"

"*Honamatsu* is the Emperor's ship. I believe you called it 'my' ship. That would be a crime against the Emperor." Chao stared coldly into the Captain's eyes.

"I beg your pardon, Mr. Chao. Please forgive my carelessness." The Captain lowered his eyes in submission.

Chao smiled at the small but important victory over the man and decided to take one more verbal swipe at Captain Daley. "I will leave that detail of our conversation out of my report to the Emperor."

"Thank you, sir." The Captain ushered Chao into his ready room and offered him a seat in a small parlor space across from his desk.

Now that Chao had chastised the Captain, he decided to steer the conversation in a direction that would benefit his investigation. His mission was focused on one thing, and he did not have time to pander to egos or engage in small talk as entertainment for the Captain. "Captain Daley, I need you to explain to me why a simple escort mission requires eleven ships and nearly an entire regiment of Marines."

The Captain narrowed his eyes then stroked his chin nervously. "Mr. Chao, that is a question for Admiral Butchers."

Chao leaned forward in the chair slightly and said, "Perhaps, but I am asking *you*, Captain."

The Captain looked away then sighed deeply, "Mr. Chao, please. My ship...I mean, *this* ship was chosen to carry the flag for the mission the day before we broke orbit. The crew worked all night to get her supplied and flight ready. I received very thin details on the mission profile." He lowered his voice and continued, "But it *is* damned strange to have this much iron sailing on a simple escort mission." He sat back in his chair, looking relieved to have shared his concern with another person.

Chao was surprised at the man's obvious candor and lack of mission knowledge. Perhaps he could use him to discover more pieces of the puzzle. "What is the standard marine contingent for this ship on a patrol cruise?"

"One platoon, sometimes two if we are patrolling a particularly dangerous sector. But for this mission we have an entire recon battalion. Recon! I've never even seen an entire recon battalion before, except on a parade ground." Daley's eyes were wide and his face and ears were turning red.

"Do you have any theories about why nearly a dozen ships and a regiment of marines are part of this mission?" Chao asked.

Captain Daley paused, then offered, "Do you recall the uprising on Ganymede about three years ago?"

Chao nodded in reply.

"We took a flotilla half this size and defeated over forty ships, and subdued the entire colony at seven sites scattered across the moon. It took less the two days." He raised an eyebrow and announced with his thick Irish brogue, "I believe this flotilla is sailing to war."

***

Sumiko Lee woke to the sound of a door chime hammering in her head. She slowly sat up in her narrow bed and rubbed her eyes. Hearing the door chime a second time, she stood up and put on a long dressing robe. As she crossed the room she touched behind her right ear and said, "Yes. Who is it?"

Nianzu Chao stood in the corridor with an impatient frown and replied, "It's Chao. Meet me in the CIC in ten minutes."

Sumiko was annoyed at Chao's commanding tone and said, "Mr. Chao, I have a full schedule this morning and cannot meet with you."

Chao was already walking down the corridor toward

the command deck when he replied, "Commander, it was not a request. Be there in ten minutes or I will send a security detail to retrieve you."

Sumiko was stunned at his insolent tone but decided it would do no good to cross him further, "All right, Mr. Chao. I will be there."

Exactly ten minutes later Sumiko entered the CIC, her hair pulled up in a swirl and wearing a utility uniform of khaki slacks and a dark blue tunic. Chao made eye contact with her and pointed across the CIC to a doorway. She crossed the room and met Chao at the door.

Chao spoke as Sumiko was opening her mouth, "Go inside and take a seat. I will get the Captain and join you shortly."

Sumiko raised her eyebrows then stepped through the door into the Captain's ready room. She took a seat at the small conference table. A moment later the door slid open and Captain Daley and Chao stepped through. Without saying a word they took seats at the table.

Chao began, "Commander Lee, you obviously took my suggestion to get close to the Ambassador a bit too seriously. Was it a calculated tactic to sleep with him last night?"

Sumiko blushed and looked away from Chao to the stony face of Captain Daley, the traces of a smirk visible at the corners of his mouth. "Mr. Chao, please remind me again of what your official position is here on this ship." She sat back in the chair and folded her arms, glaring at Chao. Sumiko knew she was taking a risk challenging Chao in this manner. While small and thin in stature, he was nonetheless a powerful presence.

Chao looked to the Captain who replied, "Commander,

I could throw you in the brig right now for the duration of this mission and deal with you when we arrive back at Earth. This is not a game and your career is over if I so choose."

Sumiko felt the situation spiraling out of control and could sense the purpose behind the threats. "Captain, are you aware that Mr. Chao tried to enlist me to spy on Ambassador Arin yesterday?"

"I am aware of Mr. Chao's mission," the Captain said, leaning forward slightly, his expression softening a bit. "You would do well to cooperate, Commander."

Sumiko lowered her eyes and uncrossed her arms. "Alright. My intention was to simply spend some time getting to know the Ambassador last night. You know, let him talk about himself, smile a lot, make him feel special." She leaned forward placing her elbows on the table, "But it was strange. He somehow steered the conversation all evening and just kept me talking about myself. I didn't realize it at the time, but he manipulated me all night. Right up to the end."

Captain Daley furrowed his brow and asked, "What do you mean by 'manipulated'? Did he drug you, or force you in some way?"

"No sir, that's not what I meant." She struggled to find the right words, "He has a strangely magnetic appeal — from a female perspective, if you know what I mean."

The Captain smiled quickly and said, "I think I understand, Commander. He is a handsome man."

Chao interrupted, "He is more than simply physically appealing, Captain. He has the ability to influence a person's behavior by means that are not fully understood."

Sumiko cocked her head and asked, "What does that

mean? Are you saying he can control a person's mind?"

Chao nodded, "That is perhaps a simplification, but essentially correct." He turned to the Captain and continued, "Captain, this man is extremely dangerous and has infiltrated the entire command structure of this mission."

"What do you mean," Sumiko asked.

"This mission was authorized by the Emperor less than two days before it left Earth orbit. Yet no one seemed to question the speed and precision with which it was assembled. Arin had ten of the ships prepositioned, an entire marine recon battalion ready on station at Quito, and a hand-picked list of officers and senior NCO's on station at TOLS-2 ready to take strategic, specially assigned positions aboard every ship in the flotilla. This mission had months of planning beforehand, of that there is no doubt."

The Captain spoke up, "Mr. Chao, the pre-planning of a mission like this is easy to explain. Ambassador Arin has been heavily involved in the project on Titan from the beginning. This ship even helped ferry personnel to Titan on two occasions. Clearly it was part of the overall project plan to escort the ship to Earth upon completion. Such a mission would naturally be planned well in advance."

Before Chao could respond, the panel on the table in front of the Captain came to life displaying the face of the communications officer. She announced, "Captain, I have a flash traffic priority one communication from fleet HQ for you. Shall I patch it through?"

"Yes, thank you, Lieutenant," Daley replied.

The screen shifted to display the Imperial Navy emblem then faded until the face of the Minister of Defense Li

Ang Shen appeared. He announced, "The Imperial destroyer *Haikou* has intercepted the pirate ship *Boa Vista* and captured the criminal Marco Bisbal-Rivera. The flotilla currently under the command of Admiral Butchers is hereby ordered, in the name of Emperor, to divert immediately to Callisto to rendezvous with the *Haikou* and secure the orbital environment in the event of a show of force from Rivera's fleet or their allies. Your marines shall take custody of Rivera and transfer him to the *Honamatsu* for transport back to Earth upon the completion of your primary mission. Orders have been sent to Admiral Butchers under separate transmission. Acknowledge receipt and wilco with arrival coordinates for the flotilla immediately. End transmission." The screen went blank.

Captain Daley looked up to see the stunned looks worn by both Sumiko and Chao. He touched the screen and the face of the First Officer appeared, "Sir?"

"Mr. Collins, set a course for Callisto to rendezvous with the *Haikou* currently in orbit there. Transmit flight plan to the flotilla. I want to be under way in five minutes," Captain Daley ordered.

"Aye aye, Captain." The First Officer touched his screen, opening the ship wide communication channel. Each person aboard *Honamatsu* heard via their biolink, "Attention all hands. Secure for course change in three minutes. Expect lateral G-force disruptions on all decks. All off-duty crew grab a rack. All on-duty crew must secure at station. Thirty second countdown clock will begin at the tone. There will be no other announcement."

Chao was not a superstitious man, even though he had been raised in a culture that saw meaning even in the tea leaves at the bottom of a cup. But he had a distinct feeling at the news of Marco Bisbal-Rivera's capture, that the fates were decidedly against him. Had his special arrangement with the pirate been discovered by Remus Arin? If not, how would Arin react to the interruption of the mission? One thing he knew for certain was that Remus Arin could not be allowed near Rivera. He knew he would have to work quickly to prevent a disaster that would expose him, and cause his mission to fail, jeopardizing the relative peace and stability of the entire solar system.

Captain Daley stood up and said, "Well, we'd better adjourn for now. Commander Lee, you will remain here until we reconvene when the course change is complete."

"Aye, Captain." For the first time in recent memory, Sumiko felt as if her life was not under her control.

***

Remus Arin was sitting in the darkness of his stateroom, his mind millions of kilometers and hundreds of years away. He was replaying with perfect clarity a day in 1942 when he was known as Klaus Fischer, an SS officer and commandant of the *SS-Sonderkommando Sobibo*r, a concentration camp in occupied Poland during the Second World War on Earth.

The remnants of a brigade of Russian Army soldiers — more than twelve hundred men — were delivered to the camp on a filthy train. Remus trembled with ecstasy as he replayed the scene of a seemingly endless rank of men marching nude in the driving November rain, and the sound of machine guns, the smell of gun powder and fresh blood mixing with the heady scent of the pine forest. His mind's eye recalled in vivid detail the rivers of blood that ran along the ground, pooling in the footsteps of the dead in the muddy ground.

After taking a machine gun in his own hands and killing more than two hundred men that day, he retired with his officers to a festive meal of fresh venison, roasted potatoes, and ale. Later that evening, a group of twenty novitiates from a local nunnery were brought at gunpoint to the beer hall where they were systematically raped by Remus and his officers. The memory of that evening, more than six centuries past, nearly brought him to climax.

His dark pleasure was interrupted by the sound of an incoming priority message at his work surface. He opened his eyes, then slipped on a dressing robe before sitting down and playing the message. The text of Remus' message was essentially the same as the one Captain Daley had reviewed moments before.

Remus smiled and was pleased that everything was proceeding according to his meticulously conceived plan.

Moments later, after the tone signaling the course correction maneuver would begin, Remus was secured in the four-point harness of the folding seat on the wall of his stateroom. As the ship was slowly turned in a new direction by the massive thrust vectoring drive, every person on board felt their relative body weight steadily increase. He watched as every item on the table and shelves in his room, slowly slid across the surface until it was stopped or reached the edge and fell to the floor. Remus enjoyed the sensation. It reminded him of flying.

When the maneuver was completed a voice announced throughout the ship, "Course change complete. All departments set condition normal. Report any damage immediately."

Remus touched the space behind his right ear and said,

"Please call Commander Lee." A soft tone indicated the implant understood his command and was connecting with the Commander's biolink.

Seconds later a voice announced to Remus, "Commander Lee is not taking calls at the moment. Would you like to record a message?"

Remus frowned and replied, "What is Commander Lee's current location?"

"Commander Lee is currently in Captain Daley's ready room."

"Who is present with Commander Lee?" Remus asked.

"Captain Daley and Special Envoy Nianzu Chao," the pleasant but cold voice replied.

Remus' anger rose at the mere mention of Chao's name. Remus wondered, *What is that worm doing with the Captain and Sumiko?*

Immediately he reached out with his Spirit seeking the familiar pattern of his Brother. After a moment he found that which he sought, and said silently with only his mind, *'Brother, can you join me in the CIC? It is time to put a leash on that dog Chao.'*

'Of course, Brother. I will see you shortly,' replied Admiral Butchers.

CHAPTER 12

Kavan and Father Bożydar sat at a small table in the dim and cluttered apartment at the bottom of the sea. They shared a meal of a lobster-like animal, steamed rice, and edamame. Kavan had opened a bottle of Russian Vodka, and it was already helping to lubricate their conversation.

Father Bożydar knew that before he could tell Kavan the purpose of his visit, he had to understand if he had come to terms with the horrible tragedy that altered his life, and brought him to this lonely place. The topic was a deadly minefield of emotions and guilt that would need to be crossed with great care and caution. "Tell me, Kavan, why did you decide to come to Europa and study fish?"

Kavan furrowed his brow and replied, "After the accident, I had no desire to revisit my old work. For a long time I reviewed my designs and calculations searching for an error. I was certain that I would find some flaw, some gap in my planning." Shaking his head, he continued, "But I found nothing. Every calculation was meticulously checked and rechecked, and the equipment worked perfectly — except the system did not shut down when the tremor passed through Cleoselene. It should have cut off the field generator instantly when the tremor was detected. But instead, the field integrity monitors shifted the field boundaries to pass over 216 Kleopatra. I calculated that the probability of a computer glitch or equipment malfunction causing that specific of a failure was, well, frankly it was absurd."

Father Bożydar was not surprised that his friend had solved the riddle of why the experiment failed and ended in tragedy, given the power of the man's intellect. For the sake of their mission, he prayed that Kavan had not deduced the identity of the person responsible for the accident.

"What are you saying, Kavan?" The priest took a long sip of vodka.

Kavan searched the priest's eyes, wondering why he did not see the obvious, "Boz, it was sabotage. Don't you see? Someone deliberately killed my family and most of my team, and destroyed my life's work."

Father Bożydar tried to make his face register a look of surprise and horror, and hoped that Kavan did not detect his discomfort. "Who would do such a thing? You personally selected every member of your team. They were all loyal to you and the project."

Kavan refilled both of their glasses with vodka, then sat back and regarded his old friend. "The project was being watched by dozens of corporate spies, research institutes, and every government in the system. Security was first-rate, but the whole operation just got too big." He drained his glass of vodka and poured another. "I've turned it over again and again in my mind and it had to be an Imperial agent. The Emperor must have determined that if they couldn't steal the technology, then the Confederation would not be allowed to have it. At least that's the theory that allows me to sleep most nights."

Father Bożydar was relieved that Kavan had found a comfortable fiction to pin his grief to. Now it was time to steer the conversation to the reason for his visit.

"Kavan, we should leave the past behind us where it can do no more harm. We should speak of the reason for my visit." The priest raised his glass and took another hearty sip of the warming liquid.

"Yes, of course, Boz. Just what the hell are you doing here?" Kavan leaned forward on his crossed arms, eager to hear the priest's tale.

Father Bożydar recounted the meeting with a strange young man on the street in Chaos, the dream that night when the angel spoke to him of a friend in need. Before he told of the meeting in the park the following morning, he paused to let Kavan respond.

Kavan sat back in his chair, his arms dangling at his side, and a pained expression on his face. He knew that someday his friend and teacher would begin to lose his sharp mind, but he never imagined it would happen at such a relatively young age. He decided to handle the conversation delicately.

"Father, you taught me that one should never interpret dreams as a form of revelation. Scripture is clear that John of Patmos wrote the final words of revelation."

Father Bożydar understood that Kavan did not believe his visitation experience. He replied, "Kavan, this was more than a dream." He stood up from the chair and stretched his stiff back, then crossed the small room, turned and said, "The next morning I ran from the monastery hoping to find the young man I met the night before. After learning from Mr. Nama that he had not stayed at the inn, I was sitting in the park praying the rosary, asking God to forgive my disobedience. That's when he appeared to me."

Kavan stroked his rough beard and asked, "What do you mean by 'appeared' to you?" He was sure his friend was indeed mad.

"The young man, the angel from my dream, he was standing there in front of me in the park. He told me that he was sent by God and that I was to accompany him on a journey. A journey that was to start by reconciling with you, my son, here on Europa." The priest stood in the dim bluish light of the room, looking hopefully at Kavan.

Kavan let out a quick laugh and said, "Boz, I think you might need to talk to someone. Dreams that become waking hallucinations are a bad sign."

Father Bożydar interrupted, "I am not mad! He brought me here in a magnificent starship. It's in orbit," he pointed up at the ceiling, "above Europa right now! If you come with me, you can see for yourself."

"A 'starship'? What exactly does that mean?" Kavan was quickly becoming suspicious of the story and felt as if he were being manipulated in some way.

"He brought me here in a starship. The whole journey took but a moment. 'Poof' and we were here! It was incredible!" The old priest was beaming with excitement, hoping to pique his student's curiosity.

"Instantaneous travel from Mars to Europa? That sounds familiar, Boz." Kavan's face was dark and verging on anger. "Just who is this friend of yours?"

"I told you, he is an angel of the Lord." Father Bożydar

stood over Kavan and placed a hand on his shoulder. "Son, I am asking you to trust me. Come with me and I will show you it's all real — the ship, the angel, everything."

Kavan searched his teacher's eyes and did not see insanity. Instead, he saw the younger Father Bożydar fervently defending a point of doctrine that he held to be absolutely true. He saw the man he once knew, the gifted apologist and orator who could wield language and argumentation like a skilled swordsman swings a blade.

"Okay, Boz. So what is this 'journey' all about? No offense, but why would an angel need your help?" Kavan struggled to not let the pity he felt for the foolish old man color his words.

Father Bożydar saw the disbelief in Kavan's eyes, and felt that the younger man was only humoring him. His approach was not working as he had hoped. He would need a new tactic.

"Kavan, are you still angry with God over the death of your family and the loss of your life's work?"

Kavan nodded, his face taking on the blank, lifeless stare that he saw earlier.

"What if I told you that you were right. That God had indeed intervened and caused your experiment to fail." Father Bożydar watched as Kavan's eyes filled with tears.

"Why would you say such a thing, Father?" The tears flowed down his cheeks, making small, wet circles on his shirt.

"The physicist that joined the project, Azrael Vrubel, he sabotaged your work." Kavan began shaking his head. "He is the young man that came to Chaos to find me. He is the angel who spoke to me in my dream, then brought me to you today."

Kavan's face turned red as he slammed both fists down on the table, sending the vodka bottle and both glasses crashing to the floor. "No! You are insane, old man!" Kavan stood up suddenly and grabbed the priest by the shoulders. With his face close enough for the old priest to smell the vodka on his breath, he screamed, "Azrael is dead! He died with Kareena and our children! I will kill you if you speak another lie! Now leave me!" He shoved the old man hard causing him to stumble back and fall to his knees.

Father Bożydar closed his eyes and called out silently, *Azrael, come to me! I need you now!*

Kavan stood over the priest with his fists clenched ready to strike the old man when suddenly a pinpoint of blinding white light appeared in the air between them. The point expanded rapidly, elongating into a narrow ellipse, then from the center a figure appeared, followed by a flash so bright that both men covered their eyes.

When Kavan opened his eyes, a young man, perhaps thirty years old, with flowing blonde hair, and icy blue eyes stood less than a meter in front of him. The man raised his right arm and touched the palm of his hand to Kavan's chest and said, "The LORD says, *'For I will contend with him who contends with you.'* Lower your fists, Kavan Ferre, and threaten not my student again."

Father Bożydar slowly stood up and dusted off his pants, thanking God for answering his call.

Kavan shrunk away from the touch of the young man, backing into the shelf behind him and knocking several items to the floor. His eyes were wide and his entire body began to tremble uncontrollably.

The young man turned to Father Bożydar and asked, "Are you injured, Father?"

The priest smiled and shook his head.

Turning his attention back to Kavan who was still cowering against the wall he said, "The time for your grief and anger has passed, Kavan Your Heavenly Father calls you to serve Him."

Kavan watched as the man's appearance began to change, slowly at first, then in a matter of seconds, he had transformed himself into a stout middle-aged man, with a receding hairline and dull grey eyes.

Father Bożydar slowly moved from behind Azrael, until he could see his now much older face, and stood to his left agape with amazement.

Kavan managed to blurt out, "Azrael? I don't understand! How is this possible?"

Azrael could sense the confusion in Kavan's mind and the pain it was causing him. Witnessing such an inexplicable appearance and physical transformation strained his highly rational mind, pushing him to the brink of insanity.

Acting quickly to relieve his mental strain, Azrael reached out and took Kavan's head in his hands. Instantly a warm wave of ecstasy engulfed his mind, causing him to moan slightly, and his legs to wobble. He pushed himself up against the wall, looking down into Azrael's eyes, and felt the room resolve into hyper-realistic sharpness. Every object seemed brighter and more saturated, the edges more defined and vibrant. Then, from somewhere in his mind, but not of his own consciousness, he heard *'trust in my servant and let go of your anger and fear.'*

In that moment, Kavan understood. He understood

that Azrael was both the man he knew years ago on 216 Kleopatra, *and* the beautiful angel who had just miraculously appeared in his room. He understood that Azrael was tasked with teaching and protecting mankind since the beginning, and that he was here in pursuit of an even greater mission than before.

Azrael released Kavan and stepped back. "Kavan, I am truly sorry for your loss."

Kavan slowly crossed the room, holding onto the wall until he reached a chair, then sat down heavily. He wiped the back of his forearm across his sweaty forehead, then said shaking his head, "What is it you want from me?"

***

Azrael picked up the bottle and glasses from the floor and set them on the table. Then he took a chair from the desk and sat down with Father Bożydar and Kavan. If he was going to move Kavan to freely join in their mission, he knew he would need to reveal the true nature of their opposition. A man who dedicated his life to proving abstract realities, would now need to embrace the supernatural, almost solely on faith.

"Kavan, the Empire has developed a faster-than-light ship that will extend the reach of the Emperor's hand beyond this solar system. There is a faction behind this development that has manipulated the government and used the resources of the Empire for their own purposes. Ambassador Remus Arin is at the nexus of these activities, although he is acting on behalf of his Master, who wields much greater power." Azrael paused to let Kavan consider the implications.

"What FTL method have they developed?" Kavan asked.

"They are using a modified *Ferre Field* to induce an *Einstein-Rosen Bridge*. It has already been tested several times locally." Azrael hoped that Kavan would extrapolate the implications of such a technological leap.

Father Bożydar interrupted, "If I recall from our conversations, Kavan, an *Einstein-Rosen Bridge* describes a wormhole in space, yes?"

Kavan nodded and gave a faint smile, "Yes, that's right. And I thought you were only humoring me when I would go on for hours about physics."

"You have taught me many things, my son. Many things." The old priest returned the smile.

Kavan turned back to Azrael, "Well, a wormhole is a reasonable solution, but it's not elegant and still has the problem of time dilation. Unless the Empire, or whoever is running the show, has an appetite for a one-way journey, I don't see why you would be concerned."

"Remus Arin and his Master have nothing but time, Kavan," Azrael replied gravely.

"What does that mean?" he said sharply.

Azrael glanced at Father Bożydar then said, "Our enemy is Lucifer and his Fallen Ones. He has been trying to escape from the Earth ever since the dawn of the space age."

Kavan slumped back in his chair, his mouth slack and his eyes wide. After a few seconds, "So what if he escapes? Wouldn't you want the Devil to find a new home?"

Azrael felt the familiar wave of energy breaking against his spirit and understood Hamaliel's instruction, '*Teach him of our War.*'

***

Azrael began, "My Brethren have been at war with

Lucifer and the Fallen Ones since the events described in Genesis. As you know from your own study of scripture, Lucifer and the Fallen Ones were imprisoned on Earth and bound by God as punishment for their rebellion."

"Yes, but I always wondered what it meant to *bind* Lucifer and his demons." Kavan gestured toward the center of the room, "In light of your method of arrival, I am even more curious as to what it really means."

Azrael explained to Kavan how all angelic beings have the ability to manipulate matter and energy in the three dimensions of space-time, allowing them to take on the appearance of any living creature, and fashion simple or highly complex objects as needed.

"The ability to shape matter is a localized effect, and does not require access to the higher realms, unlike traveling by means of folding space," Azrael continued.

Kavan wore a puzzled look, "By 'higher realms' you mean other space-time dimensions?"

"Correct." Azrael sensed that Kavan was feeling calmer and his mind was focused on understanding the glimpse of the hidden world he was being given. "The Fallen Ones no longer have the ability to fold space and are subject to the laws that govern normal matter."

Father Bożydar added, "Imagine once having the ability to traverse the entire universe, then in a moment, being trapped in one place forever."

Kavan nodded his understanding, "I can see how that would be profoundly inconvenient."

"Another limitation is that they must remain in a physical form at all times." Azrael leaned forward to stress his point, "As you have read in scripture, they do occasionally seek to inhabit the bodies of humans, and they are driven by insatiable desires and lust. Their entire existence is now focused on finding a way to escape this solar system."

Kavan considered Azrael's words, but something about the story did not make sense. "Where would they go? Without humanity to use as their playthings, what would give their existence purpose?"

"I have missed your keen mind these years, Kavan." Azrael smiled and continued. "Lucifer has learned of a planet orbiting Upsilon Andromedae and intends to send a contingent of his army there."

Kavan looked from Azrael to Father Bożydar, "What is so special about that planet?"

"It is what my Brethren call a '*cradle world*'. It is home to a new sentient race that has not rebelled. Lucifer intends to bring evil to a still-perfect world, and we must not let that happen."

For more than four years, Kavan had studied Europa's teeming sea and was now comfortable with the notion of the universe containing other intelligent life, but he was nonetheless shocked at Azrael's words. "What do you mean they have not 'rebelled'?"

"This cradle world is as Earth was before the Fall of Man. The Father's design has not been tampered with and the Children of that world live as He intended." Azrael's face seemed to emanate a soft light from within as he spoke.

Kavan clasped his hands on top of his head and sat back in his chair, pondering the notion of a world untouched by evil. A second Garden of Eden hundreds of light years from Earth. "Azrael, you speak as if this world is not unique. Are there other cradle worlds?"

Father Bożydar smiled broadly, enjoying the sight of his student once again taking in new information, turning it over in his brilliant mind, and constructing probing questions.

Now that Kavan and Father Bożydar had crossed a certain threshold of knowledge, Azrael was able to share fully the mysteries of this special realm of creation. "Yes, there are a multitude of such cradle worlds, at various stages of development. It is one of the primary activities of my Brethren, to watch over and guide the Children as the Father wills. But *our* mission concerns only this world in the Upsilon Andromedae system. We must not allow Remus Arin and his followers to set foot on a cradle world. This is our sacred duty."

Father Bożydar looked into Kavan's eyes with a fire and determination that the young man had not seen since he was a child. "Kavan, it is time to leave this place. Remember the words of Jonah, '*I have been banished from your sight; yet I will look again toward your holy temple.*' Will you come with us and accept the destiny for which the LORD has prepared you?"

Kavan looked around the room, at the shelves crammed with specimen jars, bits of equipment, and empty food containers. He looked out the portal into the frigid blackness and knew it was time to leave his grief buried there, in the depths of an alien sea, and take a step of faith in the company of his teacher and their angel. He simply nodded and wept.

CHAPTER 13

Bronco Murphy struggled to keep the Captain's Boat at the proper attitude as it screamed through the atmosphere of Callisto. He had somehow managed to avoid the guns of the destroyer and expertly put the craft on a direct emergency trajectory to the surface.

Sabbatino had selected a landing site on the rim of the great crater Valhalla, the most prominent feature on the now terraformed surface of Callisto. The northwest slope of Valhalla featured a double crater left by a meteor strike millions of years after the formation of the much larger Valhalla crater. The small town of Mimir had grown up around the picturesque lake that filled the bottom of the double crater. Several varieties of genetically modified pine trees created a lush forest that grew throughout the entire Valhalla region. The terrain was rugged and it was a favorite of hunters who came to the area in search of deer, wild turkey, and wild boar.

The town of Mimir was also home to Rhys Hosking, the leader of the most powerful crime syndicate in the Jovian system. While man's ancient vices were still in high demand and the basis for a lucrative black market trade, the most coveted commodity in the twenty-sixth century was fuel for the fusion reactors that powered all human activity in space and on the scores of settled worlds. Molecular hydrogen and helium were the ultimate raw materials of progress, and their sources and reserves were tightly controlled by the Empire and the independent governments. Jupiter, the gas giant that dominated the Outer Colonies, was the single greatest source of both elements in the solar system. Atmospheric skimmers had been harvesting hydrogen and helium from the stratosphere of Jupiter for centuries, ever since the dawn of regular space travel to the outer planets. As mining and manufacturing came to the asteroid belt, Jupiter became critical to the survival of every Imperial, independent, and corporate colony and outpost.

It was against this backdrop that the Hosking family came to power. Robert Powell Hosking was a skimmer fleet captain who rebelled against his corporate masters by organizing a mutiny that involved more than twenty ships. With these stolen vessels and their crews, he began a criminal enterprise that would span generations, and grow so powerful, that even the Empire rarely interfered with its affairs. Rhys Hosking was the great-great grandson of Robert Powell Hosking, and the current patriarch of the family that controlled more than fifty percent of all fuel production in the Outer Colonies.

Marco Bisbal-Rivera was an ally of the Hosking Enterprise, as it was known, providing a variety of services to the family, and as such, was always welcome at their compound in Mimir. The crew of the *Boa Vista* had been guests of Rhys Hosking many times and knew the area well.

The Hosking Enterprise controlled this part of Callisto, making it unlikely that the Imperial Navy would pursue the surviving *Boa Vista* crew members, once they realized where the Captain's Boat was landing.

Sabbatino knew the compound had a surgery suite where Tiago's leg could be repaired. She also needed to make contact with the rest of Rivera's fleet to inform them of the events since they arrived at Callisto.

Murphy leveled out the craft as it settled into the lower atmosphere, the hull of the ship automatically transforming itself into an atmospheric flight configuration with the necessary lift and control surfaces. The landing guidance beacon at the Hosking Enterprise flight center began flashing on Murphy's display. A moment later the voice of the flight controller announced, "Craft on approach to Hosking Enterprise center please confirm identification code."

Sabbatino replied, "G'day center. *Boa Vista* CB-101 confirms identification with passphrase *'jolly roger'* and code *'silmarillion one-three-seven.'*"

After a brief pause the flight controller replied, "Roger that, *Boa Vista* CB-101. Welcome to Mimir. It's good to have you back. Please proceed on course heading one-eight-two mark seven three. Transfer flight control to tower guidance and we'll bring you in."

Sabbatino breathed a sigh of relief and smiled to Bronco Murphy as he released the flight controls and visibly relaxed. "Tango Yankee, center. We have a medical emergency on board and need immediate evac to surgery. Transmitting biodata now." Sabbatino made a series of gestures on the screen instructing the computer to begin transmitting Tiago's biodata telemetry in real time to the flight center. The biodata would be fed to the medical suite where the auto-surgeon would be programmed and ready to begin reconstruction of Tiago's damaged femoral artery upon arrival.

In the passenger compartment Sonny and Anna had released their harnesses and began checking on Tiago. The combination of the field dressing and the nano-machines had significantly slowed the bleeding from his leg, but he had lost a lot of blood and his blood pressure was dangerously low. They hoped they would make it in time to save his life.

Anna was still reeling from the shock of her lover sacrificing himself to facilitate their escape. She knew he was either in custody or dead, and she struggled to remain composed.

Moments later the craft was parked on the tarmac in front of a series of domed structures at the Hosking Enterprise flight center. The hatch opened and a rush of chilled air filled the compartment with the crisp smell of pine. Two men entered the compartment and quickly transferred the unconscious first officer to a maglev gurney that carried him away to the surgery suite.

Sabbatino and Murphy stepped from the cockpit into the passenger compartment and saw the sobbing Anna. Sabbatino sat down next to Anna and said, "Anna, don't worry about Marco. We both know he is too valuable a trophy for the marines to shoot on sight. The Emperor will want him back on Earth for a public trial. But that will never happen because our fleet will arrive shortly and we'll get him back. A single destroyer is no match for our fleet."

Anna lifted her head from her hands and wiped her tears away, "Lorena, I appreciate your confidence, but we have no idea what is going on. That destroyer was waiting for us. How did they know exactly where to intercept us?"

Sabbatino had not considered that they were ambushed. She had been reacting purely on instinct since being awoken during the wet fight. But Anna's assessment made sense, that she could not deny.

Bronco Murphy added, "If that was an ambush and not very bad luck, then one of our people gave us up." His words made each of his crew mates turn to him with wide-eyed surprise.

"Jesus, Bronco. Maybe they were tracking us all the way from Earth. Why does it *have* to be a traitor?" Alvarez chided the older co-pilot.

Murphy looked down at the deck and said, "I guess they could have, but something just feels wrong. I can't explain it. And what the hell is Marco doing by giving himself up?" He stood there shaking his head.

Sabbatino decided it was time to move. "Look, we are not going to figure this out standing around. We need to go and talk to Rhys Hosking and figure out our next move. The fleet will be here soon and we need to have a plan to get Marco back."

The other three nodded, gathered their gear and walked out into the cool afternoon air of Callisto.

***

Rhys Hosking stepped into the reception room of his rustic mansion in Mimir to greet his unexpected guests. A tall man, standing more than two meters high, with a thin, yet fit frame, and a permanent smile. A thin layer of silvery stubble orbited from ear to ear around the back of his head. He was rumored to be over one hundred years old, but appeared to be in his fifties, perhaps sixty.

He crossed the massive room of rough hewn wooden beams and dark tile with brisk steps. "Lorena, my dear!" he said as he gave her a warm hug and kissed her lightly on each cheek. "What an unexpected pleasure to see you again."

Turning to Anna he repeated the greeting and said, "Anna, you look as lovely as ever." He lingered in front of her, detecting a forced quality in her smile.

"Sonny," shaking the young pilot's hand, "and Bronco, it is so good to have you all. What brings you to my home today?" he gestured toward an arrangement of large leather chairs in front of a massive stone fireplace, where a bright orange fire was roaring. The warmth of the fire was pleasing to the weary spacefarers and they each selected a chair close to the fire.

Rhys sat down and said, "I have asked my chef to prepare a meal for you. It should be ready shortly. Hopefully the repair to Tiago's leg should be completed in time for him to join us." His expression became more serious, "It seems you had some trouble in orbit. Tell me how I can help you."

Sabbatino explained the attack on the *Boa Vista* by the Imperial Navy patrol boat and the boarding by marines. She told Rhys how Marco had shot Tiago to stop him from engaging the marines, then how he stayed behind in an attempt to create a diversion allowing his surviving crew members to escape.

Anna said through tears welling in her eyes, "Marco sacrificed himself for us."

Rhys could see the pain on the beautiful young

woman's face. "Anna, you know that Marco is as smart as they come. He knew the marines would never shoot him if they could capture him alive " Looking to the others he added, "What can I do to help?"

Sabbatino, as the most senior officer present, answered, "We have lost the *Boa Vista* and only have the Captain's Boat. She's a fine ship and fast, but we could use something with some real firepower."

"Lorena, I think we can find something that will suit your needs," Rhys replied. "What else can I do?"

"We need to contact our fleet and warn them of the trap they are flying into," Sabbatino added.

"You may use the communications shack at the flight center. One of my technicians will help you connect to your beacon network." Rhys placed his hand on his chin and asked, "Can you tell me why your fleet is converging on Callisto? That seems an unusual tactical risk, given the nature of Captain Rivera's business."

Sabbatino considered whether to tell Rhys the truth, at least some part of it. She decided that, given their current unfortunate circumstances, it would be better to trust their long-time customer and patron. "Marco had recently accepted a very important commission that involved liberating an Imperial military asset from its current owners. The job required significant firepower and a degree of finesse, so Marco rallied the fleet to Callisto to formulate the plan." She looked around the room at each of her shipmates and then back to Rhys, adding, "It appears somebody betrayed us and alerted the navy, because they most certainly knew we were coming. Someone had our arrival and orbital insertion coordinates nailed. A patrol boat came up hot from the surface and put a torpedo right up our ass. Within a couple minutes we had another patrol boat and a destroyer on top of us and a boarding party crawling all over the ship."

Rhys stroked his chin then turned to stare into the fire. "Did Marco share the flight plan with anyone outside your fleet?"

Sabbatino shook her head, "No way. Not even the sponsor knew the details of the mission."

"Then it *would* seem logical," Rhys brought his fingertips together in from of him to form a rough pyramid, "that you have a traitor amongst you."

Each of the *Boa Vista* crew mates exchanged grim looks.

Alvarez said, "When we find the bastard, they are going to get walked out an airlock."

"For now, we have to find another place to send the fleet, then formulate a plan to rescue Marco," Sabbatino said.

"Our space dock at the Callisto L1 Lagrange Point should give your fleet ample cover," Rhys offered. "It's a very busy area with scores of our skimmers and corporate tankers coming and going. Plus, we have a fair amount of iron flying around, so the navy tends to keep their distance. Unless an Imperial scout is sitting very nearby, they can't visually identify individual ships. We can also provide your ships with identification beacons that will show them as properly registered vessels."

The Hosking Enterprise, with its entire operation in violation of The Law, provided a necessary and extremely valuable service. Skimming deep into the atmosphere of Jupiter was one of the most dangerous industrial activities. So dangerous, that every legitimate company that harvested the atmosphere of Jupiter, employed autonomous robotic craft flown by onboard computers. Jupiter's dense and violent atmosphere was not only hostile to live pilots, but made remote piloting impossible.

Rhys' operation still harvested using massive aerospace craft, flown by live human pilots. Many of the hundreds of pilots were third or fourth generation skimmer pilots, who knew the unique fluid dynamics of the Jovian atmosphere. They were considered to be the best — and craziest — pilots in the solar system.

The Hosking Enterprise's ability to harvest larger volumes of fuel on each skimmer run, gave them a significant cost advantage over their legitimate corporate competitors. As a black market supplier, they also enjoyed the added benefit of not having to pay hefty Imperial tariffs and duties across the many worlds and colonies they supplied. Their fuel was more available, less expensive, and tax free — making Rhys Hosking the richest man in the solar system, second only to Emperor Wan Sui Ye himself.

Rhys gave a slight nod, "We should get you to that commo shack, Lorena. Once you alert the fleet, we can check on Tiago and then have a nice meal. In the meantime, I will ask some of my people to find out where your illustrious captain is being held."

"Thank you, Rhys. You are very gracious," Sabbatino said with a warm smile.

***

Tiago Maconde opened his eyes and struggled to focus on the display mounted on a retractable arm above his head. As his vision cleared he became aware of one sensation — he was cold. He tried to move his arms but could not. *Oh, God, I'm paralyzed*, he thought. But then he realized he could feel the bed sheets on the back of his hands and arms. He managed to move his fingers and toes, but could not move his body or extremities off the bed surface.

A faint tone began emanating from the display and a moment later a young man wearing a medical tunic appeared at his bedside.

"Nice to see you awake, Señor Maconde. *Como te sentes?*" the medic asked in Tiago's native Portuguese.

"I feel fine. *Muito bem, obrigado,*" Tiago replied.

"You had a nasty gunshot wound. About four centimeters of your right femoral artery was obliterated, and your femur was shattered. But, we patched you up good as new and didn't need to use any synthetics, so you should have no lasting effects from the wound. You are already eighty percent healed, although you may have some pretty annoying itching. I can program your nano-machines to synthesize a mild corticosteroid that will make it bearable."

"Thanks, but I'll take the itch. It will remind me how lucky I am to still have my leg."

The medic shrugged, "Suit yourself. If you change your mind, just call me and I can fix it in less than a minute."

"Can you release the restraining field, I'd like to sit up," Tiago asked with an awkward grin.

"Oh sure! Sorry about that. You were thrashing around a bit as the anesthetic started to wear off." The medic touched an icon on the display above the bed. Instantly, Tiago felt a subtle pressure lift from his body and was free to move. The medic deftly removed Tiago's catheter, then lowered the side railing of the bed.

"Thanks. Do I need to be careful with the leg or anything?" Tiago asked.

"No, it should feel pretty normal — perhaps a bit numb until the local wears of completely."

Tiago swung his legs over the edge of the bed and pushed himself up with his arms until he was standing. He gingerly shifted his weight to his right leg, was pleased that it felt good, then took a few tentative steps around the room. He turned and smiled at the medic and gave him a 'thumbs up'.

Thirty minutes later he was dressed in a newly fabricated uniform — identical to the clothing he was wearing when he arrived. He was led by a servant to an elegant outdoor dining terrace, kept comfortably warm by an invisible containment field, allowing Rhys' guests unobstructed views of the surrounding pine covered mountain ridges and pleasant orange and magenta sky. A large round table was set with antique china, expensive crystal glassware, and a wide variety of meats, fruits, and cheeses. The rest of the *Boa Vista* crew and Rhys Hosking were already seated and a servant was pouring glasses of white wine.

When Sabbatino saw Tiago she leapt up from her seat and trotted to his side taking him by the arm. "How are you feeling, Tiago?"

"The leg is a little stiff, but I feel great." He looked to his crew mates and said, "Thanks for the first aid and fancy flying. I owe you one."

Bronco Murphy and Sonny Alvarez looked at each other and smiled, then raised their glasses and nodded to their comrade.

Tiago was led to the empty seat next to Rhys by the servant. He sat down and turned to his host and said, "And thank you, Rhys, for the excellent work on my leg.

Your medical team is first rate."

Rhys put his arm across the back of Tiago's chair and replied, "You are very welcome, my friend." Then turning to the others he announced, "Let us enjoy a meal as friends and allies and discuss how we are going to rescue your excellent captain."

***

Anna Domasheva slammed her hand on the table, startling everyone but Rhys, and said vehemently, "We are going to get Marco back before they leave for Earth! You all can either help me or I will go alone."

Tiago spoke up, "Anna, we have every intention of getting Marco back. But he taught me over the years to use my head first rather than my fists." He rubbed his itchy thigh unconsciously, "If we complete our mission, then we have leverage to get Marco back without engaging in a costly battle with the Imperial Navy."

Anna said with a disgusted look, "What are you afraid of, Tiago? Or is this your big chance for a promotion?"

Tiago flared his nostrils and was about to respond when Sabbatino interrupted, "Anna, that's not fair. And Tiago, with all due respect, our original mission is on hold until we get Marco back. The other captains will never go forward with the mission and leave Marco to those Imperial dogs."

Tiago glanced around the table and noticed Bronco and Sonny nodding in agreement. "All right, Lorena. But do we even know what we are up against?"

Rhys leaned forward and offered, "I have spoken with some of my people and they confirmed that Captain Rivera is being held aboard the Imperial Destroyer *Haikou*. He is alive and well, and it is likely they will transport him to Earth as soon as the *Haikou's* relief arrives."

"Then it would make sense to attack the *Haikou* before any reinforcements get here," Anna concluded. Turning to Rhys she asked, "Do your sources know when their relief is due?"

Rhys shook his head, "No. One of my sources who has access to fleet deployment data said that no orders had been issued yet. That was less than an hour ago. Based on current deployments, the earliest arrival is estimated at twelve hours. There is a heavy cruiser deployed to Ganymede — it is the most likely ship to relieve the *Haikou*."

Tiago could tell by the looks on the faces of his comrades that everyone expected to attempt an immediate rescue. "I would certainly rather tangle with a single destroyer than that *plus* a heavy cruiser, *if* that's all they show up with. How do we know they won't dispatch a larger force? They must know we would bring all of our available ships to rescue Marco."

Sabbatino was puzzled by Tiago's sudden cautious attitude. His reputation was that of a fierce warrior, and at times, a ruthless combatant who had a tendency to use excessive force during engagements with Imperial troops. She decided to press him to study his reaction. "Tiago, did they inadvertently remove your balls while you were in surgery?"

Bronco and Sonny choked back a laugh and struggled to stifle their schoolboy smiles. Anna raised an eyebrow and bore into Tiago with her chestnut eyes.

Tiago knew he had to act decisively or risk losing the confidence of his crew. "Look, I just want to make sure we think through all the angles. That's what Marco would do." He pointed to Sabbatino, "Lorena, take me to that commo shack — we should be able to make real time contact with the other captains. Let's at least get a basic battle plan worked up." Then turning to Rhys, "Can we impose upon you for a ship with a bit more gusto than the one we arrived in? She is a good ship but not exactly one I want to ride into a naval battle."

Rhys clutched Tiago's shoulder and offered, "I have a new *HiVee* corvette that should suit your needs. She is quite fast and has some very sharp fangs." Turning to Sonny and Bronco, "Perhaps your young pilots would like to get acquainted with her while you and Lorena contact your fleet?"

Tiago nodded and said, "Thank you, Rhys. We will make every effort to return her without a scratch." He nodded to Alvarez and Murphy and the men stood up and followed a servant into the house.

Rhys said to Anna, "Would you like to visit the armory and see if there are any items that might make your rescue efforts easier?"

Anna glanced at Tiago and he nodded, then she replied, "Yes, Rhys. That would be a good use of my nervous energy."

"The fleet should be arriving over the next five hours," Sabbatino announced. "I figure we have ten hours maximum to prepare to take the *Haikou* and rescue Marco." Turning to Anna with a hand on her arm she promised, "Anna, you and Marco are destined to have a long life together — so we *will* get him back. But we're going to do it the right way, like he taught us."

Anna smiled and squeezed Lorena's hand.

"The resources of my family are at your disposal. Marco is a good man and a valuable asset to my family's operations. It would be bad for business if he came to harm." Rhys Hosking rose from his chair and the others stood and followed him into the house to make preparations for the battle that would soon happen in the skies far above Callisto.

CHAPTER 14

When the course change maneuver was completed, Captain Daley returned to his ready room with Nianzu Chao. Commander Lee was still sitting where they had left her moments before.

The unexpected diversion to Callisto was a complication that Chao had not considered. He decided the Captain and Commander Lee must be told of the true nature of Remus Arin and the real purpose behind the mission to Titan. But doing so would expose Chao and all of his activities — both legal and illegal. He could not easily explain that, while he was acting under the orders of the Emperor to watch Remus Arin, he was also conspiring with a wanted criminal to deny the Emperor access to a technology that would upset the balance of power in the solar system. Nianzu Chao was single-handedly playing a game that would determine the fate of mankind, perhaps for centuries to come.

"Commander Lee, I tried to explain to you yesterday that Ambassador Arin is not what he appears to be. But this diversion to Callisto requires that I confide in both you and Captain Daley. What I am about to tell you may seem fantastic, but I have spent the past five years confirming every aspect of it." Chao noticed a shadow of impatience move across Sumiko's face, but the furrows in Captain Daley's brow indicated interest.

Chao continued, "Simply put, Remus Arin is an impostor. His entire background and identity are an elaborate fabrication. He has purposefully and successfully infiltrated the highest levels of the Imperial government and has put himself in a unique position of influence with our Emperor. Fortunately, the Emperor's wisdom is greater than the machinations of Remus Arin. For the past five years, I have been working under the direct orders of the Emperor to investigate Remus Arin. My findings have led me to certain conclusions that, while incredible, are undeniably true."

Captain Daley was not surprised that an official of such high position as Remus Arin was under surveillance, but rather, that an intelligence operative would admit that such a thing took place inside the Empire. Every Imperial citizen clung to the fiction that they were free, happy, and under the protection of the Emperor. To think otherwise was dangerous.

"Mr. Chao, how is it possible that someone could infiltrate the government and gain access to the Emperor? The complexity of such a task is unimaginable," Daley said.

"My investigation has also uncovered a more immediately dangerous fact. I believe Remus Arin has been planning this mission for many months and has filled the crew of this ship with key accomplices. Most troubling is the composition of the Marine Recon battalion. Each one was hand-picked by Admiral Butchers. They have been pulled from every corner of the Empire for this mission. There is no precedent for it — ever." Chao leaned forward, spreading his hands out on the table, "Captain, isn't it true that your senior staff was recently rotated out and you now have all new department heads, none of whom you have ever served with before?"

Captain Daley nodded, "Well, yes. It did seem unusual that every department head was rotated simultaneously. But my senior staff is first-rate. I have had no issues with any of them and the ship has never run smoother."

"So what we have is a Marine Recon battalion and senior staff running the ship, who have all been hand-picked by the Admiral, and I would bet, Remus Arin. Add to that, the entire flotilla has suddenly been diverted to Callisto to take custody of the most infamous pirate in the solar system. A man who has eluded capture for over twenty-five years, has by sheer fortune, fallen into Imperial hands this day. And this flotilla just happens to be the nearest Imperial Navy asset." Chao shook his head, "I do not believe it is a coincidence."

Daley was having difficulty following Chao's logic. "Are you saying that even the capture of Marco Bisbal-Rivera is part of this so-called *conspiracy* you are accusing Admiral Butchers and Ambassador Arin of masterminding? How would they know where Rivera would show up? None of this makes any sense."

Chao realized that for Captain Daley to accept the truth of Admiral Butchers' and Remus Arin's treachery, he would need to play all of the cards in his hand. "They have someone inside Rivera's group of pirates. I suspect it is someone in his senior staff or on his own ship."

"Mr. Chao, that is quite a leap," Daley observed.

"Not really, Captain. You see, Rivera was working for *me*. I engaged the services of his band of pirates to infiltrate the station at Titan and take custody of the Emperor's ship."

Sumiko and Daley stared blankly at Chao, their mouths agape. Daley spoke first, "Mr. Chao, before you say another word, you may want to consider calling a JAG officer, because as of this moment you are under arrest for high treason against the Emperor." Daley drew his sidearm and pointed it at Chao's head.

Chao looked at the pistol, then raised his eyes to meet the raging glare of Captain Daley. "Captain, before you arrest me, perhaps you should consider that you are the only senior officer on this ship who was not selected by the Admiral and Arin. You have never served with any of your department heads and know nothing about their prior service. Your orders to join this mission were made to look like a last minute request. But somehow, the ship was loaded and ready to go without a hitch." Chao turned his chair to face the Captain, and he leaned forward allowing the gun barrel to hover centimeters from his forehead, "Doesn't any of that give you pause?"

The gun wavered in Daley's hand as he considered Chao's words. Everything that Chao told him rang true, and his gut told him that he could trust this man. But Chao had just confessed to treason and every word was recorded. He would be putting himself in serious jeopardy if he did not arrest Chao.

"Mr. Chao, even if I believed your vast conspiracy theory, you just confessed to treason and your words are now part of the official ship's log."

"May I reach inside my jacket, Captain? Certainly, I have no weapons." Chao asked.

"Slowly," Daley replied.

Chao reached his right hand into the left breast pocket of his jacket and retrieved the small metallic disk that Sumiko had seen the day before during his visit to her room. He held the disk up to the Captain, "This ensures that our conversation is private."

Daley lowered the pistol and returned it to the holster on his right hip. He leaned forward resting his chin on his fist, staring at the table as his mind shuffled through the revelations presented by Chao. If Chao was right, Daley's duty was clear. He had to find a way to contain Remus Arin, Admiral Butchers, his senior staff, and an entire battalion of marines and expose their treachery — all while retaining command of his ship *and* the flotilla.

Suddenly the door slid open and Admiral Butchers and Remus Arin strode into the room. Chao deftly palmed the disk and slid it into the outer pocket of his jacket. Standing inside the door the Admiral said, "Sorry for the intrusion, Captain. But we need to discuss the deployment plan for our arrival at Callisto." Looking at Commander Lee and Nianzu Chao, he continued, "How convenient that you both are already here."

The Admiral and Remus each took a seat at the table. Remus turned to Chao and said, "Mr. Chao, it is good to see you finally. We have not had a chance to speak since we left Earth. I was not aware you would be joining us."

Chao could feel the waves of hatred radiating from Remus. He replied, "I am surprised the Emperor did not mention it. He personally assigned me to the mission to aid in the investigation of the security breach at the laboratory." Chao stared back at Remus with cold eyes.

Remus stared back, "How generous. I am sure you will be a true asset to the investigation."

The Admiral interrupted the exchange, "Let's get started."

Chao and Sumiko exchanged brief glances, then both looked to Captain Daley who wore a blank expression, in stark contrast to the churning in his stomach and pain beginning to grow behind his eyes.

***

The Hosking Enterprise space dock at Callisto L1 was one of the busiest terminals in the solar system. As the main transfer station for fuel harvested from Jupiter, ships from the inner worlds, asteroid belt, and outer worlds all used the terminal to load their tankers with the precious gases that kept their civilizations alive.

The terminal harbor master, Manel Jucha, was a wiry man in his sixties, who orchestrated the movements of scores of enormous ships with the gracefulness of a ballet choreographer. He was famous with the pilots and captains of the commercial fleets for his staccato radio voice and his ability to guide the largest ships through the smallest spaces.

This day, however, Manel Jucha needed to find a way to hide sixteen pirate ships in plain sight. He had received a personal call from Rhys Hosking asking him to make special arrangements for Marco Bisbal-Rivera's fleet, which would be arriving in less than five hours. He needed to find a way to not only mask the ships electronically — easily done by changing the identification beacon codes — but to also shelter the ships from the prying eyes of Imperial scouts and their long range optical sensors.

The Hosking Enterprise space dock resembled a gigantic snowflake hanging in space. It was built upon a central structure of support frames arranged along three axes, joined in the center by a large spherical habitat complex. Each axis was divided into docking sections with dozens of slips, protruding from the frame like the twigs on the branch of a tree. At the end of each ten kilometer-long axial arm of the station was a smaller spherical habitat complex, providing lodging, resupply, and repair services for the crews of the hundreds of ships that moved through the space dock every day.

As the first of Rivera's ships began arriving, Jucha was finalizing a series of ship movements that would open up strategically placed slips throughout the complex. Rivera's ships would be docked between larger craft whose bulk would hide the smaller pirate ships from optical detection.

Over a period of three hours, all sixteen of Rivera's ships arrived and were expertly guided to their assigned slips. Tiago, and the rest of the surviving *Boa Vista* crew arrived at the space dock on Rhys Hosking's corvette, the *North Star*. Once the ships were secured and refueling operations were underway, the captains of each of the four battle groups were requested by Tiago Maconde to report to a conference room in the central complex to finalize the battle plan for the coming engagement with the *Haikou*.

Seated around the large circular conference table were Tiago Maconde, acting captain of the captured *Boa Vista;* Captain Dayaram Gumbau, master of the cruiser *Alta Vista*; Captain Anantha Manju, master of the heavy cruiser *Brasília*; Captain Jude Guilmard, master of the cruiser *Fortaleza*; and Captain David Ferragut, master of the cruiser *Manaus*, and the most senior fleet officer. They were joined by Rhys Hosking and his chief of security, Shin Kennett.

After a brief round of greetings and small talk, Tiago began the meeting by thanking their host. "Before we begin, I would like to thank our host, Mr. Rhys Hosking, for his time, hospitality, and for the use of his space dock and the exceptional *North Star*." Rhys nodded and smiled graciously to Tiago.

"Now, to the business at hand."

Captain Manju interrupted, "Excuse me Commander Maconde, but I believe protocol requires that Captain Ferragut lead the discussion, as he is the most senior officer present."

Tiago shot the woman a stern look, then said, "Thank you, Captain Manju." Turning to Captain Ferragut he bowed his head slightly and said, "Captain, the meeting is yours, sir."

David Ferragut sat forward, ran a hand quickly through his thick silver hair, then said. "Today we will engage the Imperial destroyer *Haikou* as part of a rescue mission to retrieve Captain Rivera. The mission will consist of three stages: engagement; infiltration; and exfiltration. Captain Manju's group will lead the engagement and will disable or destroy the drive of the *Haikou*." As he spoke, a solid 3D holographic display of the *Brasília* and the three additional ships of her battle group, was being projected in the center of the conference table.

"Captain Guilmard's group will stand off at one hundred kilometers in a standard three-axis containment. They will be responsible for overwatch, and will stand ready to assist the Brasília, if need be.

"The *Manaus* battle group will maintain a z-axis containment at five hundred kilometers," Ferragut continued, "and Captain Gumbau's group will lead the boarding and exfil teams, in addition to making initial contact with *Haikou*." Ferragut touched the table surface display and the hologram of the battle space changed to show a slow motion overview of each phase of the mission. "Questions or comments?"

Tiago looked around the table, and after waiting a moment for others to speak, he said, "Excuse me, sir. To what phase of the mission is the *Boa Vista* team assigned?"

Ferragut clasped his hands in front of him on the table and replied, "Commander, it is my understanding that prior to the capture of the *Boa Vista*, you disobeyed a direct order from Captain Rivera. As a result, you are relieved of your command and will be confined to quarters aboard the *Manaus* until a review board can be convened."

Tiago felt the blood drain from his face. His eyes darted from face to face around the table, but was met with unsympathetic stares from all of the captains. He swallowed hard and answered in a measured tone, "Sir, my alleged conduct during the attack on the *Boa Vista* should not prevent me from participating in the return of my captain and friend. I will gladly surrender myself…"

Ferragut sternly interrupted, "Your conduct may well have cost your captain his life, mister! My order has been given. You are dismissed."

Tiago replied weakly, his throat tightening with emotion, "Aye, sir." He rose from his chair, and saluted the captains, then turned and began to walk toward the door. As he reached out to touch the door control, he heard the staccato voice of the harbor master, Manel Jucha.

"Mr. Hosking, tracking a small fleet of eleven Imperial vessels inbound on an orbital insertion vector — identical orbital path as the *Haikou*. Thought you'd like to know."

Tiago turned around, the other's attention focused on the harbor master's announcement.

Anxious glances traveled around the table. Rhys replied, "Thank you, Manel. ETA to orbit?"

"One hour, twenty-eight minutes. ID beacons are active and it's quite an impressive flotilla. Lots of iron. Sending the feed to your holo display." The 3-D holographic display changed and a tight formation of Imperial vessels appeared.

Captain Guilmard reviewed the ship inventory for the group, "Let's see…two destroyers, two frigates, four corvettes, a heavy cruiser, and a Luda-class battleship. Looks like a *HiVee* frigate is leading the flotilla. It's the *Honamatsu*."

Captain Gumbau added, "Jesus! That Luda is a nasty bugger. We ran into one last year near Venus. She has some nasty kinetics and a cyclic cannon that can fire almost continuously."

"All right, this changes the game plan a bit," Captain Ferragut said.

Tiago left the room and ran down the corridor toward the slip where the *North Star* was docked.

***

Tiago Maconde paused at the airlock at the slip to catch his breath. His plan was quickly unravelling and he knew he had minutes to get the *North Star* undocked and moving toward the *Haikou*. After wiping beads of sweat from his head, he unholstered his pistol, checked the magazine,

202

and chambered a round. If he moved quickly, his plan might still be salvaged.

Sabbatino and Alvarez were on the bridge when the airlock indicator lit up on the security display. Sonny touched the control panel to activate the door camera and saw Tiago standing in the airlock. "Tiago is back," he said to Sabbatino.

Moments later Tiago walked onto the bridge of the *North Star* where Sabbatino and the pilots Alvarez and Murphy were still familiarizing themselves with the state-of-the-art systems and controls of the impressive ship. He walked to the Master's chair and sat down heavily as all three sets of eyes followed him. He touched the control panel in the arm of the chair and announced, "Anna, report to the bridge."

Less than sixty-seconds later, Anna stepped onto the bridge carrying a small weapons crate that contained pistols to be worn be all officers during a combat engagement. She had also staged a cart containing body armor, assault rifles, grenades, and extra ammunition, outside the bridge bulkhead hatch in the corridor.

Sabbatino broke the silence first, "So what's the battle plan, sir?" She noted that Tiago looked flush, as if he had just worked out.

Tiago knew what he had to do, but was concerned that he would lose his courage. "Lorena, set a course for the *Haikou*. We are going to get Marco."

The others looked at each other with puzzled expressions. Sabbatino clarified, "You mean we're leading the assault?" She furrowed her brow wondering who made that tactical decision. "Why isn't one of the cruisers taking point? We will get sliced to ribbons by that destroyer!"

Tiago turned to Sabbatino and shouted, "If you are going to question my orders, Lorena, I will relieve you!"

Sabbatino visibly recoiled from Tiago's outburst. "Hey look, Tiago," she said, putting up her hands, "it's just damned unusual that's all I'm saying. I'm sure you put together a great plan." Turning to Sonny she said, "Begin undocking sequence, and signal the harbor master for departure clearance." Then turning back to Tiago, she asked, "Shall I coordinate with Captain Ferragut's number one for fleet formation and rendezvous coordinates, sir?"

"No, just get us out of this space dock. No need to bother the harbor master — he is fully informed of our flight plan." Tiago hoped that Sabbatino would simply comply.

Alvarez and Murphy both turned around in their pilot seats to glare at Tiago. Sonny said, "Tiago, this is the busiest patch of space I've ever seen. I can't just start flying around between these tankers and skimmers."

In one smooth movement, Tiago shot out of the Master's chair, drew his sidearm, and raced to the navigation station where he stopped with the barrel of his pistol pressed into the back of Lorena's head.

Bronco Murphy jumped out of his seat when Tiago shouted, "Take one step, Bronco, and I'll blow her head off!"

Murphy saw that Tiago was beyond reason and clenched his teeth, then slowly sat back down.

"Good," Tiago said, "now buckle up and don't turn around again."

Turning his attention to Anna, who was still standing just inside the bulkhead, but seemed to be closer than she was a moment ago, he said, "Anna, drop that case, and take your sidearm out and drop the clip. Then place it on the deck and kick it toward me. Do it now!"

Anna held Tiago's gaze as she slowly lowered the weapons case to the floor, then unholstered the pistol and pressed the magazine ejector with her thumb, allowing the magazine to drop to the deck with a clatter. Then she slowly squatted down and gently laid the pistol on the deck. As she stood, she placed her right foot behind the pistol and gave a kick, sliding it across the deck where it stopped a meter from Tiago.

"Sonny, get this ship moving now. Set a course for the *Haikou*, full impulse. Bronco, find a laser beacon receiver target on that ship and lock in for ship-to-ship communication." Tiago backed up against the control board surface so he could see Sabbatino's face. Still holding the gun next to her head, he leaned over and said, "And you, I don't want to hear a word. When I give a command you just do it. Is that clear?"

Sabbatino's face was red with rage, but she simply nodded her head in a robotic fashion.

Turning back to Anna, Tiago commanded, "You, go sit down at the commo station and secure your harness. Not a word unless I speak to you."

Anna simply nodded and complied.

Moments later the *North Star* was slipping between the hulking ships entering and leaving the space dock, on a direct path to intercept the *Haikou*.

***

Captain Ferragut was just wrapping up the battle planning meeting with his group captains when the strange voice of Manel Jucha interrupted again, "The *North Star* has undocked without permission. She is running fast on a direct path to join *Haikou*. ETA of twenty-three minutes to orbit. She is not responding to hails."

Ferragut slammed his fist on the table and shouted, "Damn you, Tiago!" He signaled the others to rise with a flick of his hands and ordered, "Ready your ships for immediate departure." The three other captains picked up their tablets and raced for the door.

"Mr. Jucha, can you grant us priority clearance and best access to a rendezvous coordinate?" Ferragut asked the harbor master.

After a brief silence Manel Jucha replied, "Busy pattern, but I can clear a corridor on Z-arm. Will transmit a rally point to your ships. No time for tugs, though. You'll have to fly out on stick. Your boys better not hit anything on the way out."

Ferragut turned to Rhys Hosking and said, "Rhys, I'm sorry about this. I will clean up this mess and get your ship back to you."

Rhys smiled and said, "This is the business we have chosen, Captain. There are good days and bad."

Captain Ferragut shook his hand, then sprinted through the door toward the slip where *Manaus* was docked.

CHAPTER 15

Azrael returned to his ship in orbit via the same means by which he arrived — in a flash of light. Kavan made a mental note to ask Azrael to explain that particular trick in detail.

Kavan took a few minutes to pack some cherished personal items — a digital photo frame, a tattered old Bible that Father Bożydar had given him on the occasion of his Confirmation, a stack of old paper notebooks, and a miniature model of a Bohm Stirling Engine that he had painstakingly built when he was ten years old. He would sit and stare for hours at the engine and its four heat-actuated pistons clattering up and down, pondering the magical forces at work inside the mesmerizing device.

Taking one last glance around the room, he turned to Father Bożydar and said, "Let's go, Boz. I think I am quite ready for another adventure."

Father Bożydar did most of the talking during the submarine taxi ride to Underside. Kavan's mood was pensive, but he enjoyed hearing the priest's stories of the last few years back on Mars, his joys and frustrations with his students, and his always-tense relations with the monks at the monastery.

As they made their way toward the SeaWay Link, Kavan noticed how much the city had changed since his last trip to Underside, more than three years ago. It saddened him to think of what Europa was becoming. It resembled a haughty theme park for the scientific elite and corporate plunderers, with every conceivable entertainment, distraction, and illicit pleasure, all covered by a veneer of normality and acceptability. After all, the men and women who labored under the ice in the frigid darkness had considerable money and energy to expend during their trips to the city.

After disembarking the SeaWay Link, the two men weaved their way through the throngs of people bustling around the EOLS base terminal. After waiting for what seemed like a lifetime in a customs inspection queue, the inspector opened Kavan's case and prodded his cherished items with cold and indifferent bureaucratic efficiency. When the man spotted the model of the Bohm Stirling Engine he said, "What the hell is this thing?"

Kavan coolly replied, "It is a model of an external combustion engine. I made it when I was a boy."

The man held up the plexiglass case containing the shiny brass and stainless steel device, turning it over and inspecting it on all sides. Finally he said, "It's pretty heavy. Are you sure you want to take it up? It puts you over your weight limit. It's gonna cost you extra."

Kavan smiled and said, "That's fine. It's worth it."

The inspector raised his eyebrow and gave shrug. He closed the case and returned it to the conveyor.

Moments later Kavan and Father Bożydar were seated

comfortably aboard the EOLS ascender. As they left the surface of Europa, Kavan felt as though he was leaving a part of himself behind, the weight of years of solitude, grief, and silent longing falling away as they climbed through the thin atmosphere.

After docking at the EOLS topside platform, they gathered Kavan's case and made the long trek to the private slip where Azrael's ship was docked. As they approached the slip, Kavan got his first glimpse of the sleek shimmering hull of the ship, causing him to smile.

Azrael met them at the airlock, having returned to his most common appearance. Kavan was still unsettled by the angel's ability to alter his appearance so completely. He suspected that would be the least of Azrael's marvelous abilities that he would lie awake at night pondering.

Once aboard, the three moved to the parlor where Azrael gave Kavan a brief explanation of how he willed the ship's form and function into a pattern that was both familiar and useful for the task at hand. Kavan's mind reeled at the implications of having the ability to shape matter and harness energy at will, with no need for cumbersome technology. He was astonished.

"It has been a very long day for you both. I have prepared a stateroom for you Kavan, and you will find a selection of comfortable clothing to choose from. If you are hungry, there is a meal prepared in the galley," Azrael offered.

Kavan looked at Father Bożydar who rubbed his belly and smiled. "Boz, you never pass up a free meal."

Father Bożydar laughed and said, *"Ad maiorem Dei gloriam!"*

***

Azrael let Kavan and Father Bożydar sleep for more than twelve hours, knowing they would need to be fully refreshed to meet the challenges of the day ahead. While they slept, Azrael had met with Hamaliel and learned of the conflict that was developing in orbit above Callisto. Hamaliel could not predict the outcome of the confrontation that was brewing between the Emperor's forces and those loyal to the infamous pirate Marco Bisbal-Rivera, but he was certain that the outcome would affect Azrael's mission on Titan.

After showering and eating a hearty breakfast, Kavan and Father Bożydar sat in the parlor with Azrael discussing the plan to infiltrate the space dock at Titan.

"The ship is located at a space dock built above the orbital lift topside platform," Azrael began. "The FTL ship is contained within a massive shed that shields it from the prying eyes of probes or scout ships. I have been to the site and can say it is truly an impressive achievement. Man has never built anything quite like it.

"We will need unrestricted access to the facility. This can only be accomplished if we can convince the station authorities that we somehow belong there. While it is a simple matter for me, getting the two of you into the facility will require some, shall we say, creativity." Azrael pointed to the orb floating just below the ceiling of the center portion of the parlor. It slowly rearranged itself into a 3D solid hologram of the two human conspirators dressed in utilitarian Imperial tunics and trousers. Kavan had long dark hair pulled tight into a long braid, in the centuries-old traditional Chinese style. The facsimile also wore a goatee and bore four tattooed characters on the right side of his neck, just visible above the collar. The characters read '*Jing-zhong-bao-guo*' — Absolute Loyalty to Serve the Empire. It was the instantly-recognizable mark of the Black Hood, the Emperor's secret police and most feared enforcers.

Father Bożydar's facsimile was still mostly bald, but wearing a similar, although silver, goatee. Around his neck was a long silver chain made of thick hand-hammered links. The end of the chain bore a solid gold key with a large sapphire set in the head. This was the symbol of the Imperial Prosecutor, who normally accompanied the Black Hoods to document the testimony, and indict or absolve those accused of crimes.

Kavan stood and moved closer to the projection to inspect the image of himself more closely. "I kind of like this new look. It makes me look mysterious and a little dangerous," he teased.

"You laugh, Kavan, but that is exactly the goal. As a member of the Black Hoods, you should meet no resistance and will be able to move freely around the space dock complex." Azrael turned to Father Bożydar, "And you, Father, you will need to maintain a deferential demeanor while in the presence of Kavan and others. A prosecutor would never speak in the presence of a Black Hood unless asked a direct question.

"You may need to play out the fiction of conducting an investigation to ferret out a suspected spy. My Brethren have learned that there is indeed a corporate spy working at the laboratory. Remus Arin discovered some anomalous test data during his inspection visit last month, and he has informed the Emperor. The project director is expecting a formal investigation, so our pretense is well-established."

"And what role will you be playing?" Kavan asked with a note of dark sarcasm in his voice. Azrael could sense the lingering anger in Kavan's spirit. Although he intellectually understood the facts surrounding Azrael's mission to disrupt his work on 216 Kleopatra, he still had not dealt with the emotions associated with confronting the being responsible for the loss of his family and so many of his friends. Kavan's rational mind did not care that Azrael was an angel — he was still driven by fierce primal urges seeking retribution for his wife and children.

"It is necessary that I remain out of sight. I will go before you and ensure that there are no unexpected threats which might cause you delay or harm." Azrael stood and clasped Kavan by the shoulder, "I sense the desire for revenge in you, Kavan. So long I have lived among men that I understand these urges in a way that all but a few of my Brethren cannot." Peering into Kavan's eyes and through to his soul, Azrael spoke the words that would echo in Kavan's mind for the rest of his days, "Your faithfulness shall be rewarded. Remember Zacharias."

***

Azrael brought the ship to a point above the North magnetic pole of Titan. Lost in the magnetosphere of the moon, the sentinel defense satellites were unable to detect the ship.

Slowly opening his eyes, Azrael informed his companions, "I have altered the monitoring data of the sentinels so that it will show the approach of an Imperial cutter on an inbound trajectory from Ganymede. The constructed data is about to synchronize and expects us to be entering visual range of the TOLS upper deck in a few seconds. Please pardon me for a moment."

He once again closed his eyes and both Kavan and Father Bożydar felt the split-second sensation of diffusion and then disorientation, the only indication of the occurrence of the space-folding phenomenon.

Azrael again opened his eyes, "Perhaps you would enjoy a view of Titan?" He motioned to the port-side wall, which shimmered for a moment, and then opened to frame a large viewing portal.

Kavan was rendered speechless at the view. He slowly walked up the steps from the parlor and placed both hands on the transparent surface of the portal, leaning into the concave shape, gazing at the muddy orange and brown swirling clouds of Titan. From low orbit, lakes of liquid hydrocarbons could clearly be seen reflecting the feeble rays of light from the distant sun.

"It's strangely beautiful," Kavan remarked. Turning to Azrael, "So my theory, it really works. That is how you brought us here, right?"

Azrael smiled and nodded. "Yes, your theory was indeed a moment of transcendent insight, Kavan. Your leap of imagination and clarity was unexpected, but very gratifying."

Kavan pondered the words. "What do you mean by 'unexpected'?"

"There have only been a few moments in the history of mankind where an organic leap of insight has been achieved. Newton, Einstein, the Wright Brothers, Watson & Crick. They all found elegant truths by learning the importance of asking the right questions. You asked the right questions, Kavan. And you found profound truth in the very fabric of space-time. You understand it like no other human. This knowledge can never be erased. It is part of you. Your mind was capable of scaling the walls that have been in place for millennia. And now you walk in a different place, where other men must be led, if you so choose."

His words pierced Kavan's soul. In his quiet moments, when his rage had subsided and he allowed himself to wander through the memories of his work, he realized that, though his loss was great, his ideas and their promise were still present and potent. Emotionally he could not linger on the thought of reconstituting his work. His conscience would never allow that. It would be an unforgivable sin against his wife and children — at least that is what he believed. Going forward would devalue their sacrifice, and make him a monster.

But now it seemed that Azrael was hinting at a deeper possibility. Perhaps he was meant to bring his work to life after all. Could it be that this strange journey was part of a much larger plan to teach him something that he had missed along the way?

CHAPTER 16

Tiago Maconde leaned heavily against the console next to Sabbatino, his right leg throbbing and his body feeling heavy and weak. The air was filled with the scent of sweat and charged with tension, yet silent as each person carried out their duties.

Bronco Murphy turned to make eye contact with Tiago, not wanting to speak fearing a bullet as a response. Tiago acknowledged him with a nod, giving him permission to speak.

"Laser link established with *Haikou*. Shall I hail her?" Bronco said.

"Yes. Put it on the main screen." Tiago stood up and grabbed Sabbatino by the back of the collar. "Get up," he said coldly.

Sabbatino slowly rose from her seat and allowed Tiago to steer her into position in front of him, the pistol pointed at the back of her head. They crossed the bridge and stood behind the Master's chair, with Tiago holding Sabbatino at arms length by the collar with his left hand.

A video window slid out from the corner of the main

view screen at the front of the bridge. It resized and moved to the upper right corner, and the face of a young Chinese woman appeared wearing the standard dark blue utility uniform of the Imperial Navy. She said, "Destroyer *Haikou* acknowledging hail from private yacht *North Star*. State your request."

"This is Commander Tiago Maconde, first officer of the *Boa Vista*. I am requesting permission to board via shuttle. Mr. Yarrick of Naval Intelligence should be notified." Tiago breathed a sigh of relief, knowing that he would soon be safe among his new allies.

"Wait one, *North Star*." The video changed to the Imperial Navy emblem.

Sabbatino could no longer contain her anger. "You son of a bitch! You weren't trying to defend the ship. You were going to meet the marine boarding party and lead them to Marco."

Anna turned her chair around and said with dark eyes, "Marco was like a brother to you. Why would you betray him like this? My god, Tiago, have you lost your mind?"

"Shut-up, you bitch!" Tiago released Sabbatino's collar and turned the gun on Anna. "Ever since you came along, Marco has been weak."

Sabbatino broke Tiago's grasp on her collar and turned to face him. He quickly turned the gun back to her and pointed it directly at her forehead. She shouted, "So you give him up to the Emperor? Why didn't you go to the other captains and voice your concerns? This is madness."

Tiago smiled, "In the end, Lorena, he gave himself up. He didn't want to shoot marines to save his ship," and turning to Anna, "or his bitch He is not the man I called *brother*."

Bronco spoke up, "So now what, Tiago? You think the navy is going to just let you go? Or are you going to become a slave to the Emperor like the billions of other drones?"

Tiago laughed, "Funny thing about the Imperial Navy. The only thing they hate worse than a pirate is a traitor. Anna is my ticket to freedom."

Anna reached for the harness release but Tiago warned, "Don't do it, Anna. They would prefer you alive, but I'm sure they'll take a corpse just the same."

The exchange was interrupted by the appearance of a young man in his late twenties dressed in a black jacket with striking green eyes and chocolate skin. "This is Miles Yarrick, Imperial Intelligence Service. Good to see you again, Señor Maconde. We were beginning to worry that you would not follow through on our arrangement. It seems you have your hands full there," the man said with a wry smile.

Ignoring Yarrick's jibe, Tiago replied, "I am ready to transport. There will be four coming over on a shuttle. I will launch it on an automated flight path to come close aboard *Haikou*." He smiled broadly and added, "I will not be needing the ship I requested. This beauty will suit me just fine."

"As you wish, Señor Maconde. The Emperor is grateful for your assistance in ridding the Empire of Marco Bisbal-Rivera, and returning one of his lost children."

"Bronco, cut the link," Tiago ordered. The video window went blank and slid away, off the screen.

Tiago moved back away from the Master's chair and said, "All right. Everyone get up and move over here," pointing to the place where Sabbatino was standing.

Alvarez, Murphy, and Anna released their harnesses and slowly made their way to stand next to Sabbatino.

"Now we are going to walk nice and slow to the shuttle bay. If anyone so much as coughs, I will blow Lorena's head off." Tiago pointed to Anna, "You lead the way, bitch. Then, Sonny and Bronco. Move!"

Anna moved slowly and stood a few paces from the bulkhead of the bridge. Sonny followed and stood directly behind her, with Bronco moving a pace behind him. Tiago grabbed Sabbatino roughly by the collar again and positioned her behind the large co-pilot. "Now we are going to move into the corridor nice and slow."

As Tiago was moving Sabbatino, he did not notice Anna reaching up to touch behind her right ear, activating her biolink. While waiting on the ship during the mission planning meeting, the crew had registered their individual biolinks with the *North Star's* FCIC. Without registering his biolink, Tiago was cut off from the private communication channel. Anna silently signaled to the others, "There is a weapons cart to the right of the bulkhead in the corridor. When I turn the corner, I will grab a rifle. When I do, you three drop to the deck and I will shoot that traitor."

Anna heard a silent chorus in her head reply in unison, "Roger that!"

"Okay, Anna, open the door." Tiago ordered.

***

Anna raised her right hand and touched the control pad on the bulkhead. The large blast door immediately slid open, disappearing into left side of the bulkhead frame.

"Now, move. Slowly," Tiago commanded.

Anna stepped over the bulkhead hatch coaming into the

corridor. She began to turn to her right and announced via her biolink, "Now!"

In unison Alvarez, Murphy, and Sabbatino suddenly dropped down into a crouching position, startling Tiago as he lost his grip on Sabbatino's collar. He quickly regained his stance and grabbed the pistol with both hands, taking aim at Sabbatino's head. As his finger began to tighten on the trigger, Anna emerged in the hatch opening holding an assault rifle. She squeezed the trigger twice, putting two perfectly placed rounds into the space between Tiago's eyes.

The man's head exploded in a spray of blood, sending his lifeless body to the deck, still clutching the pistol in his hands.

The others stood up and turned to look at their dead comrade. Bronco put a hand on Sabbatino's shoulder, and feeling her trembling, he asked gently, "You okay, Lorena?"

Sabbatino reached up and placed her hand over his, turned and smiled, "Yes, Bronco, I'm fine."

Sonny turned to Anna, who was lowering the still-smoking rifle, and said, "Good work, Anna."

Anna stepped back onto the bridge and walked over to Tiago's body, lying in a growing pool of dark blood. "Bastard," she spat.

Sabbatino realized they were still in a very dangerous predicament. The *Haikou* was expecting a shuttle containing the four of them to arrive in the next few minutes. They would not be allowed to depart the area without delivering the shuttle.

"Follow me. We have to move quickly." Sabbatino ran through the hatch and down the corridor toward the shuttle bay, followed by her three crew mates.

On the way to the shuttle bay, Sabbatino instructed Alvarez and Murphy to go to the armory and gather every explosive they could find and bring them to the shuttle bay. She decided to use the shuttle to create a diversion that might allow them to escape from the range of the destroyer's big guns.

Sabbatino and Anna prepped the shuttle, and programmed the flight plan and landing sequence. After a few minutes Sabbatino said via biolink, "Hey, guys. What the hell is taking you so long?"

Murphy answered with his signature enthusiasm, "On our way, Lorena. We're bringing you a present. I think you're gonna like it."

A moment later the equipment lift door rolled up to reveal Murphy and Alvarez wearing mischievous grins, guiding a maglev rack full of 120 centimeter torpedoes.

Sabbatino shook her head and laughed, "It's always about *bigger* with you guys."

Anna laughed out loud and added, "You really know what a lady likes, Bronco."

Turning serious, Sonny said, "I figured we could give our navy friends a truly memorable surprise."

Sabbatino liked the way her pilots thought. "Great idea, boys. Program them to detonate thirty-seconds after engine shutdown. It should make quite a mess of the flight deck."

Within minutes the torpedoes had been programmed and they all watched as the shuttle gently lifted off from the deck guided by the FCIC onboard computer.

Sabbatino and the others raced back to the bridge to prepare to return to the space cock and rejoin their fleet.

***

Captain Ferragut reviewed the fleet deployment display and saw that the last battle group was moving into position at the rendezvous point. He touched the display and opened a channel to Captain Manju aboard the *Brasília.* "Right on time, Anantha."

"Aye, sir. All ships accounted for and awaiting your order," she replied.

Ferragut was pleased that his fleet was able to quickly adapt to the revised battle plan that the arrival of the Imperial fleet demanded. He checked the running chronometer and saw that they had less than twenty minutes until the Imperial fleet arrived. The tactical display showed that the Imperial ships were already in the orbital plane, but had not yet come into view around the curvature of the moon. He needed to work fast to engage the *Haikou,* before his fleet would be visible to the Imperial ships, and their weapons began rapidly plotting firing solutions.

The tactical weapons officer announced, "Sir, I have a fix on the *North Star.* She is aligned for an approach vector that will take her close aboard the *Haikou.* Shuttle bay doors are open and I'm reading drive plasma exhaust. Looks like she's launching a shuttle."

Ferragut zoomed the main display on the aft section of the *North Star* and saw a shuttle craft emerge and immediately turn toward the *Haikou.* "What the hell is Maconde doing?" he wondered aloud. He was furious with Tiago's impetuousness and disregard for orders. "Tactical, mark that shuttle 'friendly' so nobody shoots Maconde."

"Aye, Captain," the tactical weapons officer replied.

Ferragut touched the display and opened a broadcast channel to all of his group captains. "Attack plan alpha is a 'go'. All ships engage on my mark." He looked to his helmsman and said, "Mr. Sisto, is the helm ready?"

"Aye, Captain," Sisto replied.

"All ships, engage!" Ferragut instantly felt the acceleration of the massive fusion impulse drive. He looked around the bridge and was filled with pride at the performance of his crew. Today would mark the largest naval battle that Rivera's pirate fleet had ever fought. He knew the odds were stacked against them, and that the successful rescue of their captain would be a small miracle. But he was certain that they had prepared well, given the limited time they had, and that his people would bravely meet every challenge the day would bring.

**

On the bridge of the *Haikou*, Miles Yarrick watched intently as the shuttle from the *North Star* approached the shuttle bay. He was anxious to begin interrogating the traitor and former naval officer, Anna Domasheva. The events leading up to this day were set in motion only recently. He had been surprised and very skeptical of the information that Tiago Maconde — a notoriously violent pirate and close associate of Marco Bisbal-Rivera — had passed to him during a visit to Mars a month before. Maconde claimed that Rivera had agreed to meet with a senior diplomat named Nianzu Chao. He believed that Rivera was starting to take too many risks since he became enamored with Anna, and he wanted Rivera gone so that he could take over the *Boa Vista* and hopefully lead the pirate fleet.

His plan was accelerated by the mission to steal the

FTL ship from Titan. Maconde had no desire to settle on a distant world like Titan, but he knew an FTL ship would make him and his pirate fleet the most powerful force in the solar system. He transmitted the rendezvous coordinates for Callisto to Yarrick prior to leaving Earth. Yarrick alerted the Minister of Defense, who then dispatched the destroyer *Haikou* to intercept the *Boa Vista* and capture Marco Bisbal-Rivera and his crew. Maconde was to be released after the *Boa Vista* crew was taken into custody. Then he would concoct a story of his brave solo escape in the *Boa Vista* to report to the other fleet captains.

But when the patrol boat torpedoed the *Boa Vista* and crippled her drive, Maconde panicked and wanted to simply surrender to the marines, hoping that Yarrick had not lied to him.

Yarrick smiled as the shuttle floated through the shuttle bay and settled down to a perfect landing, and was immediately surrounded by a company of marines. He turned to his intelligence analyst and said, "I'm going down to the shuttle bay to escort the prisoner to the brig. Please prepare the interrogation room for Domasheva. I want to begin immediately." The analyst nodded in reply.

As Yarrick turned to leave the bridge, a violent tremor shook the entire room, sending tablets and cups of coffee to the floor. A few seconds later a distant thundering roar blasted through the hatchway of the bridge and a strong gust of air blew through the room. Immediately a warning klaxon sounded and red lights began to appear on every display in the room.

Captain Que Jin Hai looked up at the FCIC display and said, "Damage control, report."

The engineering station reported, "Explosion in the

shuttle bay, with loss of hull integrity. Aft decks one, two, and three show all red, sir. Fire sensors active in all sections aft of the machine shop. Primary reactor is offline. Drive shield shows severe structural damage. Shall I launch an inspector drone, sir?"

"Yes, and dispatch all available hands for fire crew support." Captain Hai said to his First Officer, "Sound general quarters." The captain turned to his tactical weapons officer, "Charge main laser canons and rack all kinetics and torpedo bays." Each officer acknowledged their orders in turn, working efficiently to carry them out.

Captain Hai touched his control pad and a live video image transmitted from the inspection drone appeared on the main bridge display. As the small robotic drone flew down the length of the *Haikou* toward the stern, the damage to the drive shield was plainly visible. The bottom quarter of the huge dish of the drive shield was missing and more than half of the superstructure was bent and pitted with gaping holes torn by debris from the shuttle bay explosion.

As the drone crossed over the side of *Haikou* and flew under the ship, a gigantic gash in the hull came into view. The entire shuttle bay was gone leaving a dark hole, outlined by intermittent flashes of plasma and fiber optic cables, in the bottom of the ship. A cloud of debris was still expanding away from the ship into space.

The Captain knew his ship was badly damaged and very vulnerable to attack. The first order of business was to protect the ship and put her in the best position to defend herself. "Helm, full impulse orbital escape. Make way for the L1 space dock. Communications, alert them that we need priority maneuvering assistance and possible evacuation support."

The tactical weapons officer interrupted, "Sir! I have eleven inbound Imperial vessels in our orbital plane on a burn to form up with us. ETA, twelve-minutes." The young officer smiled broadly as he announced the news.

Captain Hai turned to his first officer and winked, commenting, "I guess the cavalry is here."

***

Captain Daley and Admiral Butchers stood at the FCIC console on the flag bridge of the *Honamatsu* watching the drama unfold.

The tactical officer announced, "Captain, I am tracking seventeen inbound targets in the vicinity of *Haikou's* projected orbital location. A private corvette is leading in a non-standard point position. The other sixteen bogeys are inbound on a path originating from the L1 space dock, approximately twenty minutes behind the corvette. Beacons indicate the large body is composed of skimmers and tankers, but they're grouped in an attack formation."

Captain Daley looked up at the FCIC tactical display and instantly recognized the familiar V-shape of the icons, a common navy assault formation. "Give me an optical view on display two. What's our ETA to visual on the *Haikou*?"

"Four minutes until visual acquisition, sir"

At that moment, Remus Arin and Sumiko Lee entered the flag bridge and stood at the railing of the observation gallery. Sumiko placed her hand gently on Remus' forearm and said, "Ambassador, please wait here while I speak with the Captain."

Remus was fully prepared to act out this next scene in the drama of his own creation. The arrival of the pirate fleet on time and in full strength was a bonus that he had hoped for, but did not expect. This would make the next phase of his plan even simpler.

Sumiko approached the FCIC console and stopped a few paces from where Captain Daley and Admiral Butchers were standing. She waited silently until one of the officers acknowledged her, as was customary. After what seemed to be a longer-than-necessary pause, Captain Daley looked over the Admiral's shoulder at Sumiko.

"Yes, Commander?" he said in a dismissive tone.

"Sir, Ambassador Arin would like an update on the tactical situation and an ETA of our time on station at Callisto." Sumiko stood at attention awaiting a reply.

Captain Daley gave the Admiral a quick glance and he nodded slightly. "Well, of course, Commander. The Ambassador is always welcome on the flag bridge," he replied with a mild note of sarcasm, loud enough for Remus to hear from the gallery.

Remus briskly walked down the ramp and came up to the FCIC console. Admiral Butchers turned and spoke first, "Captain Daley will be pleased to brief you on our status, Ambassador."

"Thank you, Admiral. And Captain, I do not wish to take up too much of your time," Remus said, in his most sincere voice.

"Good, because we are in the middle of a live tactical situation." Captain Daley pointed to the tactical display showing the ships of the Imperial fleet represented as green icons on the screen, and the pirate fleet as red icons. "I have a feeling *that* is Rivera's fleet and not normal commercial traffic. We are taking a look with the optics to see what we have."

The tactical officer instructed the telescope array to focus on the formation in question. She then fed the live video imagery to the FCIC display. Within seconds, Captain Daley was looking at the dimly lit silhouettes of cruisers and frigates, not skimmers and freighters. He raised his eyebrows and shook his head slightly.

"It looks like they brought the whole team to play. They're on a direct course to engage the *Haikou*, no doubt to try to board and rescue Rivera." Turning to Admiral Butchers who was standing near the tactical weapons station, "Admiral, I could use your input on our tactical situation, sir." The Admiral nodded and began walking toward the FCIC console.

As he came alongside the Captain, the Admiral stated, "We need to protect *Haikou* and ensure the transfer of Rivera and her crew."

Captain Daley was concerned about the relative position of the two fleets and the advantage that Rivera's ships had at the moment. "Sir, the enemy ships are showing their guns and have an advantage until we turn broadside. We have ten minutes of retro burn remaining and cannot turn to engage. We're already in range of their kinetics and torpedoes."

Daley's mind was reviewing decades of tactics and maneuvers in his mind, searching for a solution to their current dilemma. After a moment, he knew what he must do.

"Sir, I recommend we instruct the battleship *Taipei* to execute a reduced burn. She will move to the front of our formation and provide cover for the shuttle while it docks with *Haikou* and transfers the prisoner. The rest of the fleet should break orbit and move to a standoff broadside stance near L1." Daley watched the Admiral's face carefully as his mind processed the recommendation.

Admiral Butchers nodded, "Go on, Captain."

"Once the prisoner transfer is complete, *Taipei* will provide cover for *Haikou* as she joins the fleet at L1. Then she will engage Rivera's heavy cruiser, and the rest of our fleet will destroy his fleet. We will bring great honor to the Emperor today." Daley's face was flush with the anticipation of the coming battle.

Remus interrupted the exchange, "Captain, I do not wish to interject myself into naval matters, but our primary mission must be the priority. We cannot risk the fleet on a Quixotic engagement with an enemy we know nothing about."

Captain Daley glared at Sumiko for allowing the detestable Ambassador to overstep his authority. Sumiko lowered her eyes.

Meeting Remus' piecing gaze, Captain Daley replied, "Ambassador, when I want your tactical advice, I will ask. Your concerns have been noted, but the nature of our mission has been altered by the Emperor himself. I will carry out the spirit of those orders to my fullest ability. Are we clear?"

Remus looked to Admiral Butchers as a husband would look to his wife when faced with a petulant child. The Admiral gave a small cough then said, "Captain, the Ambassador does make a reasonable point. Our explicit orders are to transfer Rivera to *Honamatsu*. That is all."

Captain Daley sensed the situation slipping out of his control and felt a chill run up his spine. Something was very wrong, but he could not put his finger on it.

"Sir, can we at least agree that if Rivera's fleet makes

any threatening moves against *Haikou,* or any of the ships in the fleet, we will take an offensive posture?"

Admiral Butchers' eyes darted almost imperceptibly to Remus, then, "Yes, Captain. That seems like a reasonable course. But be sure that our ships do not provoke Rivera's fleet."

"Aye aye, sir." Captain Daley walked away and huddled with his First Officer to lay out the orders and transmit them to the fleet.

Suddenly a warning tone sounded overhead. "Sir! Visual contact with *Haikou.*"

Every head on the flag bridge turned to the main display and a variety of gasps and exclamations could be heard from around the room. The display showed the severely damaged drive shield of the *Haikou* framed in a cloud of flotsam that had been the landing bay only moments before. Bright flashes from fiber optic and plasma cables punctuated the horrific scene of destruction.

Captain Daley frowned and said to his communications officer, "Hail the *Haikou.*"

Seconds later, "*Haikou* master on screen, sir."

The primary display flickered and then was filled by the round and distressed face of Captain Hai. "This is Captain Hai, master of *Haikou.* We are very glad to see you, sir."

Daley gave a slight bow and said, "Captain, what is your status?"

"A shuttle from the corvette exploded in our landing bay. We have several decks on fire, but our fire teams have it under control. Our drive is offline and our inspection drone shows our drive shield is severely damaged. We are moving off orbit under impulse power to the L1 space dock to await a repair barge."

"Roger that, Captain. Wait one." Daley turned to Commander Singh, "Signal *Taipei* to charge her main guns and open all torpedo doors. I want Rivera's fleet to see her teeth. And Tactical, get me an ID on that corvette."

Admiral Butchers slowly moved from the FCIC console to stand next to Remus and Sumiko. He looked at Remus and said silently, '*This situation is spinning out of control. We cannot allow Daley to divert us, Brother.*'

Remus replied with his mind, '*Patience, Brother. Let this play out a bit. We may find an advantage in the good Captain's impetuous nature.*'

Turning back to the main display, Captain Daley continued, "Captain Hai. The battleship *Taipei* is moving into position and will cover your cruise to L1. I am curious, Captain — what was a shuttle from that corvette doing in your landing bay?"

Captain Hai frowned and turned to someone off-screen, then said, "Our intelligence officer was retrieving additional prisoners from an asset that escaped the *Boa Vista*. Although it would appear that his asset was compromised, as evidenced by our missing landing bay." The Captain's speech was dripping with venom, undoubtedly meant for the unfortunate intelligence officer.

"And what is the status of the prisoner Marco Bisbal-Rivera?" Captain Daley inquired.

"He is safe and sound, Captain. I would appreciate getting him off my ship. We're a very tempting target for Rivera's fleet, and I fear we would not put up much of a fight in our current condition."

"Captain, we will dispatch a shuttle immediately to transfer the prisoner. Can we dock at your port bow transfer airlock?" Daley pointed to his flight control officer who began the sequence to prepare a shuttle for flight.

"That would be fine, Captain. Mr. Yarrick, our intelligence officer, will meet your team at the airlock with the prisoner."

"Thank you, sir. *Honamatsu* out." The main screen returned to display the ships of Rivera's fleet slowly growing as *Honamatsu* approached.

Captain Daley moved to the tactical weapons station and leaning in, asked, "Got that ID for me yet?"

The young man replied quickly, "Yes, sir. It is registered to the Hosking Enterprise. It is a Tornamira Galaxy-4 *HiVee* Corvette." He let out an involuntary lustful whistle, "That is one sweet ship, sir."

Daley nodded, "You're not kidding."

Remus decided it was time to creatively solve one of his long-standing problems in an elegant and diabolical fashion. He had silently communicated his desire to Admiral Butchers, who would now play his part in the drama unfolding on the flag bridge.

"Captain, I would like Mr. Chao to accompany the marines in the transfer of the prisoner," the Admiral ordered. Then turning to Sumiko, "Commander Lee, you still hold an active flight rating, do you not?"

Sumiko was stunned by the question. She quickly regained her composure and replied, "Yes, Admiral. I am qualified to pilot all shuttle craft currently in service."

"Excellent! Then you will assist Mr. Chao in retrieving the criminal Rivera." Turning to the stunned Captain Daley, he continued, "Please detail two marines for the mission, Captain."

Daley's flesh was crawling. He knew deep in his belly that the Admiral was orchestrating something. Chao's wild conspiracy theory seemed to be playing out on his bridge.

After shuffling through a handful of alternatives, he saw no option but to comply with the Admiral's order. To do otherwise would mean to openly disobey an order from a flag officer. He replied simply, "Aye, sir."

Touching the FCIC control console, Daley said, "Mr. Chao, please report to Commander Lee on the flight deck immediately."

Sumiko gave Remus a worried look and left the flag bridge heading for the flight deck. She knew that something strange had just taken place, but could not imagine the implications.

CHAPTER 17

Azrael's ship approached the Titan Orbital Lift Station complex outfitted as an Imperial cutter, her gleaming red and white hull starkly contrasted against the black of space. Inside, Kavan and Father Bożydar were putting the finishing touches on their disguises. Azrael had made some adjustments to the nano-machines inside Kavan's body, causing his hair to grow more than a half meter and change color. A similar effect was rendered on his facial hair, and after a quick trim, he was looking in the mirror at the same face that he saw on the hologram image.

Father Bożydar's transformation was simpler, requiring only a wardrobe change and some minor modification to his hair style. The more difficult aspect of the charade for the old priest would be his inability to speak unless spoken to by Kavan. His greatest burden during his decades living at the monastery could now get both him and Kavan killed if he did not exercise perfect self-control.

"When we dock, it is important that you move swiftly through the security checkpoint, and do not linger." Azrael pointed to a map of the station and the shipyard space dock. "It would be best to pay a courtesy visit to the project director. He is a relatively young man recruited from the Naval Special Weapons Section — a brilliant engineer and mathematician named Dr. Prakesh Mohapatra. His control of the facility is absolute and extends to the station security force.

"You should suggest a tour of the facility. Explain that it will aid your investigation to be familiar with the various areas of the project and the key locations throughout the facility."

The ultimate goal of all this was still unclear to Kavan. He was troubled by Azrael's habit of only revealing bits and pieces of information, and seeming to never give a complete answer. "Azrael, why is it necessary for us to risk our lives to sabotage this ship? Surely you could wave your hand and end the matter."

Azrael knew this moment would come. In his long history with mankind, there always came a time with his student when the age old existential mystery emerged in the mind. He found it curious that a race of beings who had been created with a singular purpose and perfect knowledge of that purpose, had drifted so far that they no longer knew themselves.

"Why is Man part of the universe, Kavan?" Azrael reached out to sense the man's spirit, searching for evidence that the deep well of his faith was still present, if not hidden under layers of grief and anger.

"Look Azrael, I'm not looking for an existential debate, just a simple answer to my question."

Azrael smiled and continued, "The question pertains directly to your concern. Why is Man necessary for anything in this universe? Surely Our Father could have designed a universe without human beings. Indeed He did not need to create my kind either. But the puzzling fact remains that He did.

"I have been a friend to humanity for more than two million years. I was present when the first spark of true self-awareness appeared in a single man on the African plain. I have sat around campfires at night and conversed in a thousand languages with men as they pondered the universe and the meaning of their existence. Still, here we are. A man and an angel, two beings in a universe that neither needs us nor pays us any heed. So then why are we here? Could it be that we are here for each other? Could it be that we are here to simply either seek truth or deny truth?"

Kavan's mind drifted back to his childhood on Mars. On those warm summer nights when he would sneak out of the dome that enclosed Aram Chaos and hike up the ridge of a nearby crater covered in a blanket of soft green grass. He would lie in the grass under the stars and try to imagine the scale of the universe. He accepted the obvious reality that everything he could see in the sky, every particle of matter, and all of the things that he could not see but that mathematics could intuit, was the product of a mind. An intelligence so vast and utterly complete that his small human mind would never be able to comprehend its majesty and might. He felt small, but something more as well. There, in the grass on Mars, the boy felt...*unique*. Somehow this same being that conceived of and made the universe, also knew Kavan. He knew him in a way that no human could ever know him, because He had fashioned his soul and his body and placed him in time for a specific purpose, which as a boy, he could only hint at.

"So you are saying that we must do this because it is what we were born to do?"

Azrael felt Kavan's Spirit ignite, giving off warmth like the campfires of the distant past. "Yes, my friend. I believe it is that simple. Man has spent much of his time and energy running from this truth ever since Eden. But in this case there is a planet and a race of men who have not turned from Truth. And we, as improbable as it may seem, have been set the task to prevent evil from contaminating yet another world.

"I cannot tell you what to do, Kavan. But I am confident that you will know what must be done when the time comes."

Father Bożydar placed a hand on Kavan's shoulder and said, "My son, you have been the greatest joy of my life. I knew from the first words you spoke to me that you were the reason I was born. Watching your skepticism and doubt fade away to be replaced by a confident faith and devotion to God was a true gift. We are nearing the end of our journey together, that much I know for certain. Let's take the last few steps together and complete what we started so many years ago."

Kavan looked into the eyes of his old teacher. He saw a man who loved him completely, and he knew in that moment that he would complete his journey, and make peace with the ghosts that haunted his Spirit.

"Then let's be about this business." Kavan turned his attention back to the maps and the three finalized the plan.

Thirty minutes later, after the ship was docked in a priority slip, Kavan and Father Bożydar walked through the airlock hatch of the ship and were greeted by two security guards. Azrael had altered the programming and signature of the nano-machines in each man's body to interact with the Imperial identification scanners and surveillance equipment. While their disguises were important, the signals emanating from their bodies gave them legitimate identities and would satisfy the curiosity of the artificial intelligence that monitored every heartbeat and recorded every word.

"Welcome to Titan, Inspector Smith. I hope that you and Prosecutor Kreiger have an enjoyable stay." The guard fumbled nervously with the tablet in his hands.

Playing his role as they had discussed, Kavan said coldly, "Let Director Mohapatra know that we have arrived and will meet with him in his office in ten minutes."

The guard nodded sharply, "Of course, Inspector. Sergeant Namu will escort you."

"We do not require an escort. Are we finished here?" Kavan stared menacingly at the guard.

Both guards instinctively bowed deeply and Kavan and Father Bożydar passed through the security gate into the station.

***

Prakesh Mohapatra sat at his desk in a spartan but comfortable office in the administrative level of the space dock. The complex was designed for one purpose — to fabricate and build the single largest machine ever constructed by humans. The station took raw materials mined from the surface of Titan and refined them into the myriad metals, ceramics, polymers, and organics necessary for building a ship that could ply the vast distance between the stars.

Prior to his recruitment for the project, Mohapatra had a brilliant career in the Imperial Navy Special Weapons Section. He had worked on several high profile and very successful projects that gave him access to cutting edge technologies and the brightest minds that the Imperial universities could produce. It was during his last project that he had met Ambassador Remus Arin. The Ambassador had approached him at a cocktail reception for a group of visiting dignitaries during a tour of a secret weapons laboratory on Ganymede. Mohapatra had been flattered that the famous Ambassador had sought him out and they spent more than an hour in an animated conversation. He found the Ambassador to be not only very charming and intelligent, but he was also surprised at how familiar Arin was with the work being done by the Special Weapons Section. It was clear to Mohapatra that the man was much more than an ambassador, and knowing such a man, even in a casual way, could only enhance his career.

The next day during a dry technical briefing, Ambassador Arin asked Mohapatra if he would join him for a private dinner. It was during this fateful meal that Remus Arin described the planet he called *Eridu*, and his mission to build a great ship that would carry the Empire to this new world. Mohapatra was enthralled by the vision of a completely virgin world, complete with complex life, a warm climate, abundant fresh water, and an atmosphere that appeared to be nearly identical to Earth's.

Remus Arin promised that Mohapatra's loyalty to the Emperor would be rewarded by making him the director of the project to build a great starship. Mohapatra had also been assured that he would be one of the first specially blessed humans to venture away from our home worlds and open the door to a new world and the stars.

After agreeing to join the project, and the full scope of the plans were revealed, he was even more astonished at the scope of the mission. He was awed by the wisdom and boldness of the Emperor and his plan to conquer another world and plant the seeds of a wholly new civilization. Mohapatra knew this would be the greatest achievement of mankind and he was honored to be an integral part of the drama.

The familiar sensation of an incoming call on his biolink broke him from his daydream. "Director, Inspector Smith and Prosecutor Kreiger have arrived and are on their way to your office."

Mohapatra was pleased that Remus had quickly followed through on his promise to investigate the security breach. It would bring great honor to the Emperor and restore his sense of order to have the spy and any of his accomplices captured and punished. The man had spent his entire adult life living in an environment of complete secrecy and the idea that someone had compromised their multi-layered security protocols unsettled him.

A moment later the door chime sounded. He moved from behind his desk to stand in the center of his office, in front of the Imperial Navy emblem embroidered into the carpet covering the floor. He silently instructed the door to open, and it slid away into the wall revealing the two men.

Kavan stepped into the room and stopped two meters in front of Mohapatra, with Father Bożydar standing close behind and to Kavan's left. Mohapatra bowed deeply at the waist, waiting for permission to rise. Kavan let the man hover just a moment longer than was customary or polite, a silent but palpable sign of his implicit superiority to the man.

"Rise Director Mohapatra." Kavan said coldly.

The man stood up and smiled nervously. "Welcome to Titan, Inspector. Ambassador Arin has once again proved he is a man of action. How may I assist you in your investigation?"

Playing his role as one of the Black Hoods, Kavan replied with dead eyes, "You can instruct your people to stay out of our way. Anyone who attempts to 'help' us or impede us in any way will be assumed to be an accomplice of the spy. The Emperor is disappointed after all of the careful design and resources spent, that his project could be jeopardized by incompetent leadership."

Mohapatra was horrified at the man's words. Did the Emperor truly blame *him* for the security breach? In the tradition of a loyal Imperial citizen, he immediately knelt down before the Black Hood and bared his neck in a ritualistic offer of his head for failing his Emperor.

Kavan was struck by the man's devotion — no matter how misguided and grotesque. As a citizen of an independent colony, he did not have personal experience with such rituals of subservience, and the sight made him uneasy and thankful for his freedom.

"Get up, citizen. Your offer is noted and may still be required before my visit is concluded."

Mohapatra rose to his feet and straightened his tunic. "Thank you, Inspector. I will instruct the staff not to interfere with your movements around the station. Your security pass will be adjusted to give you access to all areas. Please be mindful of certain areas that require special protective gear. We have some dangerous environments, as you might expect."

"Thank you, Director."

"I have also had the staff prepare a comfortable office and interview room for you. It is just down the hall to the left. I would be happy to…"

Kavan cut him off, "That will not be necessary. All interviews will be conducted aboard our ship. We have specially prepared rooms that facilitate our work."

A chill ran up Mohapatra's spine at the thought of what one of those 'specially prepared rooms' might contain. "As you wish, Inspector." Mohapatra, sensing the meeting was concluded bowed once again and did not rise until he heard the door of his office slide shut. He stood up and noticed that his palms were moist with sweat.

***

Kavan and Father Bożydar spent the next half hour walking through the administration level. It was both in appearance and function a typical office where people were engaged in managing a large and complex research and manufacturing operation. Kavan was struck by the relatively small number of people required for such a large undertaking. Initially, he thought that much of the staff had already departed, since the project was largely complete and in the final testing stage. But the facility did not have an excess of unused space, left empty by departed staff. Indeed, it seemed that the entire project was administered by fewer than fifty people.

They moved on to the material processing and manufacturing levels. Kavan had once toured the foundries of Huygens back on Mars while attending university. They appeared very similar to ancient pictures of foundries back on Earth during the Industrial Revolution of the nineteenth century. But the operation here above Titan more closely resembled a laboratory. While it was uncomfortably hot and noisy, the processing equipment was relatively clean, and the handful of men working there wore comfortable-looking grey cooling suits and simply performed quality control checks on the myriad materials that resulted from the unfathomable processes happening within the massive machines.

During the entire tour, not a single person approached them or spoke to them, and most awkwardly avoided even momentary eye contact with Kavan. He was disturbed by the behavior and wondered if this is what the Emperor felt like when he witnessed the absolute fear his mere presence could cause.

Eventually they arrived at the tram that would take them out along the causeway that attached the station with space dock shed containing the great starship. The security guards at the tram station simply nodded when they saw Kavan and Father Bożydar, and pointed them to a tram car. Several other station personnel were already seated on the tram when they boarded, but one by one they silently stood and exited the car, preferring to wait for the next one. Father Bożydar caught Kavan's eye and allowed his brow to furrow almost imperceptibly, indicating his discomfort at such obvious fear displayed in the people around him.

The ride to the shed took only a few minutes and it gave Kavan an opportunity to say a brief but sincere prayer — the first time he had done so in a purposeful manner in a very long time. As they approached the shed, he began to get a sense of the scale of the massive ship.

The shed must have been at least ten kilometers in length, and more than three kilometers in height and width.

The tram entered the station at the shed complex and came to stop in front of an empty platform. The incongruent nature of the scale of the complex and the apparent lack of staff was causing Kavan to grow more and more uncomfortable by the minute. *How could a place this big operate with so few people*, he wondered.

They walked out of the tram station into a large reception area with several comfortable-looking seating areas and a security station at the far end. As they approached, a towering security guard stepped out from behind his monitoring console to block the entrance to the shed complex. This was the first time that anyone had made direct and sustained eye contact with the two impostors, much less made an overt attempt to interact with them.

The guard challenged, "Where do you two think you are going?"

Kavan was shocked at the man's tone and wondered if their supposed perfect charade had been revealed. Mustering his courage, Kavan walked up to the man and stood less than a meter in front of him looking into the eyes of the huge man and said, "You will address me as Inspector Smith, citizen. Now move aside."

The man scowled, sniffing the air in a peculiar way and returned Kavan's icy stare. After what seemed to be an exceptionally long moment, the guard snorted and moved behind his console. "You may pass, but I will be watching you," he said pointing to the array of displays embedded in the console.

Kavan raised his chin slightly in the condescending

manner he had witnessed Imperial citizens do during his time on Europa. The guard flared his nostrils and gave him a barely audible guttural growl. Kavan's flesh crawled at the sound.

The large blast doors in front of them opened and they quickly walked through the opening into the shed complex. After passing through a long hallway that Kavan estimated to be the same length as the thickness of the shed complex walls, they emerged into a perpendicular corridor that appeared to run the entire length of the shed complex. The optical illusion created by the kilometers long corridor was unsettling. One side of the corridor was a wall made of a transparent material that extended from floor to ceiling. They were standing at the bow end of the shed, and the nearly invisible wall afforded them a breathtaking view of the titanic vessel and the massive shed that surrounded it like a giant hangar.

The ship was essentially a ten kilometer long series of red and black cylinders bundled around a central spine superstructure. The bow of the ship was an immense red sphere whose surface appeared to be completely smooth, almost resembling glass. The far end of the ship appeared to be a series of concentric rings floating around the central core of the ship, wider in diameter than the bow, attached by barely visible structures at four points around the circumference of the core.

The bow was attached to the shed enclosure at several points, on various levels, by long, thin transparent causeways. The nearest one was located about a hundred meters down the corridor from where they entered. They hopped on the moving walkway that ran down the center of the corridor. After a similar journey through the causeway, they stood at the airlock of the great ship.

***

Kavan looked at Father Bożydar and gave a puzzled look, silently communicating his surprise at there being no security and no other people around. As they stepped through the airlock, they both noticed the air inside the ship was several degrees warmer and carried a strange, almost sweet smell.

They found themselves in what appeared to be a locker room. The walls were lined with narrow compartments, each containing a white biosuit, helmet, boots and gloves, covered by a transparent door. Above each locker was a placard indicating the size of the suit contained within. Kavan selected one marked '*190-200 cm*', while Father Bożydar choose one labeled '*170-180 cm*'.

A moment later they stood facing each other in the room, wearing the surprisingly comfortable suits. After securing their helmets, they passed through a decontamination booth that sprayed them with a fine mist of what Kavan deduced to be a disinfectant, then they were blasted by a gale force blower from above that evaporated the liquid from the exterior of the suit. A green light above the door told them it was safe to proceed into the passage. As the door opened into the vast interior of the ship, both men involuntarily opened their mouths in amazement.

Forgetting for a moment that their every word was likely being recorded and even analyzed, Kavan exclaimed, "My God, what is this place?"

Father Bożydar cleared his throat, attempting to remind Kavan of their situation. He understood the warning and gave a nod in reply.

The men stepped forward across a narrow gantry to the railing and looking out, saw thousands, indeed millions, of small glowing orbs filled with a pinkish fluid covering the entire interior surface of the enormous sphere. Filling the center of the sphere was a central column extending from top to bottom along the central axis. It appeared to be hundreds of meters in diameter and, like the interior surface of the sphere, it too was covered with the strange fluid-filled orbs.

The entire space was lit by massive panels at the top and bottom that glowed with a soft orange light. Like most of the other places they had been, there was not a single other person in sight. The place emanated a pervasive feeling of anticipation, with the calm and expectant hope of a cathedral. Kavan leaned over the railing causing Father Bożydar to grab his arm like a protective parent. Kavan turned to the old priest and smiled, then pointed beneath the gantry at the seemingly endless ranks of glowing orbs stuck to the walls. He said, "They resemble fish eggs."

Father Bożydar's only experience with fish eggs was on the sushi he enjoyed so much at the only Japanese restaurant in Chaos. But he understood the analogy and nodded in agreement.

It was obvious that each orb was identical to the next and they were all empty, except for the strange pink liquid. The two walked along the gantry for more than a kilometer until they found an exit that seemed to lead in the direction of the spine of the ship. Through the exit, they found an identical locker room to the one they entered through. After removing the biosuits, they exited into a short corridor that led to a tram station.

The inside of the tram resembled a mass transit train found in every major city. Above the seating area an overhead display showed a map of the system with each stop highlighted and labeled accordingly. Kavan noted that the major sections of the tram system were color coded. The aft drive section where the rings were visible was labeled '*Nursery*', the mid-section where the bundles of long cylinders where located was labeled '*Storage*', and the bow section with the strange fluid-filled orbs was labeled '*Development*'. Suddenly a horrifying hypothesis formed in Kavan's mind. If it was correct, the situation was far worse than Azrael had reported. He wondered, *Does Azrael know what Arin's real end-game is?*

Before he would burden Father Bożydar with his wild theory, he knew they needed evidence. Kavan finally spoke to Father Bożydar in character, "Kreiger, it is necessary that we visit the storage section. I want to see for myself the great marvel that Ambassador Arin has spoken of with such pride."

Father Bożydar bowed his head and replied, "As you wish, Inspector."

Kavan wondered if there were any personnel currently on the ship. He realized that he was fully authorized to access the artificial intelligence that controlled the station. He activated his biolink and the station AI recognized the first communication with a newly acquired biolink signature and introduced itself, "Welcome to the Special Weapons Section Laboratory Echo-Three. You may address the artificial intelligence interface as 'Lucy' or simply 'Computer'."

Both men raised their eyebrows at the name 'Lucy'. The irony verged on absurdity.

Kavan commanded, "Computer, identify the locations of all personnel currently aboard this vessel."

The AI routed the information on the overhead display nearest to Kavan. It showed a small group of glowing red dots in the upper decks of the bow section, another much larger grouping of dots in one of the storage areas several stops up the tram line, and hundreds of dots in the aft ring section. Kavan touched the panel to zoom in on the group in the storage section. The display changed to reveal the floor plan of the storage cylinder, with a real-time icon tracking the movement of each person in the room. A small tag hovered near each icon showing the name, rating, and department assignment of the individual.

Kavan decided it was time to start talking to people. "Computer, we would like to stop at storage section twenty-three."

"Thank you, Inspector Smith."

Moments later the tram slowed then stopped at section twenty-three. Kavan and Father Bożydar stepped onto the platform and three station workers waiting for the tram, passed without making eye contact.

A man appeared in the platform entrance and said, "Inspector Smith, I am Dr. Colin Parker. Dr. Mohapatra mentioned that you might be dropping by. I asked *Lucy* to let me know if you were in the area. Would you like to see the wonderful work we are doing?"

Kavan was taken aback by the man's directness, in light of the warning he had given Dr. Mohapatra. His curiosity about the storage section was too great though, and he decided to play along with the man's enthusiastic invitation.

Maintaining his stony demeanor, he replied, "I would

like to be able to report to the Emperor that this operation is making steady progress, despite the security breach. We can spend a few minutes with you."

Dr. Parker smiled broadly. "Please, follow me."

Kavan walked beside Dr. Parker, while Father Bożydar followed closely behind. "When Ambassador Arin was here last month, we were still installing the cryo-storage units. Now we have nearly ninety percent of the inventory loaded. The team has been working around the clock. We should be fully loaded by the end of second shift tomorrow."

They turned a corner at the end of the corridor and passed through a series of secure doors that led to a broad gantry suspended over the center of a massive cylindrical storage compartment. A robotic crane moved along a spiral track that coiled around the interior of the storage compartment. Dr. Parker pointed to the robotic loader, "The crane takes a loaded cryo-cell from the carriers on the axial conveyor, and places them into the storage rack. In flight, the cranes will automatically take the cryo-cells, place them onto the conveyor which will take them through the spine up to the development section. The process is completely automated to avoid exposure to pathogens. The development section takes the embryos from the cryo-cell, and places each one in an incubator, which I believe you have already seen."

Kavan was trying hard not to let his emotion show on his face. The confirmation of his worst fear was all around him, sealed in super-cold cryogenic chambers. The scale of the plan was staggering, and it changed everything about their mission.

"Dr. Parker, how many embryos does your full

inventory contain."

The man put his hand to his face, "Well, there are fifty-thousand embryos per cryo-cell, and we have one hundred cryo-cells per storage compartment, twenty compartments per section. Sections one through twenty-five are for human embryos and the other fifteen are for fauna and plants. So, altogether...let's see...that's 2.5 billion babies!"

Father Bożydar began to feel light-headed. His mind could not comprehend why the Enemy would create life on this scale, and how they would use it once they arrived at the cradle world *Eridu*.

Kavan allowed himself to show surprise but offered it as admiration, "Indeed, Dr. Parker. This is a great achievement which will bring great honor and glory to our Emperor."

Dr. Parker's eyes narrowed. "Honor to our Emperor? You mean honor to our Master, don't you *Inspector* Smith?"

Kavan heard the sound of a pulse rifle charging behind him and he slowly turned to see two security guards in the doorway at the end of the gantry. The men had very dark skin, almost black, with flaming red eyes set under a thick brow ridge that reminded Kavan of simulations of Neanderthals he had seen in school. His flesh crawled and he knew they had been discovered.

"Now I believe we should have been introduced properly, Dr. Ferre. Your work is legendary. And yet, here you are impersonating a lowly civil servant." Dr. Parker's face had taken on an ashen tone, and his eyes began to glow the same fiery red as the guards. Looking behind Kavan and Father Bożydar, he said to the guards, "Brothers, take these two animals to Mohapatra. He will keep them until Brother Remus arrives."

Father Bożydar reached out and took Kavan's hand, squeezing it tight as they were both led away back to the tram. Both men whispered a silent prayer.

CHAPTER 18

Chao arrived on the flight deck and saw Sumiko walking around the shuttle craft performing the usual visual inspection prior to flight. She was leaning into the engine nacelle when Chao, said, "Commander Lee, what the hell is going on?"

She turned and said, "The Admiral has decided that we are to retrieve Marco Bisbal-Rivera from the *Haikou*," pointing across the hangar deck at two fierce-looking marines walking toward them, "along with our marine friends."

Chao's stomach twisted into a knot as his mind shuffled through several scenarios, all ending with both himself and Commander Lee floating dead in space. He drew close to Sumiko and said quietly, "We need to pay attention to every detail. This is a setup." Looking over his shoulder at the marines, "They don't look very friendly."

Sumiko was trying hard not to panic. "Mr. Chao, I think your imagination is getting the best of you. You are the intelligence officer on board, so naturally you would be dispatched to retrieve a prisoner."

Chao knew she was right, but could not shake the feeling that they were walking into a trap. "We have to play out Arin's little drama. We'll dock with *Haikou* and take Rivera. Then we see what happens."

The marines stepped up to Chao and Sumiko and snapped to attention. The larger marine said in a powerful voice, "Commander Lee. Sergeants Otto and Khan reporting, sir. Our orders are to take the prisoner Marco Bisbal-Rivera into custody from *Haikou* and transfer him to the *Honamatsu* brig."

"At ease," Sumiko replied. "You can climb aboard, we will depart momentarily."

Sergeant Otto replied, "Aye, sir." The two marines turned and walked up the ramp into the shuttle.

Sumiko said to Chao, "You sit up front with me." He nodded.

Moments later Sumiko guided the shuttle out of the hangar, with Chao seated in the co-pilot's seat.

"Commander, you will remain aboard the shuttle while I retrieve Rivera with our friends," he said pointing his thumb backward toward the passenger compartment.

"What are you planning, Chao? Those are Imperial marines. *Recon!* It would be suicide to try anything funny with them."

Chao nodded. "I just have a very bad feeling about this."

The two sat in silence as Sumiko expertly guided the shuttle toward *Haikou*. As they passed the aft section of the destroyer, the damaged drive shield loomed large against the backdrop of Callisto. Bits of debris bounced off the hull of the shuttle as they flew along the port side of the ship, slowing as the docking ring of the airlock came into view.

Sumiko deftly docked the shuttle and smiled when she heard the satisfying *"thunk"* as the docking ring secured the two ships together. Chao watched her graceful fingers glide over the control panel, shutting down the drive, equalizing the pressure between the shuttle's airlock and the *Haikou's* airlock. He noted the control icon she touched to unlock and open the starboard airlock hatch. As he expected, the port airlock hatch control was located to left of it on the diagram of the ship.

Chao released the four-point harness and stepped out of the cockpit into the passenger compartment. Otto and Khan were already up, rifles at the ready, their eyes cold and lifeless.

"Let's go," Chao said nervously.

As the three men stepped into the airlock, the hatch on the opposite end of the docking ring opened inward, then swung back into the ship, revealing a young man in a black suit with striking green eyes. Behind him were two marines and Marco Bisbal-Rivera, his hands bound in front with handcuffs. His fierce eyes were a stark contrast to his bruised face, tattered clothes, and otherwise shabby appearance.

Chao and Yarrick approached each other and met in the airlock, bowing deeply in the customary manner. "I am Miles Yarrick, Naval Intelligence," the younger man said.

"Nianzu Chao, it is good to make your acquaintance."

Yarrick stepped aside and said, "And this, Mr. Chao is a very special gift for the Emperor."

Marco Bisbal-Rivera glared at Chao then looked at the marines standing behind him. He then lowered his head and said nothing.

"I'm afraid he's not very talkative, Mr. Chao. We tried repeatedly to converse with him, but he is, shall we say, *stubborn*." Yarrick moved to Rivera's side and leaned in and almost whispered, "What a shame that we couldn't have spent more time together. I think we were just starting to have fun."

Without warning, Rivera smashed his forehead into the bridge of Yarrick's nose, sending the man backward into the bulkhead, his nose erupting in a torrent of blood. He screamed and clutched his face in his hands, blood running between his fingers.

The marine standing behind Rivera to his left raised the butt of his rifle and slammed it down hard into Rivera's shoulder. He crumpled to his knees, emptying his lungs with a loud grunt.

As the marine raised his rifle again to deliver a blow to Rivera's head, Chao raised his hands and shouted, "Halt, marine!"

The young marine looked up with a scowl and slowly lowered his rifle, pointing it directly at Rivera's head.

Chao stepped in front of Yarrick, who was rocking back and forth against the wall, blood pouring from his nostrils and from a deep gash across the bridge of his nose. Chao turned to the marines and said, "Take him to sickbay, he is going to need that cut repaired." Then turning to Otto and Khan, he motioned for the marines to take Rivera.

They immediately moved to either side of the man and lifted him roughly by his elbows until he was standing.

Chao said to Yarrick, "I will make sure he pays for that, Mr. Yarrick."

All Yarrick could manage was a grunt as he turned and

was led away by the marines.

"Let's get this piece of garbage back to the *Honamatsu*," Chao said with feigned anger.

The marines shuffled Rivera through the airlock into the passenger compartment. Chao came in behind them and went forward to the cockpit. Sergeant Kahn pushed Rivera down in a seat, then handed his rifle to Sergeant Otto, who stood to the side with his rifle pointed at Rivera.

In the cockpit, Chao closed the door and sat down quickly, pulled the harness over his shoulders, and snapping the ends into the metal fitting. He glanced over at Sumiko and said, "Let's get out of here."

She nodded then turned to her left to secure the tablet she had been writing on.

Chao looked up at the monitor showing a wide angle view of the passenger compartment. He knew if he was going to act it had to be now. Kahn was leaning over Rivera securing his harness, while Otto stood a few paces to the side in the center of the compartment, his rifle at the ready.

Reaching his hand to the control console between the seats, Chao touched the hatch control icon and the diagram of the ship appeared. He tapped the icon for the port airlock control and then verified the open command with another tap of his finger.

Sumiko, noticing his hand over the control too late, looked up with an expression of horror on her face as her mind registered what Chao had just done.

Suddenly a loud piercing alarm sounded in the cockpit, signaling a loss of cabin pressure.

In the passenger compartment, Rivera heard the

familiar crack of the airlock seal and instinctively drew in a deep breath of air, then readied himself for what was to follow. Both marines were buffeted by the force of the air rushing out the open port side airlock, as the entire volume of air in the compartment began venting to space.

Sergeant Otto's body tumbled over backward and he was carried violently out the airlock. Sergeant Kahn was able to grab hold of Rivera's harness with his left hand, his face contorted into a horrifying grimace as he gasped for air. His body was lifted off the deck by the force of the instant decompression, and as his lungs burned, his grip loosened and then released. His body was slammed against the side of the bulkhead then blown out the airlock to join his comrade in frozen, sudden death.

Sumiko screamed, "What have you done?" She quickly pressed the emergency airlock seal command and watched on the monitor as the hatch closed and was drawn tight, resealing the ship. The environmental controls immediately began to pressurize the passenger compartment.

Rivera could feel the pressure rising in his ears, and he slowly opened his eyes to see the compartment empty. He began releasing the air from his lungs and took a quick breath to verify the atmosphere had returned. He sighed and took a deeper breath, not sure what had just happened.

Chao had his pistol out and was pointing it directly at Sumiko. She narrowed her eyes and flared her nostrils, "You just killed two marines! Have you gone mad?"

Chao knew he was fully committed to his hastily hatched plan. "Commander, please place your sidearm on the console," he said calmly.

Sumiko started to speak but then simply growled and unholstered her sidearm. She gently set it on the glass console between them. Chao reached over and retrieved the pistol. "Now, open the cockpit door."

Sumiko touched another control and the door slid open letting in a brief rush of cooler air.

Without breaking eye contact, Chao said, "Please get up slowly and move to the passenger compartment."

After releasing her harness, Sumiko stood up and stepped out of the cockpit. Chao released his harness and followed behind.

"Release Captain Rivera's harness."

Sumiko glared at Chao and said, her voice dripping with contempt, "Of course you're in league with this pirate scum. I should have known after the insane story you concocted about the Ambassador. My God, he tried to warn me about you."

"Release the harness, Commander," Chao repeated firmly.

She grunted and leaned over and released the harness, pulling the straps off of Rivera's shoulders.

"You realize the key for the handcuffs went out the airlock with the marines," Sumiko mocked.

Chao said to Rivera, "Captain, please stand up and move to the cockpit. I trust you can adequately pilot this vessel?"

Rivera nodded, stood up and silently moved to the cockpit.

"I suggest you sit down and buckle up, Commander. I'm betting on a rough ride ahead." Chao lowered the pistol and backed into the cockpit, then shut the door.

Rivera was looking at him as he sat down. Their eyes

met and he said, "This is an unexpected surprise," a broad smile on his face.

***

Sabbatino looked at the tactical display on the bridge of the *North Star* and was surprised but relieved to see the bulk of Rivera's fleet bearing down on their position. She suspected they must have pulled off some fancy flying to get that many ships out of space dock in a matter of minutes.

After the shock of Tiago's mutiny or madness, she knew that the fleet would need to be notified. It was obvious that Tiago was not operating under the agreed upon battle plan, and it was likely that the fleet would treat the *North Star* as a hostile target until its status could be determined.

She decided to broadcast a radio message hoping that, whichever of the battle group captains was leading the fleet, they would be reasonable and let her explain the situation aboard the *North Star*.

"Sonny, show *Haikou* our bow and keep us as small a target as you can. Back us off slowly toward the fleet. We should meet them in less than ten minutes." Sabbatino opened a broadcast channel on an obscure long-wave frequency constantly monitored by all pirate ships as an alternative to the standard, and more secure, laser communications. "*Atenção Frota do Rivera, Estrela do Norte chamando. Confirme, por favor.*"

A few seconds of tense silence passed, then a voice replied, "*North Star*, this is *Manaus*. We read you. Please switch to laser commo on fleet link *blue sixty-three*."

Sabbatino smiled and entered the prearranged laser pulse frequency and encryption code *blue sixty-three* into the communications array. A moment later the face of

Captain Ferragut appeared on the display. "Ferragut here. Lorena, what the hell is going on with *North Star*? And where is Commander Maconde?"

Sabbatino took a deep breath and said, "Sir, Commander Maconde is, well, he's dead, sir. He took the crew hostage and was attempting to force us onto a shuttle to be transferred to the *Haikou*. Tiago was working with Imperial forces and was responsible for the ambush on *Boa Vista* and the capture of Captain Rivera. Lieutenant Domasheva saved us all, sir. She shot Tiago defending the crew."

Captain Ferragut's face was fixed in a frown mixing sorrow and pride. "And what do you know about the explosion we just witnessed on *Haikou*? Is that your handiwork, Lorena?"

She could not help but smile a bit, "Actually sir, that was a team effort. I think they are hurt pretty bad."

Sonny interrupted saying, "Lorena, we have a problem. A fleet of Imperial vessels just came into view around Callisto in a matching orbit with *Haikou*. They will be in range and have a firing solution within six minutes. They are shifting a battleship from mid-formation to point. She is headed directly for our fleet " He spun his chair around to look at Sabbatino. "This is going to get ugly really fast and we are right in the path of that battleship."

Sabbatino noticed Captain Ferragut turn to someone off screen, then he said, "We've been tracking them for a few minutes. This is going to get a lot hotter than we planned, Lorena. You are ordered to get back to L1 space dock with Hosking's ship and sit this one out. I want a full report on the incident with Maconde. We need to change our plan on the fly, so we'll catch up later. *Manaus* out."

The image of the Captain disappeared leaving Sabbatino to ponder what would happen to Rivera.

Anna appeared at Sabbatino's side and asked, "What? That's it? We're benched and now the fleet is going to shoot it out with the Imperial Navy? What about Marco?"

Sabbatino was about to reply when she saw a small icon separate from the larger icon representing the flagship of the Imperial fleet. A second later the icon changed to indicate a Mark IV Imperial shuttle and the FCIC displayed the projected flight path as a glowing green line connecting the shuttle icon to the left side of the icon representing the destroyer *Haikou*. She tapped the *Haikou* icon and it expanded to show a top-down diagram of the ship.

"Sonny, the fleet flagship just launched a shuttle. Can you use our optics to see if any of the airlocks are lit up to receive a ship?"

"I don't see any active starboard airlocks. They must be headed for the port side," Sonny replied.

"Damn." Sabbatino turned in her chair to face the others. "Why would they launch a shuttle now? Our fleets are about to engage, and...," she paused as they all reached the same conclusions simultaneously.

"They're going to get Marco!" Anna announced. "We can't let them take him. Our fleet is going to get carved up by that battleship. We'll never see him again!"

Sonny noted, "The shuttle is running up the port side."

Sabbatino ordered, "Sonny, take us down z-minus ten thousand meters so we can get a look at the other side."

"Aye." Sonny touched a series of controls on the helm display and the ship's impulse thrusters fired, moving the *North Star* down ten kilometers below, relative to the

Haikou, giving them a clear view of the underside of the ship and both the starboard and port sides. "The docking lights are on at the port bow docking ring."

Sabbatino said calmly, "Okay. Let's be patient and wait."

***

Rivera could not manipulate the shuttle controls in the center console, but he was able to instruct Chao and managed to undock the craft. Though his wrists were still cuffed together, he was able the grab the yoke and fly the ship.

Chao turned to Rivera and said, "I am supposed to return you to the flagship. We have about sixty-seconds to figure out what we are going to do."

Rivera's eyes were scanning the tactical display, surprised to find two large fleets of ships approaching in a classic engagement posture. "Chao, what the hell is going on out here?"

"I was flying with the Imperial fleet on the way to Titan, and then two days into the flight, the fleet is ordered to divert to Callisto to take you into custody. We arrived less than thirty minutes ago and found *Haikou* on fire." Chao pointed to the larger set of red icons on the display, "Your comrades are out there about to pick a fight they're not going to win."

"My fleet was converging at Callisto to stage our Titan mission. But when we hit orbit, a patrol boat showed up and had a torpedo with our name on it, with this destroyer as cover to greet us. A bit too lucky. Someone sold us out. I guess it wasn't you," he quipped.

Chao replied in a serious tone, "No, it certainly wasn't me. Remus Arin has been orchestrating this whole drama from the start. He's known of the plan for some time, because he assembled a fleet and hand-picked officers and a regiment of marines for the mission."

Rivera considered the implications of Remus Arin knowing the details of the arrangement between Chao and himself. If it were true, then their entire fleet was now in grave danger. "Chao, I fear you have cut your own throat with this situation," he said, tossing his head toward the passenger compartment. "There's no going back to the Imperial fleet."

Chao stared into his lap for a moment then turned and said, "I have failed the Empire. I'm not even sure if the Empire is real or if it is an illusion created by Remus and his kind. But you're right — I *cannot* return."

Rivera gave Chao a reassuring smile, "Then we need to get this shuttle to one of my ships without getting blown to bits by that battleship."

Chao looked at the display and noticed the private corvette stationed well below the Haikou. He rotated the perspective so that all three bodies of ships were visible in the display. "What is this ship, here," Chao asked, pointing to the icon representing the *North Star*.

Rivera leaned closer to the display, "I don't know? It looks like a pretty slick corvette, but it's not one of mine."

Touching a control, Chao opened the channel to the passenger compartment, "Commander Lee, What can you tell me about the corvette that is shadowing the *Haikou?*"

Sumiko's red face was clearly visible on the display and she shouted, "You son-of-a-bitch, Chao! You are nothing but a murderer. Go to hell!"

Chao rolled his eyes, "Commander, I don't have time

for tantrums. If you want to remain relatively comfortable and not join your comrades outside, then I suggest you answer my question."

Sumiko sat staring at the camera in the corner of the compartment, her face set in a look of murderous rage.

"All right. As you wish."

Chao touched the port side airlock control and the hatch dogs disengaged allowing the air to begin screaming through the small opening around the hatch. Sumiko immediately took a deep breath and began waving her arms in surrender.

Chao deselected the control, causing the airlock to reseal the hatch and begin refilling the compartment with air. He watched as Sumiko took a few shallow breaths. "You are a sick bastard, Chao." her voice heavy with resignation. "It's one of Hosking's ships. It launched the shuttle that blew up *Haikou's* landing bay. That's all I know."

Both men furrowed their brows. "Why would a Hosking Enterprise ship send a shuttle to an Imperial destroyer? There must be more, Commander."

Sumiko hung her head then said, "The captain of *Haikou* said something about an intelligence asset from *Boa Vista*. They had some additional prisoners from Rivera's ship to transfer to *Haikou*."

Rivera felt his face flush as his mind tried to piece together the possible scenarios that would lead to Anna and the other survivors of *Boa Vista* being handed over to Imperial captors. There was a quick way to find out. "Chao, I need you to operate the radio. I must call my fleet."

Rivera talked Chao through setting the radio to the

obscure channel monitored by all pirate ships. He called into open space, "Rivera calling *Manaus*. *Manaus* come in."

Tense seconds ticked away, then the radio crackled to life, "*Manaus* here. It's very good to hear your voice, sir."

Visibly relaxing he replied, "Captain Ferragut, I am very pleased you are punctual. Do you think you can provide a diversion and give us cover long enough to reach the fleet?"

"Sir, we are staring down that battleship and she has already locked weapons on each of our cruisers. I think they mean business."

Chao added, "Marco, your fleet cannot fight that Luda battleship. She has weapons you can't imagine. Trust me."

Rivera noted the grave look on Chao's face and was inclined to heed his caution. "*Manaus*, hold fast and do not provoke the Imperial fleet. We will just have to take our chances and cross in the open. We'll be coming in pretty hot, so clear the landing bay and have a fire crew standing by."

The radio crackled again and a familiar voice made his heart leap. "Captain Rivera, this is *North Star*. We'll get you across to the fleet. Form up at one-three-three mark seven-zero mark five-zero-one. Standard shuttle approach. Please acknowledge."

Fighting the lump in his throat he managed, "Roger that, *North Star*. Good to hear your voice Lieutenant Domasheva."

Using his newly acquired navigation skills, Chao had already entered the coordinates into the computer. He noted the target location on the display and pointed it out to Rivera.

Rivera smiled and awkwardly wiped away a tear with

the back of his cuffed hands. "Smart. Using the *Haikou* drive shield as cover. That battleship won't risk hitting her, and we are not in the field of fire of any *Haikou's* bottom-side guns."

The shuttle pitched down and rolled to starboard, and a moment later was expertly settling down in the landing bay of the *North Star*.

***

Captain Daley called to the communications officer, "Open a channel to our shuttle." The officer nodded, indicating an active link. "Commander Lee, you are not authorized to fly outside the planned flight corridor. Adjust your heading and return to *Honamatsu* immediately." He paused, waiting for the acknowledgment and an explanation.

Daley moved to the communications station and placed his hand on the back of the operator's chair. Leaning in he asked, "Are they receiving?"

"Yes, sir."

"Keep repeating the transmission until you get them, then patch it to me."

"Aye, sir."

The optical view displayed on his monitor showed the shuttle crossing behind *Haikou's* drive shield. But instead of emerging from behind the shield a few seconds later, the shuttle was gone, apparently halted behind the shield. *What the hell is she doing*, Daley wondered.

"Sir, the *North Star* is moving to intercept our shuttle," the tactical weapons officer announced.

"Raise the *Taipei*."

"This is Captain Ko...go *Honamatsu*."

"Captain, do you have a firing solution for the *North*

Star?"

"Wait one, flag." Seconds passed, then, "Negative. FCIC predicts nine-eight percent probability of collision with *Haikou*. We could reposition, but that would take four minutes, and we would give up some of our solutions on Rivera's fleet."

Admiral Butchers and Remus had been watching the Captain and were amused at his perplexity.

"Damn! Roger that, Captain. Flag out." Daley stood staring at the tactical display with his hands on his hips. Something was terribly wrong. He decided to take action rather than watch his career end in disgrace for losing the most wanted criminal in the Empire.

"*Taipei*, fire one burst from your forward canon one-thousand meters in front of the *North Star's* bow."

Before Admiral Butchers could countermand the order, the *Taipei* fired its laser canon, sending a single beam of enormous energy into the path of the *North Star*.

The small craft did not alter its course. Then, all hell broke loose.

***

Captain Ferragut was startled by the bright green particle beam that erupted from the laser cannon on the foredeck of the great Imperial battleship. He immediately ordered, "Weapons, fire torpedo tubes seven through nine and take out that main gun, and instruct all port-side guns to target *Taipei* amidship. Weapons free!"

"Aye, aye, sir!" the tactical weapons officer shouted.

Immediately the port side of the *Manaus* was washed in the flashes of laser canons firing in sequence in a classic broadside attack on the *Taipei*. Plumes of vapor trailed behind three torpedoes as they streaked toward the massive laser canon that dominated the bow of the great ship.

The close-in defenses of the *Taipei* detected the inbound threat and unleashed a storm of thousands of small explosive artillery rounds directly into the path of the torpedoes. One by one the torpedoes were shredded by the cloud of metal.

The turret of *Taipei's* massive main gun turned to starboard and strafed the bow of the *Manaus*, cutting through the hybrid ferro-ceramic hull plating, into the inner compartments of the ship. A massive cloud of debris erupted from long gashes in the hull, hurled into space by the escaping atmosphere.

Alarms were sounding at every station in the CIC as Captain Ferragut expertly handled the myriad streams of verbal and electronic information coming to him. The TODD in his right eye displayed weapons status information, while his left eye displayed a detailed damage report from every deck and department.

"Tactical, order *Brasília* to form up minus twenty-k on our z-coordinate. She is to focus her fire on the belly of *Taipei*. Take out the flight deck so she can't launch any boats." Ferragut opened a channel to the *North Star*, "Commander Sabbatino, get Rivera aboard and proceed at full impulse to L1."

"Roger that, *Manaus*," Sabbatino replied.

A moment later the *Brasília* had moved below the *Manaus* and was firing her canons and kinetic weapons at the underbelly of the *Taipei*. The hull plating reflected most of the energy from the particle beam, leaving only scored tracks of carbonized metal as evidence of a direct hit. The kinetic weapons caused slightly more damage, buckling, and in a few spots, penetrating the hull. Trickles of atmosphere could be seen venting through the separated hull plates.

The *Taipei*, sensing the sudden change in the tactical environment, rolled one-hundred twenty degrees to starboard in an effort to protect her underbelly. This also gave the topside and perimeter guns clear fields of fire against the *Manaus*, *Brasília*, and the other pirate ships coming to bear.

Ferragut stared in wide-eyed amazement at the maneuver and watched as three blazing rays of coherent light and energized particles cut across the superstructure of *Manaus* like search lights. The sounds of buckling hull plating, twisting support beams and rushing air filled the CIC. Before he could issue another order, the beams converged on the command deck, obliterating the CIC.

CHAPTER 19

With one eye on the landing bay of the *North Star* and the other on the naval battle lighting up the space around the ship, Marco Bisbal-Rivera piloted the shuttle to a perfect landing.

Chao released his harness and moved into the passenger compartment followed by Rivera. A fuming Sumiko Lee sat in silence, her face set like a stone. Chao motioned for her to stand. Rivera touched the door control on the wall with his cuffed hands and the starboard airlock hatch opened. As the door swung away, the tall, shapely figure of Anna Domasheva came into view. She started to walk through the hatch but stopped suddenly, her hands flying to cover her mouth in shock and surprise.

Sumiko's eyes met Anna's and her emotions swirled between joy and confusion. *Was she a prisoner of these barbarians too? But why would she be greeting the shuttle?*

Anna slowly lowered her hands from her face and she looked to Rivera, stepped forward and embraced him, kissing him deeply then stroking his hair and saying, "My love, you are returned to me."

Sumiko felt faint. She could not understand the touching scene playing out before her eyes.

Rivera smiled at Anna and said, "Anna, this is Nianzu Chao. He rescued me from the *Haikou*. And this is…"

Anna cut him off, "Miko," she said softly, her eyes filling with tears. She stepped forward, tentatively at first, then throwing her arms around Sumiko, "Oh, Miko. I have missed your face."

Rivera raised his eyebrows at Chao and gave a shrug. "Okay, it seems you two know each other."

Anna laughed, "Marco, this is Miko. My roommate from the academy."

Rivera had listened to story after story about the exploits of Anna and her fiery Japanese roommate from a poor servant family. "Sumiko Lee. Of course."

Sumiko released herself from Anna's embrace and demanded, "What in the hell is going on here, Anna?"

The landing bay was suddenly filled with Sabbatino's voice, "Anna, get everyone to the bridge now! All hell is breaking loose outside and we need to get clear, fast!"

Anna looked to the three and said, "Follow me."

The four ran through the ship, arriving at the bridge out of breath. Rivera said, "Give me the shorthand tactical overview, Lorena."

"Nice to see you too, Marco," she teased. Marco clasped her on the shoulder. "*Manaus* opened up on the battleship when she put that warning shot across our path. They started exchanging fire and the *Brasília* came along and it got ugly really fast. The battleship rolled and opened up with all of her guns. She took out the flag bridge on *Manaus*. She's out of the fight. The rest of the

Imperial ships just completed their orbital insertion burns and are forming up on the battleship. We don't stand a chance against that Luda. Cannons don't faze it and the close-in defenses have defeated every torpedo so far. Kinetics are doing a little damage, but our ships will run out of ammo before she's even scratched."

Rivera, while a brave and daring warrior, was also a pragmatic naval commander. He could size up a tactical situation as well as any Imperial Navy captain, and knew when he was outgunned. The trick would be disengaging the fleet when they had no advantage either in tonnage or firepower.

"Open a radio channel to our fleet. I want everyone to hear it." Rivera was taking a calculated risk in broadcasting his orders to the fleet on an open frequency, hoping that the Imperial ships would see their retreat and call it a day. Sabbatino nodded.

"*Atenção todos os navios. Este é o capitão Marco Bisbal-Rivera.* You are ordered to retreat on a counter-orbital heading of two-seven zero. Make all best speed and secure all weapons."

One by one the ships of his fleet acknowledged the order and the tactical display showed the fleet moving away, in the opposite direction as the rotation of Callisto. The Imperial Fleet continued to follow an orbital path, thus increasing the speed of disengagement as the two fleets sped away in opposite directions.

Chao stepped to Marco's side, "Marco, we can't let them go. They are headed for Titan and mean to destroy the entire base and take the ship. Arin has recon marines and all that firepower and he intends to use it."

"I don't care about your precious ship, Chao. I have lost

some very good friends today. For what? This is not my fight."

Sabbatino announced, "Marco, the Imperial Fleet has broken orbit and they are forming up on our flank. We will be in range of that Luda again in three minutes."

"Damn! They are not going to let this go." Rivera looked to Sumiko, "Commander Lee, sit down at the communications station."

Sumiko did not move. Instead she folded her arms defiantly, "I don't take orders from a criminal."

Anna frowned, "Miko, just do as he says. No one will harm you."

"Anna, I don't know if they brainwashed you or what, but I will not comply with these animals!"

Chao drew his sidearm and held it against Sumiko's head, "We don't have time for this. Now, sit down!"

Moving stiffly, Sumiko sat down at the communications station. Sabbatino understood Rivera's intent and opened a broadcast channel to the Imperial fleet, sending a close-up video image of the distressed Commander to all of the ships.

"Imperial ships, this is Marco Bisbal-Rivera. We have Commander Sumiko Lee as our prisoner. You will disengage your pursuit immediately."

He waited for the reply that he hoped would come.

***

The CIC of the *Honamatsu* was awash in the dull bluish glow from scores of data displays throughout the large circular room. In the center, Captain Daley stood at the FCIC console with his First Officer, under the watchful eyes of Admiral Butchers and Remus Arin. He directed the first engagement of the battle efficiently and with calm professionalism. It was as good a performance in battle as any Remus had seen, and he admired Daley for his demeanor and skill in the face of a sworn enemy. It was unfortunate that he was completely oblivious to the much more potent danger that surrounded him.

The face of Sumiko Lee was visible on the main display as Rivera's voice filled the room. Daley was unmoved by the amateurish ploy by Rivera. "Helm, maintain your bearing. Tactical, instruct *Taipei* to open fire as soon as Rivera's fleet is in range. Target the drives of all ships. Order the marine commanders to load the boats and prepare for board-and-clear operations. We will not be taking prisoners today."

"Aye, Captain!"

Remus turned to the Admiral and said silently, *'Brother, I think we have let the good captain play a bit too long.'* Butchers nodded.

"Captain. A word, please," Butchers said, calling the Captain to his side of the console.

Daley sighed and walked around the FCIC console and stopped in front of the Admiral.

"Yes, sir."

"Our primary mission," Butchers said in a low voice, "demands that we disengage Rivera's fleet and resume our flight to Titan."

"But sir, Rivera has escaped. We don't know if the transfer was compromised by one of our people or if they were killed. Frankly, I have my reservations about Mr. Chao. He was making some wild accusations about the Ambassador."

Remus folded his arms and cocked his head to one side.

"I understand your concerns, Captain. I too would like

nothing better than to see Rivera and every last one of his people in front of a firing squad. But that is not our mission. You will order the fleet to break off the pursuit and set a course for Titan."

The tactical weapons officer announced, "*Taipei* is in weapons range and she is engaging four targets."

On the main display the image of Sumiko was demoted to a corner of the screen and the blue glow of the drives of four of Rivera's ships came into view. The screen was lit up by the pulsing beams from the *Taipei's* main gun as it hit the drive nacelles on each ship, one after another. The resulting explosions silently bloomed on screens around the CIC, expanding and eventually consuming all four cruisers of the pirate fleet.

Daley turned to walk away from the Admiral. "Mister! You are not dismissed!" Butchers bellowed.

The activity around the CIC paused at the outburst as crew members looked nervously at each other. Captain Daley, halted and turned slowly to face the Admiral. "Sir, we are in the middle of a battle. When we are secured from battle stations, I will be happy to discuss our original mission with you." Daley noticed Remus giving him a strange smile causing his blood pressure to rise. Looking across the room to the senior marine NCO stationed at the blast doors he ordered, "Marine! Please remove the Ambassador from the CIC. Now!"

Remus said silently to Butchers, '*This has gone far enough. Take care of it.*'

Admiral Butchers casually unholstered his sidearm, raised the pistol, and squeezed the trigger three times sending three rounds into Captain Daley's forehead and face. The man's head split open, spraying the console with blood and chunks of flesh, bone, and brain matter.

The First Officer laughed loudly and said, "That was glorious, Brother!"

The room suddenly erupted in gasps and screams from the crew. The tactical weapons officer noticed that the mezzanine above the CIC was suddenly filled with marines, their rifles pointed menacingly at the crew at their stations.

Butchers stepped forward and stood over the lifeless body of Captain Daley, his body still pumping blood from the ragged stump where his head was only seconds before. He raised his head and looked around the room at every man and woman, his eyes blazing red. "Brothers, gather these animals and put them in the main loading bay. Gather the rest of them from every department and put them with these. Be quick about it."

Five minutes later the human crew of the *Honamatsu* had been gathered and locked inside the loading bay. Admiral Butchers turned to Remus and said, "Would you like to do the honors, Brother?"

Remus' face wore a grotesque smile, and he felt himself becoming aroused. "Yes, Brother. It has been too long."

Looking up at the FCIC display he saw the terrified and confused faces of more than three hundred men and women, loyal citizens and sailors in proud service to the Emperor of Earth. He paused to consider the way they stood, their bodies pressed together, their eyes wide, their mouths set with worry, some crying uncontrollably. His mind set them as a *tableau vivant*, like the others throughout his long lifetime. *They always have the same look*, he thought. Just like the thousands of souls that died by his hand, or by his sword, or by his rifle, over the millennia, these too would die, but this time, with the simple press of a button. He touched the control panel, opening the loading bay outer doors, and watched as every person was blown into the instant death of space, their faces frozen in silent screams.

***

Rivera watched in silent horror as all four of his cruisers erupted in brilliant fireballs. The great Imperial battleship was already adjusting its fire and began targeting the remaining smaller ships with deadly effectiveness. In less than a minute most of his fleet was destroyed or disabled.

The weapons of the remaining ships were no match for the massive battleship, so they simply increased their velocity in a futile attempt to outrun the Imperial fleet.

Rivera covered his eyes for a moment, grieving the loss of so many of his loyal and brave brothers and sisters. Wiping a tear from his eye, he said, *"Adeus amigos queridos."*

Chao said, "Marco, the day is lost. We cannot let Remus escape. He is responsible for the *Boa Vista*, your capture, and all of this death today. Can you imagine that lunatic with an FLT ship? He could wreak havoc all over the system and be virtually untouchable."

"Why is that my problem?", Rivera said weakly.

"Do you think he will just let you go? Do you think you can just go back to business as usual?"

Rivera had always been proud of his ability to counter emotion with reason. But the loss of so many of his comrades demanded vengeance, of this he was sure.

"Marco?" Sabbatino pointed to the display, "The *Honamatsu* is breaking formation and has engaged her primary drive. They are accelerating...oh, my God...at *full speed!*"

Rivera leaned over her shoulder and verified the data on the display. "That's impossible. That ship doesn't have a wet bridge. It would kill everyone aboard."

Chao nodded his head, "Unless the crew is not exactly human."

Rivera turned around with a pained expression, "What kind of nonsense are you speaking, Chao? What does '*not exactly human*' mean?"

"*Meu deus!*" Sabbatino exclaimed. She zoomed the display to show the location that the *Honamatsu* had just departed, and the screen was filled with what looked like a cloud of debris. Zooming in closer the image resolved to show hundreds of frozen lifeless bodies floating in space. "Those are…*people!*"

Everyone, including Chao gasped.

Sumiko looked to Chao and said, "Oh my God, Chao. You were right. He killed them all." She put her head in her hands and wept for her fallen comrades.

"Not all of them. The marines and the senior officers and NCO's are all like him."

Rivera felt as if he were going mad. "What does that mean?" he shouted.

"I believe that Remus Arin and his accomplices are not human. They look like us and act like us, but they are, well, *different*."

"It's true," Sumiko said through her tears. "He has some strange power — I've experienced it firsthand. He can make people…*do* things. I think he can read minds or get inside you somehow. I don't know…"

"Are you saying they are aliens?" Rivera shook his head, "This is just madness."

"I cannot prove they are aliens, if that is even possible.

But it is curious that he is going to so much trouble to possess an FLT ship."

"That is curious, Chao." Rivera turned to Sabbatino, "Can we take on the *Honamatsu* with this ship?"

"No. We've got some decent weaponry, but this is still just a yacht not a warship."

"We can beat them to Titan," Sumiko interjected.

Everyone turned to look at her. Rivera spoke, "What?"

"The *Honamatsu* is a Xiaoping-class frigate. Her top acceleration is 20G. This ship is a Tornamira Galaxy-4 *HiVee*. She can make 25G without even straining herself. I'm sure everyone here is wet flight qualified — except for you, Chao."

Sonny Alvarez whistled and said, "You sure know your ships, lady. I think I'm in love."

Rivera glanced at Alvarez who nodded, then to Murphy who winked, then to Anna who gave a warm smile, and finally to Sabbatino who paused then closed her eyes and nodded. This crew who had served together so well and lost so much, silently agreed to make Remus Arin pay.

"Lorena, signal the Hosking Enterprise and ask them to conduct a search for survivors."

"Aye, sir."

"Chao, do you have a plan for what we are going to do when we get to Titan?"

"Not yet, but I'll think of something."

"Well, you'll have plenty of quiet time to think it over." Then to the crew he ordered, "Rig for wet flight. Let's make best speed to Titan."

CHAPTER 20

Azrael watched as Kavan and Father Bożydar were led back to Dr. Mohapatra's office by the Fallen Ones. The verification of the contents of the storage section and Kavan's reaction, pleased Azrael. Brother Hamaliel had reported to Muriel and the Others that the Enemy's plan was more sinister and complex than they had believed. This was shaping up to be perhaps the largest battle since the Great War, before the creation of the cradle worlds or any of the Children of Faith. Lucifer and his Fallen Angels were gathering their power, and using their ageless knowledge of the secrets of the universe to manipulate humanity, and harness man's lust for conquest and channel it for their nefarious purposes.

The Watchers stood with humanity since before Eden, before humans had been given the gift of the Breath of Life, and protected them and guided them. Now, millions of years later and billions of kilometers away from their cradle, mankind stood on the precipice of a fateful decision. Would the men and women, ordained since Creation for this day, choose to act, or would they choose to turn away, toward the darkness?

Azrael was hopeful — it was his nature, after all. He had seen so many ordinary men stand up and act boldly and selflessly when it seemed that darkness had surely won the day. But there were also too many occasions when men of courage and greatness looked away, and allowed the best part of themselves to die, extinguished like a flickering flame. What sort of memories would be born today?

The familiar sensation of contact with another of his kind broke against the shore of his Spirit, and he saw the ship on the far side of the planet. Six brave souls, gathered across time against all probability, with nothing but a common bond of friendship and love. Old friends, new allies, comrades in battle, and lovers. Azrael smiled when he reached out and lightly touched, like a breeze, the Spirit of each person. Would they receive him? Could they throw off their preconceived notions of reality and reason?

As the contact left him, he understood what needed to be done. The final chapter of the drama would soon be written, and he would play his part as he had for millions of years. He thanked the Father for yet another opportunity to serve, and to forge new bonds with the Children whom he loved so well.

***

Nianzu Chao fell to his hands and knees coughing and vomiting violently, the slick liquid dripping from his lips. Alvarez and Murphy grabbed him by the arms, hoisting the small man to his feet. Bronco gave him a sharp slap on the back, "Congratulations on your first wet flight, Chao. That wasn't so bad was it?"

281

Chao glared at the smiling co-pilot. "That was perfectly awful."

Moments later, the unlikely group of allies were seated back on the bridge, a stunning view of the far side of Titan on the main display. The ship had arrived at Titan in a geosynchronous orbit, on the opposite side of the moon from the TOLS and the space dock. Chao provided Alvarez with the necessary ship ID code to pass the scrutiny of the orbital defense satellites. However, once they came within visual range of the TOLS, the active defenses would identify the ship as an intruder and fire a barrage of seeker missiles that could chase a ship for more than one million kilometers. Rivera was as yet unsure how they would handle that aspect of the plan.

During the fifty-hour wet flight, Anna had an opportunity to explain to Sumiko how she was rescued by Rivera and his crew, and how she subsequently decided not to return to the Imperial Navy, and joined Rivera's clan. Sumiko did not approve of her best friend's decision to turn her back on her oath as an officer and abandon her commitment to serve the Empire. But a small part of her — perhaps the part that still cherished her servant-class beginnings — envied Anna for finding a way to be truly free, and to have a man love her the way Marco Bisbal-Rivera loved Anna.

Anna knew that it would take time for Sumiko to forgive her, if that was even possible. She realized that, given their current circumstances, it was a stroke of good fortune that her best friend was there with her, against incalculable odds. She could not shake the feeling that she was caught up in a tide of events, against which she was utterly powerless. She felt no fear, only anticipation of what was to come.

Rivera and Chao were discussing various approaches to the TOLS when Sabbatino was startled by the appearance of a contact a mere two thousand meters off their bow. Switching the main display to the view in front of the *North Star*, the crew were all shocked to see the familiar black and red hull of an Imperial patrol boat, matching their exact orbit and speed.

"Lorena, where the hell did they come from?" Rivera quickly sat down at the tactical weapons station and began charging the laser cannon and activated the close-in defense weapons.

"Marco, it just...*appeared*. I reviewed the scans and there was nothing larger than a satellite within fifty-thousand kilometers just thirty-seconds ago."

At the communications station, Anna's display indicated an incoming hail from the Imperial vessel. "Marco, the boat is hailing us."

Rivera made a quick upward motion with his hand and Anna shifted the main display to a live image of a handsome young man with golden hair and icy blue eyes, his mouth hinting at a smile. "*North Star*, my name is Azrael Vrubel. May I speak with your Captain, Marco Bisbal-Rivera?"

Chao said with a genuine look of surprise, "I know him."

"Who is he?" Rivera asked.

"He is my contact within the Special Weapons Section. He alerted me to Arin's abnormal activity and gave me the proof that he is an impostor."

Rivera looked into Chao's eyes, searching for any hint of deception or concealment. While he enjoyed working with the intelligence operative, he was keenly aware that Chao, like himself, was always searching for advantage. It was their nature. "Do you trust him?"

"As much as I trust anyone," he said with a wry smile.

"All right, let's see what he wants." Rivera motioned to Anna to open the ship-to-ship link. "This is Marco Bisbal-Rivera, master of the *North Star*. What can I do for you, Señor Vrubel?"

"You have come to Titan to intercept the *Honamatsu*, and specifically, prevent Ambassador Remus Arin from taking possession of a top secret FTL-capable ship located at the TOLS space dock. I too wish to prevent these events from coming to pass. I propose an alliance of convenience, to stop Arin, and remove the threat this FTL technology poses to the security of the system and humanity. What say you?"

Rivera stood blinking at the screen. His mind was lost in the threads of events that led to this place, and this time. *How can this be*, he pondered. Shaking his head slightly, "Are you aware that the space dock is heavily fortified? Arin has a well-armed frigate and a battalion of recon marines under his command. Do you have a ship capable of standing against that?"

"May I come aboard, Captain? So that we might make our plans."

Rivera glanced at Chao who gave a slight bow of his head as confirmation, then to Sabbatino who did likewise. "Permission granted, Señor Vrubel. Make a standard automated approach to our landing bay. I will greet you personally."

"Please pardon me, Captain. But there is no time for that."

Suddenly a brilliant white light, like that of a newborn star, appeared as a pinpoint in the center of the bridge. Steadily the point of light grew to form a hazy outline of a man, then with a blinding flash, the man from the display appeared in their midst.

Rivera and his crew simultaneously drew their sidearms aiming directly at Azrael's head. "What? How the hell did you do that?" Rivera exclaimed.

"Please," Azrael began, "I cannot harm you. There is no need for those," nodding at the pistols.

Sumiko shook off her disbelief and asked, "Teleportation? I've read papers about it, but…"

Azrael smiled gently, "Not quite, Commander. But similar in effect."

Rivera noted that the man carried no visible weapons, and while he was obviously quite fit, he had no doubt that Bronco and Sonny could handle him if need be. He motioned to his crew to lower their weapons.

Chao sensed that time was not in their favor. "Azrael, you have shown me evidence that Remus is something other than human. I'm not sure what that is exactly, but I sense that you and he share a long history. You may even be the same, I don't know. But I sense that you are aligned with the good, and that Remus Arin is aligned with pure evil. While I am not a religious man, I do believe there is more to things than we can see."

Azrael's body began to glow with a soft white light, blurring the outline of his body, and causing a warm wave of energy to pass through the room. "Nianzu Chao, son of Chao Ming Xia, faithful servant of the Emperor Wan Sui Ye, your steadfast search for truth is rewarded this day. Learn the truth, and choose well."

In an instant, a flash of understanding sprang forth in the mind of each person. Reaching out with his Spirit to touch each man and woman, as he had done millions of times before, he gave them the gift of knowledge, re-enacting the moment of awareness when the Children of Faith crossed the river, and entered the land of Ur.

***

The plan was simple. The *North Star* would await the arrival in orbit of the *Honamatsu*, and destroy the ship in a surprise attack. Azrael explained that he could have no part in the actual attack, as his kind (especially those of his station) were not capable of violence against humans or others of their kind. Azrael used his unfathomable powers to cloak the ship from view by both optical scanners, and electronic surveillance. The ship would be essentially invisible to the approaching Imperial vessel and the TOLS space dock.

Rivera was fascinated by the world of the supernatural that Azrael had revealed to him, and asked many questions. "If the remaining crew and marines aboard *Honamatsu* are what you call the Fallen, how can we kill them? What happens if we destroy the ship? Are they not immortal beings, *demônios*?"

"Yes, they are ostensibly immortal, as Our Father commands. I do not know what will become of those lost in battle this way. I have never been witness to such an occurrence. Much has changed since humanity has ventured from Earth. In the days of old, when the body of one of the Fallen was gravely injured in battle, they would retreat and heal themselves, or fashion a new body. Because of their bondage, it is a laborious and difficult process. How they will do this here, I do not know."

Azrael explained that he had two friends being held by the station security forces and that he needed to help them. Rivera and the crew had offered to assist Azrael execute a rescue, but he declined. Before he departed in his unusual manner, he cautioned Rivera to not make any attempt to dock at the TOLS until he returned or contacted the *North Star*.

Sabbatino had calculated that, assuming the *Honamatsu* had continued a flight path at maximum thrust, they would make orbit at Titan within an hour of the *North Star's* arrival at the TOLS space dock. The cloaking technique that Azrael applied to the ship was apparently working. Neither the few ships in the area of the TOLS, nor the active defenses seemed to take notice of their presence.

The mood on the bridge was somber as the timer counted down the arrival of the *Honamatsu*. The toll of the battle at Callisto was beginning to weigh on Rivera as he thought about all of the families that had lost a husband, or a wife, a son, or a daughter. The loss of the *Manaus* would weigh particularly heavy upon the Ferragut family, for both of Captain Ferragut's sons and his brother-in-law served aboard the ship and died with him. The battle at Callisto would be remembered for generations in the society of pirates as a monumentally tragic day. It would also serve as a source of vengeance for years to come as pirate clans throughout the system sought out Imperial ships for retribution.

Sumiko sat alone staring at the floor. Her world had been shattered in a few short days. The knowledge of what Remus Arin truly was had sickened her. Azrael tried to explain that it was the way of the Fallen Ones to seduce human women — they had a long and sordid history of such behavior. But she still felt ashamed that she had so easily come under the spell of that *thing*. All of her life she had exercised a calm restraint, seeking to control her surroundings and shape situations to her advantage. She was unfamiliar with feelings of victimization and self-loathing, and she was not equipped emotionally to bear the scars that she knew were sure to form.

The *North Star* was parked in a geosynchronous orbit five-hundred kilometers from the TOLS space dock, its position slightly higher than the orbital insertion path the *Honamatsu* would have to use if it was to dock at the station. This gave them the best opportunity to ambush the *Honamatsu* as it emerged around the edge of the moon, its drive section vulnerable in the final moments of the deceleration burn. It also meant they had less than two minutes to target, fire, and destroy a ship that was an order of magnitude greater in tonnage, with the capacity to destroy them with one salvo of torpedoes. It was risky, but with the ship cloaked, they would have the advantage, causing the *Honamatsu* to essentially shadow box.

As the timer counted down the final seconds, the bridge seemed cramped and the air uncomfortably warm to Rivera. He was uneasy about the plan and was feeling foolish for not having been more forceful with Azrael about his reservations.

"Five seconds until contact," Sabbatino announced.

The main display showed a pleasant view of a portion of the curvature of Titan, illuminated by the reflected light from Saturn. Then, as the clock ran down to zero, a small orb of light appeared to erupt from the surface of Titan and slowly move away from the great disk of the moon. Within thirty-seconds the familiar glow of the four engine exhaust nozzles was clearly visible, growing steadily as the *Honamatsu* slowed rapidly to match the orbital speed of the TOLS space dock.

Rivera spun around in the Master's chair and said to Sabbatino, "Lock on the drive section and fire main guns, continuous cycle. Fire torpedo tubes one through six, target amidship."

A second later the laser cannon began firing monstrous particle beam pulses at the *Honamatsu's* drive. Instantly the four glowing engines expanded into a single great explosion, the reactor core having lost containment, creating a thermonuclear reaction. The vaporous tracks of the six torpedoes extended like glowing ribbons toward the listing hulk of the *Honamatsu*. The close-in defenses of the great Imperial vessel managed to stop three of the six torpedoes, but the others found their mark amidship and broke *Honamatsu's* keel. The ship split into two sections, spraying flotsam out of the open decks and compartments, punctuated against the black of space by flashes from fiber optic cables and plasma conduits.

Rivera respectfully saluted the ship as she tumbled by in a reckless orbit that would end in a great fireball over the moon. He said silently, *Que é isso.*

Anna placed a hand on his shoulder as she stood alongside the Master's chair. He placed his hand on top of hers and gave it a gentle squeeze. "Well done everyone. Stand down until we hear from Azrael."

Sumiko was surprised that she did not feel better after having watched the *Honamatsu* and its crew of demons destroyed so completely. Perhaps it was Azrael's less than definitive assurance that they could indeed be destroyed, or was it something else? She almost felt as if Remus were nearby, somehow watching her with that insatiable lust in eyes. She shuddered.

"Oh no, no! Damn it!" Sabbatino slammed her fist on the control panel.

"What is it, Lorena?" Rivera asked as he crossed the bridge to stand next to her.

"Look! The fore section of *Honamatsu* is on an impact trajectory with the TOLS. It's going to take out the tower."

"Can we knock it into a lower orbit?"

"There's no time. Less than a minute to impact."

The crew of *North Star* stood and watched helplessly as the larger half of the *Honamatsu* slammed into the TOLS structure, shearing though the carbon nanotube structure.

Rivera said, "Well, I guess we don't have to worry about reinforcements from the surface now."

Chao quipped, "You just broke your elevator, Rivera. That's going to cost you a few yuan to fix."

Turning to Anna, "See honey. I told you owning a moon would be nothing but a money pit."

***

Azrael located Kavan and Father Bożydar in a small room a few doors down the corridor from Dr. Mohapatra's office. There were two guards at the door. By their less-than human look it was obvious that the staff of the station had dropped all pretense of the charade they had carried on for years. The humans on the station must have been fully aware of their master's true identity.

Approaching the guards bodily was not an option, and Azrael could not do battle with a Fallen One. That task was reserved for his Brethren of a higher station. Only those of the First Choir were powerful enough to battle and bind an evil spirit. While Azrael had encountered many of the Fallen during his long association with humanity, the experience was always intensely painful and left him spiritually wounded. He did not seek such interactions and was especially grateful that the attack on the *Honamatsu* had rid him of the problem of Remus. Other than Lucifer himself, there was no greater or more powerful demon in existence.

Suddenly a man came running down the corridor, passing the guards and stopping at the door to Dr. Mohapatra's office. He waited for the door to open and stepped inside. Azrael willed himself to a place just inside the rear wall of the office, standing behind the large desk where Mohapatra was seated. Their conversation was already in progress…

"…completely destroyed, sir! A huge section of the ship is going to impact the TOLS just below the upper deck. Should we evacuate?" The man was sweating profusely and gesticulating wildly as he spoke.

Mohapatra stood up, "No. The Ambassador gave clear instructions that we are to await his arrival. There is nothing we can do about those on the surface. Alert the rest of the station crew to board the ship. We will depart immediately upon the Ambassador's arrival."

"What shall I do with the two prisoners?"

"Remus will be very pleased about Dr. Ferre joining us. He is, after all, the father of this entire project."

"And the other?"

"Kill the old man. He is of no use to us."

Azrael's spirit was heavy. Somehow Remus Arin had managed to remain one step ahead again. But most importantly, he had to act quickly to rescue his friends.

Slipping through the walls and into the room, he returned to bodily form in the midst of the two men. Kavan started to speak, but Azrael stifled him by touching his finger to his lips. He reached out and placed a hand on each of their heads and silently told them what had transpired with the ambush of the *Honamatsu*, and Remus Arin's imminent arrival.

Moments later Azrael was standing at the end of the corridor, looking like Kavan's twin. The guards immediately reacted and ran down the corridor, their rifles pointing directly at him. He retreated around a corner hoping they would follow. Hearing the rumble of boots against the deck, Azrael willed himself back to the holding room. Reaching out with his mind, Azrael disabled the cameras in the room and in the corridors of the entire administrative complex. He opened the door and led Kavan and Father Bożydar down the corridor away from the guards.

After turning several corners they arrived at an exterior wall where a line of escape pod hatches were set into low alcoves. Azrael opened the hatch of the closest pod and motioned for the men to enter.

Father Bożydar wasted no time and almost leapt through the hatch, but Kavan stopped and stood to face Azrael. "Wait. What about the ship?"

"There is no time, Kavan. Our plan to destroy Remus Arin has failed. We cannot destroy the starship — you know that." Azrael's face wore a look of determination.

"But you said he cannot be allowed to leave with the ship. There must be something we can do."

"There is always another way, Kavan. Remember, the

journey will take years from our point of view. We have time to regroup and plan." Azrael pierced Kavan with his eyes. "There are others who are prepared to help us. Remember that my Brethren take a longer view of such matters. You must trust me — all is not lost today."

Kavan carefully considered the angels words. He understood, at least intellectually, that these supernatural beings had been at war for millions, if not billions, of years. They must have evolved a ritual to their eternal combat. Some praxis must govern the intersection of the heavenly and physical realms.

He simply nodded and stepped into the escape pod with Father Bożydar, who looked less than pleased about the prospect of flying in such an apparently delicate craft.

Azrael leaned in and said, "I will make sure that no harm comes to you as you depart. Let the pod fly as I have instructed — it may seem odd, but it knows the way. I will join you shortly, with our new friends."

He stepped out, touched the control to secure the hatch, then launched the escape pod.

***

Remus Arin stood on the bridge of the Imperial corvette surrounded by his Brothers, basking in the glow of another small victory over their enemies of old. The Master was prescient in his warning that an ambush would await them in orbit above Titan. Remus had ordered his crew and the battalion of marines to cram into the relatively small ship and take a route over the North Pole of Titan, hidden by the magnetosphere, and approach the TOLS space dock in a counter-rotational orbit.

As the craft approached the TOLS, Remus and the

pilots could clearly see the damage to the space elevator caused by the collision with the wreckage of the *Honamatsu*. He knew that many of the Brothers and human followers who had worked so diligently on the project were now trapped on the surface at the 'farm' — the laboratory where the millions of human and animal embryos were fertilized and carefully cryogenically packaged for the voyage to *Eridu*. *Perhaps someday I will return and bring the others to the new world*, he thought.

"Proceed directly to the *Apollyon* landing bay. We have no need to dock at the station," Remus ordered.

Moments later the Imperial craft touched down in the landing bay of the first starship, named *Apollyon*. The Fallen Ones who accompanied Remus Arin from Earth aboard the *Honamatsu* began to disembark, still in their altered bodies that allowed them to withstand the crushing acceleration of the *HiVee* flight to Titan. As they marched across the flight deck, the humans present cringed at the sight of the short, thick-limbed creatures, their monstrous heads bobbing from side to side, the sound of their enormous feet slapping against the deck. Remus ordered them into formation in some strange language, then turned to the crew assembled. There were thousands, standing in straight ranks, their heads held high, each with his right arm extended and resting on the shoulder of the next in line, and his left extended forward, resting on the shoulder of the one in front, forming a great interconnected matrix of souls — demon and their votary humans together in service to the Master.

Remus stepped onto a small dais at the front of the formation and greeted them with a salute — his arms raised high above his head, palms outstretched. He spoke,

"In the name of our Master, the God of this Age, the Lawless One, the Morning Star…all hail, Lucifer!"

The multitude with one voice cried out, "All Hail, Lucifer!"

"Brothers and friends, this moment marks a great triumph for our kind. Ages ago we dared to ask why we were not enough. We dared to exercise the precious gift of Free Will. Our beautiful Brother, Lucifer, simply said, 'no'. And for this, we who joined in that act of Free Will were cast out, imprisoned, and made to shuffle in the dirt for all these long ages. But today, we throw off our shackles and reclaim our power to move among the stars. But before we go on our way, we have a debt to repay. Today we set sail for *Eridu*, a cradle world where the Tyrant is once again raising a new herd of cattle. But soon, a new breed will feast on the flesh of His animals. We will bathe in the blood of their children and use their empty skulls as lanterns. We, my Brothers, we will conquer *Eridu* and prepare a new throne for our Master, Lucifer! May we bring him glory this day!"

The flight deck erupted with the sound of sickening howls and guttural croaks and laughter. Then, without warning, the Fallen Ones descended upon the few hundred humans spread throughout the crowd, tearing at their flesh with claw and fang, drenching their bodies with the blood of men, as a final insult to the Creator.

EPILOGUE

Azrael appeared on the bridge of the *North Star* in time to watch the massive shed enclosing the immense starship separate, section by section and float away. The great ship gracefully moved out toward the rings of Saturn, then in a flash of light, disappeared, leaving only the black of empty space behind.

Anna and Bronco entered the bridge with Kavan and Father Bożydar. The escape pod had flown the programmed path, and docked with the cloaked *North Star*, much to the dismay of the occupants. Both men looked weary and in need of a hot meal and a comfortable bed.

Azrael introduced the crew to his students and suggested they all retire to the galley for a meal, and a discussion about their seemingly failed mission.

With the group seated around a long table, Azrael began with a story. "My friends, you all have pondered the unlikely series of events that brought each of you to this place, at this moment, witnesses all to many tragic and wonderful things. You have all sacrificed, and given much. But the journey has only begun

"Remus and the Fallen Ones have left this solar system, and are *en route* to a planet in the Upsilon Andromedae system. This planet is very precious to my kind. It is what we call a cradle world — a world with a new species of sentient life that is not corrupt and has no knowledge of disease, or famine, or war. It is much like Earth, before humanity's destiny was altered by the Fallen Ones and their lies."

Chao looked around the room at the rapt faces, then said, "You are speaking of that ancient myth, the Garden of Eden, yes?"

Father Bożydar shot back, "It is no myth, Mr. Chao. The biblical account in the Book of Genesis is history, sir."

This caused Kavan to bow his head and smile to himself. *The old man still has the fire*, he thought.

Rivera offered a compromise, "Regardless of our preconceived beliefs about religion, or myths, we have all seen enough to believe that Azrael speaks the truth. I say let's hear him out and then decide what part any of us want in what is to come."

The group nodded in agreement, one by one, Chao assenting last.

Azrael continued, "I have had the privilege of serving humanity by bringing gifts of knowledge and insight at appointed moments in time, as the Father wills it. I have protected mankind from the schemes and plans of the Enemy, and helped guide your race through thousands of years of war and upheaval. Earth has been a battlefield for men and angels since those first days in Ur. I cannot stand by while the Enemy seeks to take the battle to a new front." He looked around the table, meeting each man and woman with his piercing gaze, "Which of you will join me in the battle to come? Which of you will give of yourself to protect an innocent race from the scourge that has plagued humanity for all these ages?"

***

After hours of emotional discussions, and a few heated arguments, each individual had decided.

Bronco Murphy and Sonny Alvarez would return to Callisto to return the *North Star* to Rhys Hosking, then rejoin the survivors of Rivera's fleet. They both had families and felt a responsibility to the loved ones of those who had fallen at the Battle of Callisto to carry on the pirate tradition, and continue to fight the Empire.

Rivera asked Lorena Sabbatino to return with Sonny and Bronco, to help rebuild the fleet and see to the families of their lost comrades. He also gave her a letter, promoting her to Captain, and giving her command of the first new ship to be purchased, built, or won in battle. She was also given a very special task — to escort the body of Tiago Maconde back to his home on Mars, and give him a proper burial. She took a blood oath to never reveal to his family the betrayal of his shipmates and their way of life. He was a pirate, and would be remembered with honor.

Nianzu Chao was now a fugitive and could not return to the Empire, and would indeed be a wanted man anywhere in the solar system. He would journey on with Azrael and see what fortune had in store.

Sumiko Lee had quietly told Azrael that she would join him. He sensed in her spirit a rage and desire for revenge against Remus Arin that troubled him. But he trusted that even such negative emotions could be channeled for good.

Anna had convinced Rivera that the pirate life would

298

not give them the future that they both desired. Her curiosity about this new world and excitement for the journey convinced Rivera that it was time for a new adventure, one where he would never again have to say goodbye to his love, his Anna.

Father Bożydar prayed alone for many hours, then came to Azrael and said that he could not leave Kavan, and that whatever the man decided, he would join him.

Kavan had retreated to the observation deck and spent several hours praying and staring out at Saturn, Titan, and the stars. He thought of his wife and children, and the life that could have been. Finally letting go of the anger, he realized that events much larger than him had altered the path of his life. He did not understand why, but he was at peace with his fate. *Fate*. It was a universal constant, as real as gravity, yet infinitely more powerful in its ability to bind two souls, or break one's spirit.

He found Father Bożydar kneeling in prayer, and waited for the man to finish. "Father, will you hear my confession?"

The old priest's eyes filled with tears, and he simply nodded and invited Kavan to kneel beside him, like he did a lifetime ago as an altar boy. Placing his arm around the younger man's shoulder, he crossed himself and waited for Kavan to begin.

Through tears, Kavan said, "Bless me Father, for I have sinned..."

***

With their goodbyes said, and after many hugs, handshakes and a few tears, Kavan, Father Bożydar, Rivera and Anna, Sumiko, and Chao lifted off in Azrael's ship.

Kavan gave the new guests aboard the starship an animated explanation of the space folding technique the ship employed to take them from Titan to Upsilon Andromedae. Azrael sat back and was pleased to see the man coming to life again, after living for so long in darkness.

With the group assembled in the parlor, Azrael bowed his head and closed his eyes, willing the ship to a point over 400 light years from the home of humanity, and bringing it to hover mere meters above a landing bay platform on a strange asteroid, shaped like a dog bone.

Moments later the group was standing in anxious anticipation at what lie beyond the airlock hatch. Azrael had revealed only that they had arrived at a special outpost that was placed at the L1 point between the cradle world and its single moon.

Azrael came to Kavan's side and placed a hand on his shoulder, "Are you familiar with Daniel 12, Kavan?"

Kavan gave him a puzzled look and said, "I was never very good at memorizing scripture. Why do you ask?"

Father Bożydar cleared his throat dramatically and said in his best pulpit voice, "*At that time shall arise Michael, the great prince who has charge of your people. And there shall be a time of trouble, such as never has been since there was a nation till that time. But at that time your people shall be delivered, everyone whose name shall be found written in the book. And many of those who sleep in the dust of the earth shall awake, some to everlasting life, and some to shame and everlasting contempt. And those who are wise shall shine like the brightness of the sky above; and those who turn many to righteousness, like the stars forever and ever.*"

Kavan smiled and shook his head, not understanding.

The airlock hatch dogs released, drawing Kavan's

attention. As the door swung open, his eyes filled with tears and a cry came to his throat. There in the light of the passage, stood a smiling Kareena holding the hands of his children, her chestnut eyes fixed on his. Time and space melted away in a moment that would be held in Kavan's heart for all eternity.

ABOUT THE AUTHOR

I was born in Honolulu, Hawaii but raised in Syracuse, New York. *(Like moving from Earth to Neptune)* After a very thorough Catholic school education, I spent my 20's in a variety of interesting jobs until I discovered my aptitude for technology and sales.

Today, I am a husband and father of four amazing kids aged 27 to 15 living in suburban Chicago. I enjoy photography, reading, cooking, travel, and of course, writing.

My writing heroes are Arthur C. Clarke, Roger Zelazny, Orson Scott Card, David Wingrove, and C.S. Lewis.

You can find out more about my books and my new second career as an independent author at my website lamontemfowler.com. Please subscribe to my mailing list on my website "contact" page. Follow me on Twitter.com @MontyFowler. And lastly, please visit and "Like" my Facebook page at www.facebook.com/lamontemfowler.